Walking the Knife's Edge

Elise Carlson

Faraway Fiction Press

Walking the Knife's Edge is a work of fiction. Names, characters, locales and events are either products of the author's imagination or used in a fictitious manner. Any resemblance to actual persons, living or dead, or actual events is purely coincidental.

Content Warnings: family violence and child abuse (graphic in chapter's 3, 4 and 24), family dysfunction, CPTSD and some homophobic, sexist/ misogynistic etc. refs.

First published in Australia by Faraway Fiction Press
Text © Elise Carlson, 2025
Cover illustration and design © Elise Carlson, 2025
Moral rights of the cover artist, Lawrence Mann, have been asserted.

The font used for chapter headings is called Fifa Welcome and was designed by Edwin Alenjandro.

This book uses British English spelling conventions.

ISBN 978-1-7642172-0-0 Ebook
ISBN 978-0-6454633-9-2 Paperback

Also by Elise Carlson

Dramatis Personae

Brock Heights Residents

Des & Cam, brother's, Rarkin's over the road neighbours and friends.

Trent, Rarkin's mentor and older friend.

Orange Tree Hill Residents

Glenn, Rarkin's friend, and shadower student.

Uncle Alan, Rarkin's mum's brother.

Aunt Lil, Alan's wife.

GreenHill Residents

Wac & Tac, twins, shadower students with Glenn, and friends of Rarkin.

Sythe School Trainers & Heads

Trainer Lauran, teaches History of Sorcery and Magic, and Monster Studies.

Trainer Morea, teaches Monster Studies.

Trainer Sirona (she/her), teaches Zushai (hand to hand combat.)

Trainer Dorthin (he/ him), teaches marksmanship.

Headmaster Zatrack, head of sytheren and syther students.

Headmistress Rinas, head of sytheren and syther students.

Sythe School Students

Miona (she/ her), skilled at hand-to-hand combat.

Merin, (she/her), Miona's girlfriend, outgoing, flirtatious, makes Rarkin nervous.

Rinth (he/him), also skilled, too rich for Rarkin's liking.

Amon (*spoilers*), smiles too much.

Ryan, Amon's loud-mouthed friend.

Lylez (she/ her), the most petite student.

Joe and friends; Johnny and Nick (also from Brock Heights).

Chapter 1

Life in Brock Heights

A mother smiled at her daughter as if the kid was the source of light in her world, while both climbed into their pristine motor carriage. The engine started smoothly and the carriage drove off down a road paved with rainbows. Or at least it seemed to, from where I stood; the only graduate without a single family member in attendance.

"Pass more than I did, boys?" Des called, as he pulled up in his faded motor carriage, its chassis rust-flecked from driving through puddles over too many years.

Smartly dressed parents congratulating graduates behind me looked down their noses at Des. I glared at them, as my mate Cam opened his older brother's motor carriage door and climbed inside. I climbed in after him, and Des clapped me on the shoulder, with a little sadness in his eyes. Mum had planned to be there, but Des knew I didn't have the money for the electric-way, home was over an hour's walk and neither of us could remember the last time my mum left Brock Heights.

"So?" Des asked.

"I start my building apprenticeship in two weeks," Cam replied.

Des grinned at him in the rear-view mirror. "And you Rarkin?"

"I got into Sythe School," I replied.

Des gave me the same smile. Then he eyed Cam in the mirror. "Before our mates ask why you're building houses when you could train to contain monsters, I want you to know that I appreciate Sythe employees having a decent place to sleep after protecting us from crime, sorcerers and co."

Cam smiled. Des was right, but people tended to overlook danger-free career options in our neighbourhood.

"Sorcerers and Co.'s a good name for a company," I said. "You got a new job Des?"

Des grinned. "If I had the magical talent for that… I wouldn't be using it in a way I'd want to advertise."

Cam rolled his eyes. Des had a habit of shoplifting for the fun of the challenge. Nothing expensive, just bits and pieces for the thrill of the thing. Ma Tully and Cam didn't approve, but there were worse things you could do for kicks.

Des drove us on, down a road lined with fences of well-maintained, brick, steel and wooden houses. Apparently it hadn't changed since before the Nuclear War, back when people had money and there were fashion trends, and nostalgia for more stable times didn't freeze whole suburbs development.

But this neighbourhood looked alright for a time capsule. Newly painted gates opened to carefully manicured lawns and neatly laid out gardens. It was almost *too* tidy, like a travel house, not a home.

We knew we were nearly home when the road got pot-holed, the footpaths became cracked and gardens became overgrown. The houses shrank from five bedrooms to two or three, with rusty steel, mossy slate or tarp patched tile roofs.

We parked on Des's lawn and Ma Tully strode down the front path to greet us. She gave Cam a hug and smiled proudly at him. Then she smiled and nodded to me. I nodded, thanked Des for the lift and crossed the road, hoping Mum was ok.

I walked up the lawn Mum kept neatly trimmed and opened the door in a timber wall of patchy white paint, shaved off where it had flaked. The floorboards of our small lounge were free from dust, the bench tops of the ageing kitchen behind it were clean, and Mum's bedroom door, second on the left, was open.

"Mum?" I called.

She stepped out of the kitchen wearing a fragile smile and holding a freshly iced cake on a plate. I smiled. She wasn't lying in her room depressed like I'd feared, and having failed to pick me up from school, she'd made cake. It'd been a long time since she'd baked.

My smile faded a little. It was biscuits when she'd missed Glenn's parents' twenty year wedding anniversary, and I'd only just made it in time, with a lift from Des. The effort was a nice way to show she was thinking of me, and I appreciated it. But part of me couldn't help wishing she'd been there instead.

"I got into Sythe School," I told her.

She smiled, putting the cake on the table and stood on tip-toe to peck my cheek.

"Uncle Alan will be proud! Will you join him in Monster Containment?" she asked.

I wasn't sure. Working for Monster Containment meant you had to get your sytheren *and* syther qualification and I'd struggled to remember enough to pass my General School exams...

"Maybe," I replied.

We sat at the kitchen table and my muscles tightened at the sight of three plates. Mum served a slice of cake onto each, as Dad stomped up the front path and the door swung open.

"Cake?" he called. "The boy must have passed. Not such a useless dreamer after all."

I glared at him.

"Suppose you want to go to Sythe School and work for City Government?" Dad asked, taking the piece of cake Mum offered him with a small smile and a silent nod of thanks. Would it kill him to say 'thank you' out loud?

I met his gaze and replied, "Yeah."

"Not sure I want you in the City Guard," Dad said, ignoring the fork mum had laid down, icing sticking to his fingers as he picked up his piece with his bare hand and took a bite. "Bit embarrassing, those bums standing round the gates all day. Monsters haven't got near the city for centuries," he said around his mouthful. "What are our City Rates paying for, eh?"

What would he know about it? And it would be embarrassing, if I had to arrest my father for public drunkenness as he staggered home one night. I clenched my teeth and took a deep breath through my nose, instead of eating.

"Say something boy," he ordered.

I fought down the urge to swear at him, because if I did that while he was sober, he'd remember, and he wouldn't pay my Sythe School fees. For a moment my jaw didn't want to unlock. I pried it open, eyeing the untouched cake on my plate to avoid looking at him. "I don't know which government department to work for."

Lying to his face was a small source of satisfaction. If I worked in Monster Containment, I could get called out to the National Park Zone on the edge of the Wild, as far from Brock Heights as possible. But Sythe Schools didn't just train Monster Containment, Search and Rescue or Healers; they also trained the Syther Force. Sometimes I liked to fantasise about joining the Syther Force and putting my father behind bars.

"Make a decision," Dad replied. "I'll not have my money wasted by you changing your mind and taking extra subjects."

He intended to pay the fees. I relaxed inwardly, and Mum smiled.

"Good cake," Dad said, holding the large piece up. "I'm going to the pub."

***

I heard him come home well after dark. I was sitting on my bed in my bricked up, former-porch bedroom, opposite the box my clothes lived in because I didn't have any other furniture. I glanced at a brochure pinned to my wall showing a syther team in smart, dark green uniforms. Behind them a crane lifted a carnivorous, giant torian bird out of a field and an admiring farmer-family looked on. Monsters like that mostly stayed in the Wild Zone, but I wondered what it felt like to be recognised for what you achieved, instead of discriminated against for how you looked. I had a plan for that.

I unfolded a page of handwritten notes from my pocket. The top line recorded the casual city guard's salary I could earn when I became a sytheren, the lowest rank you could get at Sythe School. That would be temporary, while I studied to become the second rank, syther. There was savings estimates, then the exciting numbers; what I could earn as a syther working for Monster Containment and how much I'd need to put a deposit on a house in Orange Tree Hill, near Mum's brother Uncle Alan and my mate Glenn's houses. I might get to test these numbers in a year's time... It was a light in the dark, a dream, but now that I was going to Sythe School, hope of leaving Brock Heights and my father bubbled inside me.

The front door slammed shut.

I froze, listening for my father's footsteps as he stumbled down the hall. It was an old habit. He hadn't entered my room for a few years, not since the final time he hit me and I punched him square in the nose. I still remember his brown eyes widening in shock. He eyed me from head to toe, as if realising for the first time how tall I was at twelve years old. As if he'd forgotten I'd grown a lot over the last two years, since the last time he'd hit me before that. He'd left my room then and hadn't come back in since. But my habit of listening intently to where he was when he came home remained.

"Rarkin?" he slurred.

I frowned. He didn't talk to me much. He talked more to mum. But even they hadn't talked much in recent years.

I stood and opened my bedroom door. Couldn't hurt to see what he wanted. It was safer speaking to him when he was drunk. Like drink stripped away the effort he usually spent pretending whatever he was angry about was my fault.

"I wasn't sure you'd..." he trailed off as he stumbled forward, then leant on the doorframe of his bedroom door, looking up at me. "You did well son."

I gaped. Were those *tears* in his eyes? They couldn't be. He never cried. He never showed any feeling but discontent, or anger. How could he be...

He was already stumbling through his bedroom door, fumbling at the handle. Then it shut firmly behind him, probably because he was leaning against it to stay upright. How many drinks had he had? It was years since I'd seen him that drunk. I'd tell mum to make sure he stayed hydrated in the morning. Or should I get her now? Was he safe on his own, if he was drunk enough to say something he hadn't said about me in *years*?

Mum's door opened, and she took me by the arm and led me out the lounge door, to the dark patch of grass lined with the one flowerbed that was our backyard.

"He wanted to be a syther," mum said quietly.

I frowned. What did she mean? He thought the Syther Force was a waste of space... Besides, with how unreliable he was, how could he get any higher rank than sytheren?

"But he failed his medical. It was his bad leg. His father wouldn't let him see a healer until it was too late, and the bones had started healing a bit deformed."

His bad leg? He always seemed to walk fine to me. Though he stumbled more with his right leg when he was drunk. And he was always more inclined to hit me when he was unsteady on his feet when I was younger... unsteady but sober. Had he been concealing an old injury all this time? Why go to so much effort in front of your own son? Was that part of why he was a prick; because he was in constant pain?

But I was distracting myself from the main point. "How's he going to feel about me succeeding at something he can't do? When I never measured up to what he expected before, and now I'm outstripping *him*?"

Mum sighed and smiled sympathetically. "He'll find it hard. But I heard what he said to you and I think he means it."

"And he'll be pissed to have cracked like that in front of me when he's sober, won't he?" I asked, my jaw starting to clench again.

Finally, something was going to plan in my life. I'd taken a single step on my road out and he was going to sabotage it, like he had everything else.

"I don't think he'll remember."

I exhaled deeply through my nose, trying to loosen my jaw. Even if she was right, neither of us had done anything he might be that angry about since...

I was six, sitting in the passenger seat. Mum clutched the wheel convulsively, her eyes on the rear-view mirror as a neighbour's 'borrowed' car sped behind us. She pulled over, trembling. He wrenched us both out, shoved us in the back seat of the stolen car and drove us home so fast I was afraid we'd crash and die.

Mum hit the floor in her room. The wind knocked out of me as I hit my floor. I heard banging, drilling and then I couldn't open my door, for hours, all night, the next day. I was hungry, thirsty. I could hear him stomping across the lounge, smashing crockery, throwing things around. I shivered and felt sick, wondering what he'd do to me when it was my turn on the receiving end of his fury.

Could mum let me out? Could we take off until he calmed down? But it wasn't mum who let me out. I heard him groaning, then the metal clunking to the ground and my door swung open.

"Lunch is on the table. Eat before it gets cold."

It was him. The living room was clean, the decorative objects missing, likely smashed to bits. But he'd cleaned everything up. And mum was sitting at the table, a brittle smile on her face, one eye swollen half shut. I rushed to the bowl of soup beside her and started shovelling down mouthfuls so quick I was lucky it wasn't hot, or I'd have scalded myself.

I flinched at a thump on the table, but it was dad roughly setting down a glass of water.

"Have a drink. We'll go for a walk later."

Mum smiled at him again. I didn't stop shovelling down food, because I was hungry. But I was old enough to know it was over. He was back to behaving like nothing had happened. Like he always did. And no one ever said anything about it, or challenged him, because why end the peaceful period of pretending to be a functional, non-self destructive family, and return it to its normal state of abuse, any faster than his lack of self control would in the end?

I shivered, but not because the night air in our backyard was cold. My days of living in fear of, or actually being his punch bag were over. I was too big, and more importantly; too aggressive for that now. But words could be sharper than swords. And his yelling could drown out the noisiest motor carriage. You had to get in fast, and cut him down with your words before his words started cutting your feet out from under you.

"He's not a bad man Rarkin," Mum said. "He made the veranda into your room because he understands that I need space. He let me have my own room for the same reason."

I stared at her in disbelief. He did two decent things in his entire life that *weren't* apologies for his otherwise shitty behaviour and that balanced out the cowardly, abusive way he behaved the rest of the time?

Light shining through my bedroom window shone harshly on the premature lines of Mum's face and highlighted the premature grey in her lank brown hair. She was tired; worn down. And with those two tiny compromises, he'd got her to stay. He'd convinced her there was some good in him. But clinging to him was like grasping a life raft that spent half its time drowning you, when *it* wasn't relying on *you* keeping both of you afloat.

"He'll still pay your school fees," Mum assured me. "It won't be easy for him. He'll have to stop drinking for at least a month to get them paid on time."

I tried not to laugh out loud, because Mum was taking this seriously, but couldn't she see the irony of that? After fifteen years as a so-called parent, he finally had to crawl out of a bottle, take responsibility and do something with his life. He'd take it out on us, like he did everything else, but it was about bloody time he developed a capacity to deal with life and started acting like an adult. I'll have grey hairs by the time I'm twenty if he doesn't...

"I know he's hard on you Rarkin, but he tries. I need you to try too. It would be wonderful to get you through Sythe School."

My breath caught. She'd been afraid of Dad since we tried to leave that time when I was six, but I'd started talking about being a syther like Uncle Alan then, and I'd found more reasons to hold onto that dream since. She knew that, and she didn't earn much cleaning other people's houses on Orange Tree Hill; not enough to pay my school fees... was that partly why we still lived with Dad?

She looked at me, her eyes imploring.

"I'll try Mum."

I'd try not to give him what he deserved; if my only chance to become a sytheren and a syther, to get out of this household, this suburb, to anywhere else, even just for a day's work now and then, depended upon it. But I'd have to add school fees into my estimates, because there was no way he'd pay if I took off, especially if I took Mum with me. That made the dark tunnel ahead longer, the light at the end smaller, but Chaos himself couldn't make me let go.

I lay awake when I went to bed, long after I was certain Dad was asleep (and still breathing in his drunken stupor). He'd give up drinking for a while, resent me for having the opportunity he either blew or never got, making him worse than ever, and I'd have to shove that aside to focus on studying and passing my sytheren exams in six months' or a year's time; whichever I was ready for. What would that take? I decided to visit Glenn in the morning and ask him what the first year at Sythe School is like.

I woke up when it was still dark, feeling lousy, but sleep evaded me, so I had breakfast and started walking to Glenn's when the sun came up. The lady next door drove past with dark eyes and a drawn face, from working around kids only to reach retirement age and keep working, because her husband died before they paid back money lenders the cost of their house. Her neighbours were in bed, sleeping it off, but Lena was lifting her baby into her motor carriage, her toddler waving as he climbed in. I waved back. They'd be off to day-care while she worked, trying to earn rent and pay bills on her own.

It was Esiraday, last of the four work days before two days of Week's End. General School exams had given us an extra day off, and I intended to use mine learning about my future.

As I walked north, towards Orange Tree Hill, everything got better. Lawns were mown, there was no rubbish in yards and people filled in potholes in roads with dirt because they cared how they looked, even if City Government didn't. The people heading to work here looked tired but had hope in their eyes. Further north, nearer City Centre, things changed again. The roads were maintained, as were fences and gardens. Houses got bigger and nicer. Glenn's place had an open yard and a big veranda around the house, which I walked towards, intending to sit on the couch at the back until Glenn got up.

"Hello Rarkin," Glenn's father Dory said with a smile, as he shut the front door. He was dressed in sturdy clothes and a blacksmith's leather apron. Gear from a craft that survived the Nuclear War, and all the weapons it produced, until long after the remaining weapons were buried, or launched into the void beyond the sky. Dory was a survivor, just like his craft. I guess I was too.

Dory studied me, and I smiled. "Yeah, I got in."

Dory's smile widened, pride shining in his eyes. He'd been a syther, before his wife was abducted, when Glenn was two.

"So Glenn didn't follow my footsteps exactly, but you might?"

I couldn't help returning that wide faced, honest smile. It made me feel good all over.

"You might surprise yourself with what you achieve there," Dory said. "They'll recognise what you can do and give you the chance to do it."

That would be a change; I was used to teachers suspecting me of being behind every act of vandalism that occurred on school grounds. Just because I sprayed the message the P.E. teacher had coming, the one that prompted him to resign in embarrassment, didn't mean I was behind all of them. I smiled. Sythe School might be harder, but I hoped it would be better.

"Hey Rark!" Glenn called from the veranda.

Dory said goodbye and left for work, while Glenn came out and read my news off my face. He clapped me on the shoulder and led me towards the old couch at the back.

"You'll love Sythe School," he said. "City government will give you an electric-way pass to travel out the city, to the Sythe Castle."

That alone was a childhood fantasy, but anxiety gnawed at me.

"What do I have to know to pass sytheren studies?" I asked.

"History of War and Sorcery is compulsory," Glenn warned, confirming that I'd need to memorise facts to get anywhere, something I was terrible at. "Countering prejudice against magic-wielders and sorcerers has been a big deal in Sythe ever since the massacres the Sorcerer Purge caused a thousand years ago, but you'll find the rest easier; Zushai; weapon-less fighting and Monster Studies. And when you get up to syther studies; you'll learn to manipulate magic."

"*You* can craft magic?" I asked.

He smiled. "I can't say much yet; they're big on secrecy protocols to safeguard Sythe from ignorance, prejudice and fear, but yeah. Shadowers start learning it in our second year. But you have to get your sytheren rank before you can learn it. You know magic's a substance?"

I nodded. Stories described magic as floating clouds of raw power in the air of the Wild Zone, especially the Miaran Wild, where the continent's first people have lived for thousands of years.

"How can *you* wield magic *here*?" I asked.

"It's in everything; you, me, the air we breathe, the food and drink we consume. It's been around since the world began. The First Sorcery War happened because scholars in different kingdoms identified magic particles and experimented with them and magic use spread. Sythe Schools teach sythers to recognise magic too and that's halfway to using it."

So if I knew how, I could turn the air into a magical shield to block my father and the poison that normally spewed from his mouth these days? Chaos, I could probably make magic in the air pick him up and throw him out the window…

"Don't people discover how to use it themselves? By accident?" I asked.

"It takes powerful motivation to connect with magic the first time. Only sorcerers are likely to have a strong enough genetic connection to accidentally manipulate magic. Do you remember that stepfather who beat his kids the street over from yours, and how the kids were taken away by Social Welfare?"

I blinked. "One of the kids was a sorcerer?"

Glenn nodded. "The kid's teachers reported suspicions he was hitting them to Social Welfare, but as soon as he hit a kid with a belt; he caught fire. It takes extreme stuff to prompt kids to wield magic in obvious ways."

Darkness rose. My heart sped up and I was terrified. Glass shattered. I was falling, flailing. I turned in mid-air. Dad's eyes blazed behind falling shards of glass. Something surged in me. I reached out and ripped at him. He cried out as glass hit the ground.

I hit the ground. I turned. Dad gasped at a deep, bloody gash running across his forearms. Make it stop. Breathe. Push it away.

My heart raced. I reached to hold my wounded knees; but there was nothing wrong with them. I reached to stop the flow of blood from my left shoulder, from the cut it got when my body broke the window, but under my shirt were old scars. I was panting on an old couch, and Glenn sat beside me, watching with his mouth open.

"When?" he asked.

"I don't remember," I replied. "But when I got these," and I tugged the neck of my shirt over my shoulder, revealing faint scars from shattered glass.

Glenn shook his head.

"Trent warned me to watch for any sign of you wielding magic after that. He beat the life out of your Dad that night. Des and me had to drag him off to make him realise we were there. The gashes on your Dad's arms, that was you?"

"Do you think a broken window could cut like a knife moving sideways?" I asked critically.

"It had to have been," I added, hugging my knees. "Nothing else makes sense."

Glenn sighed.

"How did I…"

Glenn grimaced. "You probably caused the magic particles in his skin to rip it open. Magic particles are raw energy and nasty things happen when people who don't realise what they're doing defend themselves with magic. That's why the department pulls sorcerer-children at risk of abuse out of their homes."

"And the department only have enough funds to help sorcerer-kids, who might be a danger to others, not just *in* danger, like me?" I asked.

"You're too smart for your own good mate. You'd get enough evidence for Force Sythers to put away a few scumbags if you worked as a shadower, like me."

I shook my head. "I wanna get out of the city; go someplace else."

"You will, as a student, a sytheren, then a syther."

Niether of us commented on getting to the third rank; sythe. They were the elite. No one in these parts dreamed of getting that far. We didn't even know what sythes did. I didn't even share Glenn's confidence of making it to syther, but I'd seize my chance with everything I had.

Chapter 2

Sythe School

I had to wait a full four weeks of holidays for the MijoraDay that was first of the working week and my first day at Sythe School to arrive. Uncle Alan and I stepped onto a platform beside the electric-way, my route to Sythe School and out of Bellaria City. Metal tracks ran between houses, with a central wire suspended overhead and a shiny metal carriage rattled towards us. It halted, its doors sliding open. My body tingled with nerves as we boarded the contraption. We sat by a window and Uncle Alan nodded at people in green syther uniforms. I clenched my jaw as we glided forwards, gaining speed more rapidly than a motor carriage.

"How far does the Way go?" I asked Uncle Alan.

"To Terriah City, through the National Park and Wild Zones."

"Have *you* worked in the Wild Zone?"

"Yes. Its clearest landmarks are the Electric Way and the magical shield that arches over it. There are few settlements, all of them also shielded and built beside the Way. Beyond them, its just rivers, mountains -natural landmarks- and trails not used often enough to justify the expense of proper maintenance, so that's where Search and Rescue do a fair bit of our work, locating lost or stray wanderers, and escorting them back to safety."

I shook my head, as Bellaria City's ancient stone walls towered before us. Above them rose the multi colour sheen of a shield enchantment, a dome rising high above the city, to block magical and aerial attacks. It seemed strange, given the Farm Zone ringed the city, and even it was buffered by the National Park Zone, against the strange magics and powerful monsters that roamed the Wild. Did the city walls and shield enchantment pre-date the zones? Were they from a time when monsters were a direct threat to the city?

Ahead of us, in the city walls, a tunnel for the electric-way opened up. A booth in which city guards armed with stun guns waved to the driver as we glided past.

"Those blokes have a dull shift," Uncle Alan said. "Every entrance to the city is guarded, originally in case monsters got in, but now they're watching for smugglers dealing illegal goods, or traders avoiding city taxes, which rarely happens via the electric-way."

I blinked. "Is there still organised crime in Taros?"

Uncle Alan lowered his voice. "Sythe Bases have the upper hand when it comes to International Law Enforcement, but city-states the world over are too fragmented and under-resourced to eradicate organised crime. We have to watch out for monster smuggling from the Wild Zone or National Parks, though City-Government keeps it quiet."

I shook my head at my uncle working in a world I knew so little about. Then I turned to the window for my first look at the Inner Farm Zone. Paddocks stretched across hills for leagues. Sheep, cattle and horses grazed far from where monsters in the Wild Zone could smell or hunt them. More greenery than I'd ever seen stretched to every horizon.

We travelled longer than I thought Taros could be, stopping at platforms in Farm Zone towns to let passengers on or off. Then we glided into the Outer Farm Zone where crops, orchards, vegetables or vineyards grew in rows, forming a giant, colourful patch-work blanket spreading over rolling hills. Travelling through so much open space and greenery made me relax a little. It would be good to get out here four days a week.

"Nearly there," Uncle Alan said, gesturing at high stone walls and towers rising ahead.

Bellaria Sythe Castle's walls were as ancient as Bellaria City's, but had more modern repairs or extensions, as if they had suffered more damage, or come under attack more often. The electric-way ran through countryside opposite them, and a short road led from the platform to the castle gates. I stood as the carriage slowed, lifting my satchel onto my shoulder.

"Enjoy your first day Rarkin."

"Thanks Uncle Alan."

The doors opened. I stepped into a soft world of green, staring at the wide blue skies above, as I followed the road to the ancient castle walls. Towers flanked the open gates, with a bridge joining their tops. Beyond them, a woman peered out from the window of a brick booth, turning to study me as I approached.

"First day?" she asked.

Was I gawking that much? I nodded to her.

"Head into the office," she added. "They'll get you sorted."

"Thanks," I replied, following a path beside a modern asphalt driveway to a loop before the main entrance. Motor carriages parked along the loop, dropping off young, smartly dressed students, making me conscious of my patched denim pants and scuffed leather jacket. As if my scruffy clothes and hair didn't make me stand out enough, my wavy, overgrown auburn hair was multiple shades lighter than everyone else's brown or black, like a beacon of difference blowing in the wind.

A father turned from his daughter to frown at me. The girl's mother looked down her nose and I glared at them and turned away. Would my Trainers assume I was trouble too?

I turned onto an ancient stone path, worn smooth by thousands of students over centuries. It was hard to believe that

I was a student here now. Two older boys' mock fought beside the towers, skillfully avoiding contact. A third lounged against the wall, arms crossed, coolly surveying the scene. I smiled and the boy lounging against the wall flicked his chin in reply; my people were here too.

An office lady in the tower booth gave me a map, an introductory letter and my timetable. I entered a grand room with a high domed ceiling, two upper levels ending in graceful balconies overlooking large mosaics, a central fountain on the ground floor, and corridors branching off to different wings of the castle round it. Skylights shone through the dome, bordered with graceful white shapes outlined in gold; murin birds flying against a bright blue sky, symbolising peace and freedom. No-one had mentioned how beautiful this place was.

I compared my map to reality, then followed a mosaic path depicting sythers in uniforms from different periods of history. My walk took me over tile sythers wearing full bronze armour and long red or green silk capes, others in iron suits and more coloured capes, then steel suits of armour, then bullet proof vests over the brown uniforms for the Syther Force, dark green uniforms for Monster Containment, red for Healers, black for Military, white for Peace Keepers, yellow for Search and Rescue, orange for Foreign Aid and purple for sythers who worked at Sythe Bases doing whatever they did in secrecy. I was guessing sytherens were a modern, grunt rank, too recent and not important enough for art. And that even at Sythe

School, what high ranking sythes did wasn't common knowledge.

The mosaic ended before a grand spiral stone staircase in an alcove, which I climbed. Above, a message saying, *Welcome New Sytheren Students!* hung across open double doors, leading into a corridor.

Wooden desks with two chairs at each lined my classroom in four rows, a big old-fashioned whiteboard stood at the front and shelves full of books with worn covers lined both walls, depressingly like General School. I chose a desk in the back row and waited as my classmates filed in, with Taron tan or brown skin, black or brown eyes and some hazel, the single Siroan blonde and my auburn hair standing out, making me half wish I'd worn a hood.

Most of us had athletic builds, while five broadly built guys looked older than fifteen. Everyone else sat in pairs, introducing themselves if they sat next to a stranger, but eyes scanning the room for spare seats moved on when they saw me, and I had a desk to myself.

"Welcome to Sythe School everyone," our Trainer announced when we were seated. She was tall and slim, with brown hair, rare blue eyes and a sensible, delicate face that looked out of place in a trainer's pale blue uniform.

"My name is Trainer Lauran, and I will be teaching you History of War and Sorcery to begin with, then Monster Studies. You will learn self-defence and Zushai with Trainer

Sirona and weapons training with Trainer Dorthin next half semester, and I shall take you out for field training.

"At mid-year, those of you who are sixteen or over have your first opportunity to sit exams about your knowledge of common monsters, History of War and Sorcery and practical exams in self-defence, marksmanship and basic first aid. If the examiners are happy, you will become a sytheren. If not, or you do not turn sixteen until later, you can continue sytheren studies and sit your sytheren exams at the end of the year."

Six months till I could be tested on loads of content my brain wouldn't take in...

The lights dimmed, and an ancient mosaic was projected onto the whiteboard, depicting a young woman wearing a crown, surrounded by domed buildings.

"We will start our history with the Sorcery Wars," the Trainer continued, "because at the Second Sorcery War's end, Empress Teliph, depicted here, united secret sorcerer organisations in teaching young sorcerers at the world's first Sythe Schools, three-thousand-year-old examples of which are depicted in this image."

Sythe is *three thousand* years old?

Kids in front of me opened notebooks on their desks, took up pens and started making notes. I sighed, picking up my pen before I forgot the Empress' name. The Trainer went into detail about how the First Sorcery War brought on the First Dark Age, and caused world-wide hysteria and prejudice against sorcerers and had them all living in shame, fear and hiding until Teliph's predecessor, Emperor Nartzeer brought them out.

At that point, I realised that the solidly built, dark haired girl in front of me wasn't writing notes. She'd sketched the empress and labelled her, but that was all. I kept watching as the Trainer lectured. The girl drew, writing hardly anything, with poor spelling. It dawned on me that while I had no hope of remembering my notes during exams, this girl couldn't *take* notes. How would she remember anything?

She turned back and saw me staring. I flicked my chin at her and she smiled, her dark eyes gleaming. When the Trainer asked us to share our thoughts on the First Dark Age, she turned to me.

"Writing all the right letters in the right places for today's notes would take me a week," she said, "so I use pictures and key words to remember the meanings of the drawings."

"Why didn't I think of pictures?" I replied. "I nearly failed General School because all the sentences went straight through my head, but I couldn't draw to save my life. Yours are good."

"I'd draw and get you to do the writing, but you'd write too much and have to read it to me," she replied, her black eyes shining.

"You have trouble with reading too?" I asked. "How did you get through General School?"

"I got funding from the Education Department for talking books, a learning assistant who could scribe, and sat my exams in a separate room where teachers read exam questions and a device from Bellaria Sythe Base recorded my answers as I dictated them."

She told them what was wrong, and they helped. No one from Brock Heights asked for help. You didn't admit to weakness; someone might take advantage of you.

She looked at my notes, at long sentences sprawled across my page.

"Try using headings and just enough words to make sense," she suggested. "We can ask for print outs of the images the Trainer uses, and make notes on them too."

There was no way I was asking that pretty wallflower Trainer for help, but when the lesson ended, and I packed up and dawdled out, the girl came back to me and said, "Trainer Lauran will print out the history images for tomorrow."

Someone who didn't know me from a Serenan had tried to help me? I didn't want or like help; you had to deal with everything yourself, because it was just you lying awake in bed at night… and strangers never helped *me* off their own back.

"Thanks," I replied, avoiding her gaze.

"Do you spar?" she asked.

She was broadly built and toned, almost more muscled than me. "Yeah."

"Then let's check out the Practical Training Centre."

She led the way through ancient stone corridors, using her map. "You're not worried about sparring with a girl?" she asked.

"I learnt to spar with an older mate's girlfriend," I replied. "He's seven years older than me and not good at holding back, so he coached, and she sparred."

"Was she good?" the girl asked.

"Her family's of Mavin descent," I replied. "She's a Zushai master."

She smiled. "I'm Miona."

"Rarkin."

People stared, eyeing her with concern as we collected padded gloves and vests from hooks and moved onto a painted rectangle on the Sparring Room floor of the Practical Training Centre. The five broadly built guys from class were there too, two of them pausing their sparring match as we entered. The blonde raised his brows in surprise as Miona and I put on our gear. But the brunette sneered at me, as if he thought me fighting a girl made me beneath him, or some shit. I glared at him.

Then I turned back to Miona, tingling with anticipation, crouching, ready to strike or retreat in any direction. She smiled and swung for my stomach. I sidestepped. She jabbed at my head and I ducked and landed a partial blow on her hip. She smiled broadly.

She went for my head and I used an elbow to deflect her. Her left fist came at me. I got my right elbow up in time and my heart beat faster with excitement. Then her knee pressed my hip, as her arm pushed my right elbow. I overbalanced and hit the padded floor with a surprised laugh.

"Flattened by a girl!" The brunette called. "He's useless!"

My smile didn't entirely leave me face as I flashed him a glare.

Miona gave me a hand up. "Don't mind him," she said quietly. "Thinks he's a boxing champion, but he's a sore loser."

I tried to put him out of my mind and eyed her appraisingly. Then I smiled, deciding I could strike faster. I lunged at her hip, buzzing with the thrill of challenge. She sidestepped. I ducked a head blow from her right and walked into her left fist, which knocked the wind out of me, making me laugh and cough. She let me catch my breath.

I thought about it. Then I dived at her and tackled her to the ground. She burst out laughing as she slammed onto her back and I rolled sideways off her. I helped her up, as the brunette turned to spar with the blonde behind her, having lost interest in me. Good. This could be fun.

I was more careful in my next round with Miona, conscious of not giving her an opening. I stayed on my feet for a fraction of a bell before she knocked me down. The brunette was smirking again, but his blond mate muttered, "Leave it Chareck."

Apparently I'd need to keep an eye on him. He seemed to be a smug, bullying prick.

Miona's hand clasped mine as she levered me to my feet, focusing my attention back on her. I smiled. She wasn't quite as strong as Tak, but I suspected she had the skill to give even him a run for his money.

"You're holding back," I said.

"I learnt to spar with a retired professional," she replied.

"Why did you want to learn?" I asked.

"I saw him practising against imaginary opponents when I brought morning tea to our farmhands, and I liked the grace and control. Our farm was in the Outer Farm Zone, where garls burrowed into it occasionally. I saw Monster Containment in action and knew I wanted to be a syther, so he offered to coach me."

We sparred some more after that, then went from lunch to Self-defence. Our self defence trainer was a thin woman of medium height, who paced the room gracefully.

"This lesson will become Zushai, the art of weapon-less fighting, a contrary descriptor, because in Zushai, your entire body becomes a weapon. But before you learn to use it, you must know how to defend yourselves. Who has sparring or professional fighting experience?"

Miona raised her hand, and I tentatively did the same, as did half the class.

"Before we begin, Training Centre Rules, violation of which may see you expelled. Excessive use of force and excessive aggression are serious offences. Your rules for this stage of training are; do not attack until your partner is ready. Do not hit them as hard or as fast as you can. Do not hit them repeatedly without pause. Always wear protective gloves and padded vests when sparring and attack *only* with your hands. Use of feet, knees, elbows and of course; head butting is strictly prohibited at this stage.

"First; we will build competence and confidence as we get to know each other. Then we will work towards stances and skills for ending brawls, domestic violence or in riot situations, any of which you may face as a sytheren city guard, a Syther Force syther or either rank in the Military."

Again, no mention of sythes. Did they use magic instead?

When Trainer Sirona finished her demonstrations, Miona and I practiced together. We moved gradually, for a few moments. But we *were* getting to know each other, and were confident and competent, so we pushed each other. Other pairs stared at the loud smack of her gloves against my forearms. Her blows landed hard, but not with all her strength, from my left, then my right. I stepped to counter her angle of attack, shifting elbows and forearms to meet her fists better.

Instructor Sirona's whistle blew. "Everyone sit before Rarkin and Miona's space," she said. "I want you to pay attention to the way Rarkin moves his arms to counter Miona's attacks. This is what I expect you all to do once you are experienced. Can you two demonstrate?"

I gaped. No teacher ever asked me to demonstrate anything. I was useless at school… Chareck rolled his eyes and crossed his arms, not bothering to move any closer, unlike most of my classmates, who gathered round us to watch.

Miona smiled and moved into position opposite me. My heart beat faster, muscles tensing slightly, and I drew a deep breath, feeling the pressure of many eyes watching.

I was tense and stiff at first, so Miona backed off. Then I breathed more easily, as it started to sink in that I could trust this opponent. Miona saw my comfort and she pressed me, striking harder, faster, from different angles. I braced, shifting forearms and elbows to block and took small steps, faster and faster. We danced around our fighting space in a flurry of blocked blows and footsteps, muscles tight, covered in a sheen of sweat, breathless and smiling at each other. I'd never felt so safely pushed to my limits and I enjoyed it immensely.

Trainer Sirona smiled, thanked us, then turned to the class saying, "Do not worry."

My flare of joy retreated, and my expression became guarded as I registered our class staring. Several kids looked nervously away when I met their eyes, and my mouth became a firm line as I slouched with arms loosely crossed, sizing up my class. They were amazed, not just by Miona's fighting ability, but at my defences.

And I made them all nervous. Wonderful; not only was I going to have to remember a bunch of facts to pass exams; I'd have to do it while trying not to unintentionally scare soft classmates. Shouldn't potential sytherens have more guts than this? You could join the military and hypothetically go to war as a sytheren! Sure, you could also become a city guard and weren't likely to have arrest people or combat monsters till syther rank, but city guard deal with all sorts, who were usually doing the wrong thing. Sytherens needed guts too.

Well, not quite all my class were nervous. The blond was eyeing me appraisingly. Chareck was glaring at me, standing with his arms crossed, an expensive gold watch on his wrist reflecting daylight from a skylight overhead. I noticed the tailored cut of his shirt then. The smart, polished leather shoes. He was some snobby rich kid, probably from a five bedroom house in Lakeside, or an apartment in ritzy Greenhill, a suburb of modern, Nuclear Age glass, metal and timber mansions, with riverside views, near City Centre. And he was offended someone as scruffy looking as me could be good at anything. When would I get to spar with him?

"How long have you two been sparring?" the Trainer asked Miona and I.

I blinked, realising the other kids were attacking or blocking their partners in their fighting spaces again, the blond swinging for Chareck, who side stepped.

"Five years," Miona replied.

The Trainer turned to me and I decided to pretend Trent was the beginning and my training had been consistent and replied, "Eight."

The Trainer nodded, believing the lie. Did I look that good? Sure; Trent and Sasha taught me fortnightly for eight months, and both gave me more lessons after they split up, but Miona had had proper, regular coaching. I'd had nothing but real practice against Dad without guidance, for years. How could *I* be *good*?

"Can I see you attack?" Trainer Sirona asked me.

I nodded. Miona kept her arms and elbows raised, her fists above her head, in the basic defensive stance we were 'learning'. I swung, and Miona's elbows jerked, countering blows. I struck her left. She punched with her right and I blocked instinctively with my left. I continued my attack, faster, alternating sides, trying not to let her get a blow in and she smiled, watching and defending carefully.

"Excellent," said Trainer Sirona. "I will start you on new techniques in an accelerated group after I model for the class each day."

I stared, as she went to give feedback to other pairs.

"People don't tell you you're good at things, do they?" Miona asked, and I shook my head.

"I didn't get it much at General School either," she added. "We'll have to get used to it."

The lesson ended on a high, dampened slightly by kids avoiding my gaze as we left the room, aside from the kid with fine black dreadlocks and a big goofy smile, who flashed me a nervous grin as I moved past. I was distracted by trying not to let the others averted gazes get to me, so I didn't pull away from the unexpected eye contact from that pair of big warm eyes, like I normally would. His smile and tawny skin were warm too. Like a ray of sunlight.

Now it was me avoiding looking at people, as Miona and I walked down the corridor. Not that I normally looked at people's faces anyway, because too often that became eye contact. It was bad enough they had to see me at all. So having a stranger look right at me and smile like that, such a welcoming face on someone I didn't even know, was unnerving.

Miona and I said goodbye at the driveway loop, where our classmates got into motor carriages and cheerful family members inquired about their day. I didn't feel bitter about that. I was happier than I'd been in a long time, because Miona made me feel accepted.

My happy glow lasted the whole rapid, strange-motion electric-way ride back to Brock Heights. Only when I stepped out of the carriage and walked past run-down houses did my face harden, muscles tautening slightly, and I walked tall, strutting in the confident manner that told petty thieves to go jump someone else.

I got home after Dad, now he's back earlier from not going to the pub. He was sitting in the lounge watching a nara match on our small screen. He glanced at me.

"Long day. You gonna work hard at this?" he growled.

"Yeah," I replied.

"Gonna make sure you pass your exams?"

"Yeah. I thought about how to study."

He blinked, then nodded. "Good."

I heard the dismissal and put my satchel in my room, while Mum came out to ask about my day and heat my dinner. My first day of school and at home passed without unpleasantness.

* * *

In our first class the next day, Miona moved to the vacant desk beside mine. Trainer Lauran gave us printouts of images from her lectures and under Miona's guidance I relaxed a bit, and figured out how to take notes I had a hope of remembering. I kept sparring with her and met and sparred with her girlfriend Merin too, but mostly; we studied.

Our history lessons skimmed over Old Empires and collapses, and the Monster Wars on Taros, then moved into the colonial era. The Trainer showed us photos of serpentine paintings; the Sorcery Purge in which Naydah tried to throw off Siroan colonialism by breeding an army of creatures that could paralyse sorcerer's abilities to wield magic. Puritan priests encouraged it, conservative politicians reinforced it and the Sorcery Purge swept Siro, stopping hundreds of sorcerers from using their powers with a monster's bite, a bite that was often also fatal. That was over a thousand years ago, but it made it clear I'm not the only person who gets a raw deal because of who they are.

Religious extremism lasted until deadly plague ripped through populations devoid of sorcerers, but was defeated where sorcerers skilled in healing had been sheltered or tolerated. Many claimed the Gods were punishing zealots for their extremism and called for moderation. Others pointed to the alliance of religious extremists and political leaders, and claimed religion had been hijacked, the results had been deadly and the Gods had done nothing to stop it. Were the Gods too weak to deal with humanity? Or did they fail to act because they didn't exist?

Organised religion lost credibility, allowing the Scientific, Artistic, Industrial and Technological Revolutions to kick off, in an age of enlightenment. If only there was a way to end prejudice against Brock Heights like that...

But the Modern Age wasn't a paradise of peace, wisdom and knowledge, like it pretended for decades. It was an age of colonial exploitation and ruthless nationalism, with powerful countries of the former Siroan Empire and the Mavisian Empire taking what they wanted anywhere in the world, and inventing religious, social, political or pseudo-scientific justifications after the fact.

Siro invaded what's now Taros. Bellaria City area was inhabited by Serenan's back then, tall and strong, green skinned people who evolved from a different ancestor. The arrogant Siroans decided the Seranan's were 'savages' and drove the Serenans off their land and enslaved them. Then the Siroans seized most of what's now my continent of Taros from the native humans, the black eyed Miarans, upsetting Miaran management of native wildlife, monsters and magical creatures, and drove the Miarans north. Which was stupid, because the Miarans knew how to manage some dangerous magical sites, which killed off quite a few colonists before Sythe took over management.

The Siroans, blond haired, blue eyed, porcelain skinned people, had their heads pretty far up their arses. But they screwed up, and imported too much 'cheap labour' from New Tarlah and East Timbala, until brown skinned people outnumbered white ones in Taros. The Taron Workers Uprising overthrew Siroan political and racial rule in Taros, and the least racist Siroan settlers intermarried with New Tarlahns and

44

Timbalas for self preservation, and white people, formerly greatly outnumbered, were almost bred out.

Then the arrogance of the age came to a head. The former Siroan Empire united in the Siro Block against Mavis, the largest surviving chunk of the Mavisian Empire. Their rivalry went head to head at the dawn of the Nuclear Age, as airships and powerful explosives developed. The Trainer showed us modern photos of giant piles of match wood; Siroan and Mavisian cities, coastlines bombed by bomber airships in the early phase of the Nuclear War. Then we saw photos from void-ships, which could fly through the void between our planet and its moons, showing crater trails where industrial electric-way lines were destroyed, over hundreds of leagues.

Then came the greatest tragedy, the Nuclear Holocaust; photos of swathes of an entire island nation of blacked-out, cratered nothing, obliterated as Mavis and the Siro Bloc raced to place nuclear weapons that could threaten each other's continents on it. Mavis finished first and the Siro Bloc panicked and detonated a nuclear bomb, opting to wipe out one whole island instead of risking half its continent.

The next images were photos of debris far inland; the aftermath of the tidal waves triggered by the nuclear bombing, which damaged the coastlines of both continents even further. By the end of the Nuclear War, electric-ways the world over were severely damaged or obliterated. Surviving airships had been bombed by rogue governments or peace activists. The remaining nuclear weapons had been launched on a trajectory with a void-star, which would consume them. And the greatest international age the world had ever known ended with the collapse of nations into isolated city-states, paranoid of conflict. It took a hundred and fifty years to rebuild basic infrastructure, Mavis taking two centuries to come off war-rations.

Now, four hundred years after the Nuclear War, city-states no longer live in terror of provoking each other into mutual destruction, but people are happy in small communities, and only International Sythe, organised crime and merchants have the resources and will for international relations. The Serenans keep to themselves in their own little country, the Miarans are fairly reclusive too, and our Age is the Age of Peace. The world looks so safe that beyond the Syther Force, Healers, Search and Rescue and Monster Containment, I can't see a need for Sythe. What do sythes, Sythe Bases, Foreign Aid or International Peacekeeping *do*?

I wondered if there were things City Government wasn't telling us, beyond what Uncle Alan had already implied. Things deliberately left off our curriculum. But I didn't get much chance to think about it, because Dad lost it.

Chapter 3

The Red Visor

For four weeks, Dad got up after I left in the morning and didn't come back till I'd had dinner and gone to my room. At Week's End he ignored me, making small talk with Mum and sweating, his hands shaking. I treasured every day of learning, training and returning to his absence. Though my habit of listening for his footsteps beyond my door intensified, because I knew the peace of his voice not blasting through the house wouldn't last.

The day came when my walk home became a run, because Dad was yelling; "I work hard all day and I come home, and dinner isn't even cooked! I don't care what trouble Lizzy's having —that's *her* problem! *You* should be looking after the person who provides for you; stupid woman!"

My temper flared, and my muscles tautened as I burst into the lounge room. Mum stood in the kitchen by the chopping board, shaking. Dad stood several feet away, red-faced, yelling at the top of his lungs, without a care for the wounded look in Mum's eyes.

"You want dinner?" I asked. "Why don't you cook it yourself? Or maybe you could try not terrorising Mum, so she can focus on cooking," I added, realising I'd gone too far.

Too late. The red visor came down and within seconds Dad crossed the room and bore down on me in silent, red-faced fury. I dodged, but he didn't hit me. He reached for my throat. His right hand bumped my neck and he seized it with both hands. I stumbled, and my head cracked against the front wall, blurring my vision. Thumbs pressed into my windpipe, cutting off air.

Hatred smoldered in his eyes, a foot from mine. I couldn't breathe.

I channelled my panic into my fist and punched his nose as hard as I could. My knuckles seared with pain, his nose snapped, bled; but he didn't let go. I punched his nose again, with less force. He kept squeezing, his angry eyes burning into mine, beyond black spots. I felt dizzy.

"You let him go!" Mum said quietly. "You let him go, now!"

She crossed the room, brandishing a knife with a shaking hand.

He didn't acknowledge her.

I was going to pass out...or die. A roar built inside me, a surge of protest and power. I seized it, desperate to hit him so

I could breathe. Dad cried out, letting me go. His eyes widened in shock, and he shuddered and stepped back.

I sucked in air, my lungs filling gloriously. What had I done?

I doubled over. Pain burst through my stomach, as his fist collided with it, and again. I gasped, dazed. The door creaked open. Dad froze, fist raised. His anger-crazed eyes widened. Trent stood tall before our front door, cold blue eyes burning with hatred, his pale, scarred face menacing.

On his left, the knife shook in mum's hand. Dad spotted it and trembled. Then he wrenched his gaze back to Trent. "*You*! Get out of my house!" Dad yelled.

Trent's lips twitched, as he met Dad's eyes and stepped towards him, his face asking mockingly what Dad planned to do when he reached him. Dad gasped, backing up. Trent smiled coldly, taking another step. Dad cried out and stumbled for the lounge door. He ran through it, leaving it open and took off down the street. Trent smirked, his eyes feral.

This scene was familiar... Trent had walked in before... I was on the ground, screaming, my arm bursting with pain.

I flinched away from the pain, not wanting to know what Dad had done to make me scream like that... Trent had dived across the room with a snarl, tackled Dad to the ground and beat the lights out of him.

Mum's gasp made me pull myself back to the present. She stood frozen, her knife outstretched, staring at Trent, who nodded tensely at the knife.

"You can put that down now," he said levelly.

She was in shock...confused...

"It's alright Mum," I croaked. "Trent's not gonna hurt us."

Mum walked towards the kitchen taking short breaths, and laid the knife next to her half-chopped vegetables. I glimpsed pain in Trent's eyes. Mum gasped, as Trent turned suddenly. He walked out the front door, closing it behind him, and stood with his back to us, keeping watch on our front lawn.

"I... I didn't mean to threaten him," Mum said, eyeing Trent worriedly through the front window.

I groaned. "He's waiting outside because he knows he makes you uncomfortable."

She eyed him worriedly.

"Mum; Trent bashed some bloke once because he saw him hit his girlfriend in her front yard. He hits *men* who hit women or kids because he despises *them*."

"I know he means well," she said, "But he's so cold."

She blinked, then saw pain in my eyes. She knew I thought the world of Trent. He was the only person who could eye-ball Dad with fearless contempt. He made Dad shat himself and I loved him for it.

Mum gasped, and her hand came up to her mouth. I turned to study my reflection in the mirror over our fireplace. Red patches around my neck were darkening into nasty bruising.

Tears pooled in Mum's eyes.

"It's alright Mum," I said, walking forwards to hug her, not realising I was trembling until my body touched hers, so I held her tighter to make it stop. "I'm ok," I said. "I'm ok."

Maybe if I kept saying that my heart would stop racing and it would come true.

"He saw the knife," she said, voice cracking. "He'll feel so betrayed. His stepmother was always threatening him, and I promised myself I never would. He still has scars from them, his stepmother and his father, *all over* his back. I wanted to help him move away from that. I didn't want to cause him more pain. But I failed to protect *you* and now he..." she broke off, trembling.

I stood woodenly, my arms still around her. She hadn't used force or threats to protect me for fear of hurting *him*; for ten years...

"He saw the knife when he turned away from Trent," she added. "If Trent hadn't come, I might have had to use it..."

Mum broke off, sobbing into my chest. I couldn't stop shaking. He *wasn't* going to stop. But she'd found the courage to approach him with a knife in hand... *I'd* never threatened him with a weapon; I feared he'd get it off me and attack *me* with it.

I hugged her tighter. My eyes stung, and I rubbed the tears away with my sleeve.

But my mind wouldn't let me off that easily. Because I knew it hadn't just been Trent. I'd done something. Dad had stepped back before Trent came.

I trembled and pushed the memories away, squashing them down, until I breathed normally and managed to stop shaking. I had more trouble unclenching my jaw, which was trying to lock itself shut.

"Let's go to Uncle Alan's. I'll pack for you," Mum said, stepping back and looking through the front window.

I wasn't sure if Trent was still standing there to guard us, or if he was waiting to speak to me. I took a nervous breath and stepped outside. Trent turned immediately, hyper aware of his surroundings. But Trent was always like that.

"Des called me," he said quietly, his blue eyes hard but concerned. "He heard raised voices and wasn't sure you were home. I thought your old man might get worse now you're going places. I don't know if you remember, but you've used magic against him before. I worried you might do it again."

Trent was Glenn's older adopted brother. Dory got him off the streets, but they couldn't tell him anything about magic because he'd never get into Sythe School with his record. There was no *legal* reason for him to know anything about wielding magic.

"What happened?" Trent asked.

"He strangled me. I couldn't punch him off. He ignored Mum. I lashed out with...something. Trying to cause him pain, so he didn't kill me."

"You know which magic you wielded?"

I shivered and shook my head.

"Fire magic. His shirt was singed."

I drew a deep breath and realised I was gasping for air. Then Cam was running across his lawn opposite us and Des walked out, his brows furrowed with concern. Cam stopped short, staring at the bruises on my neck. I gasped in surprise, as Cam flung his arms around me.

"You drove him off?" Des asked Trent.

Trent smirked. "He won't sleep a wink tonight."

Des's expression tightened.

"He strangled you," Cam said, stepping back, his breathing too quick, as he examined the marks on my neck. "He tried to kill you," he added, teary-eyed.

Des' mouth dropped open. Trent's eyes blazed, his fists clenching until blunt nails drew blood from his palms.

Des rushed forwards, putting a gentle arm around Cam and eyeing me worriedly, his gaze flashing from my neck to my face. We both hesitated. Trent doesn't like affection. But he was staring pointedly away. And I'd had as much as I could take. I let my head fall on Des' broad shoulder and he hugged Cam and I both.

"You going to your uncle's?" Trent asked, his gaze fixed on the distance.

"Yeah," I replied.

"When you come back, call me if he gives you trouble."

"Thanks Trent," I replied.

Trent nodded to Des's house, then walked off down the street, towards the most rundown end of Brock Heights.

Cam, Des and I stepped apart. Cam eyed me with worry, then the bruising on my neck. He seemed to think Trent wanted to know if I was in trouble, in case Dad tried to kill me again. But Des' worried gaze said it was because Trent didn't want me wielding magic in self-defence. That could end my career in Sythe before it began, and Trent must know it.

I tried to hold onto that thought. Being expelled because I attacked my father with magic was a nightmare, but it was more pleasant than the idea that my father had just tried to kill me.

My eyes burned at his hate-filled glare in my mind's eye, his hands crushing my windpipe as I failed to breathe. I knew he thought I was trouble. I got into occasional fights at General School, got average grades at best and knew I disappointed him. But the thing about having a father is that you're supposed to care about each other. Chaos; you're supposed to love each other. Most of the time, he barely showed it. I knew he didn't know how, not even with Mum.

Part of me, no matter how awful he was sometimes or how much I hated him, part of me *wanted* my dad to care about me. And he wanted me dead…

I stomped down the hurt before it got too much, keeping my shoulders straight and tried to smooth the emotions raging through my body from my face, so Cam and Mum didn't worry. I made my expression hard, unblinking, feeling Cam's worried gaze.

Then Mum stepped through the front door with my bursting school satchel and her own ancient satchel slung over her shoulders; the only overnight bags we had.

"If he gives you trouble like that again, stay with us, at least for the night," Des said quietly, placing a hand on my shoulder. "I know you worry what he'd do to her if you weren't around but…"

But he didn't want me dying protecting her. Cam's eyes pleaded the same request, but if I left her alone with him when he was like *that*…

Des and Cam squeezed one of my shoulders each and nodded to Mum, who smiled at them, then they crossed the road to their house, where a worried Ma Tully stood watching from the front window.

Mum passed me my satchel, eyeing me with a pained, hesitant look. There was a high-collared jacket on top of the clothes. It was getting dark and cool; but did she want me to hide the bruising around my neck from Uncle Alan? He'd want us to go to the Syther Station... if Dad found out... I shivered and stopped to put on the jacket.

Uncle Alan's place had a veranda at the front like Glenn's. He and Aunt Lil didn't have kids, but their big, long-furred dog Deevy rushed to greet us at the door. Uncle Alan came next, with the same prematurely lined face as Mum's, the same premature greys in his light brown hair.

What Mum said about Dad's stepmother... Mum and Uncle Alan hadn't had it any easier, had they? I shuddered, as fear and darkness rose in me and I pushed reflexively against them.

There was sadness and sympathy in Uncle Alan's eyes and he looked tired. He knew why we were here. Aunt Lil brought us into the lounge and made hot drinks from soothing herbs, and no one asked questions about why we weren't staying at home. No one wanted to talk about it. They didn't know this time was worse than usual, and while Mum glanced at me in a way that said I could tell them if I wanted; I didn't want to say the words, "Dad tried to kill me," and I didn't want her to say them either. Saying it made it real.

"Tell us about Sythe School," Aunt Lil asked warmly.

I talked about how Trainer Sirona was teaching Miona and I Zushai and a bit about the Nuclear War, but it seemed dim and distant, like things I'd done or heard five years ago. Aunt

Lil and Uncle Alan smiled about Miona, Mum began listening properly and I realised they were getting the wrong impression, thinking I'd found a girlfriend. Insane, I thought tiredly.

It was best to keep everyone back. Once you let people in, you couldn't get them out and it hurt too much; the lesson of Mum and Dad's marriage. I wasn't letting anyone else in and I wasn't inflicting myself on anyone else. I'd stay single, like Trent.

Chapter 4

The Headmaster

The uncertainty of Dad dragged. I caught guilt on Mum's face when she didn't realise I was watching. She worried she'd wounded Dad, given him a dose of his own medicine and he couldn't take it. We spent both days of Week's End at Uncle Alan's and there were no questions about how long we were staying. Aunt Lil assumed she was shopping for us when she bought groceries and Uncle Alan assumed he was cooking for four each night, until Mum told them different, so she didn't feel pressured.

On the third day, Mijoraday, I waited outside Trainer Lauran's room, my eyes unfocused, my limbs heavy as lead, because I'd spent most of the night awake. Coming to school was wonderful. I didn't want to go back to Uncle Alan's, to everyone not talking about what had happened, or wondering when we'd go home and have to face dad. More than ever, I wanted to stay at school.

I barely noticed anyone else until Miona arrived. I was leaning against the wall dozing when she nodded, and I nodded back. Her gaze was questioning.

"My father's a manipulative, abusive prick," I told her, too tired to censor my words. "The only way to be in our house is victim or perpetrator, and I don't wanna be either."

She eyed me intently, unsurprised, but concerned. "Your Mum's too scared to leave or to kick him out and he won't go?"

I nodded.

"And if *you* packed your bags?"

I blinked. If I walked out, would Mum come too?

"I worry she'd stay."

"Have you asked her?"

I shook my head. "I suspect she and Uncle Alan argued about it for years. She won't listen."

"There's got to be another way," Miona replied. "Social Welfare have allowances."

"She always ends up back with him," I replied. "And he'd drink the allowance money. My mate Cam's drunken father did that all the time. Until Ma Tully chucked him out because he failed to keep his promises to spend time with his boys. I thought Cam had it easier; because at least he had hope of his father being better. I had nothing to hope for until I got into Sythe School, but now I don't know what to do about Dad. Or how to get through school."

Miona sighed. "I can think of something, but you'll hate it."

I frowned at her.

She smiled. "You remind me of my Mum. She's in a wheelchair. Her spine got broken in an accident on our farm two years ago and she refused to let anyone help her do anything. She kept trying to reach and lift things from her chair and risking falling out, dropping things on herself or breaking more bones.

"Dad pleaded with her to let him help and she didn't listen. Until I burst into the room and ordered her to stop risking injuring herself. I also told Dad he'd have to settle for letting her do things that didn't risk injury, even if it took her so long to make a cup of tea that it got cold, because she was too stubborn to do any less."

Miona *told* her parents what to do? I was interested, despite my exhaustion. "How did they respond?"

"Mum laughed. Dad laughed till he cried. Mum knew I have a stubborn streak like hers and she decided it was best not to go head-to-head with me. Dad hovered a bit the next time she shifted boxes, checking she wasn't risking her safety, then backed off and trusted her not to endanger herself. He patiently accepted that it took her forever to get dressed each morning and undressed at night. Mum let either of us or other staffers lift heavy crates or things she couldn't reach, on shelves in the cool store they bought because she couldn't farm anymore, and she stopped risking her safety to do everything herself.

"You can't do *everything* yourself Rarkin. Every test I've taken at school with written questions a teacher reads to me, and where I dictate answers to a machine reminds me of that, and so do the things Dad and I have to help Mum with now she's in her chair."

"I *hate* needing people," I replied. "It works terribly with needing my family."

"I couldn't stand by and watch my mother attempt to do things that got her nowhere or risked hurting her, and I'd rather not do that with you," Miona replied.

She didn't want to push me, but she didn't like seeing me stuck. I respected her for that.

Trainer Lauran arrived, and the lesson was ok. I zoned out, too overwhelmed to follow the words of my favourite distraction from my screwed-up home life, and slept through half the lesson.

Miona woke me when it was time to leave and drew me a copy of her notes in the library at lunch. She insisted on sitting on a comfortable couch in the corner where I fell asleep again, as she intended. She woke me in time to eat before Self-defence and I felt better, but Self-defence was a fiasco.

"You have had plenty of time to become familiar with training partners of your choosing," Trainer Sirona said, as we stood in our usual room in the Practical Training Centre, with gloves and padded vests on. "Now that everyone has built confidence and our core strength building exercises are going well, I will choose your training partners sometimes, starting today."

She paired us off and several kids shot me uneasy glances, but Trainer Sirona paired me with someone I assume she thought would be confident facing me; Chareck. Just what I needed, for my life to get *more* interesting.

Chareck leered at me as we stepped into a fighting space on the padded floor. "No knives your type fancy here," he said quietly. "You don't stand a chance."

I blinked. He wanted to *provoke* me? *Today*?

"Nice knowing you," he said mockingly.

I almost smiled. Then he swung at me. Instinct kicked in. I side-stepped, punching him solidly in the guts, then wheeled to face him. With gloves and a padded vest, the blow did little more than surprise him. His mouth thinned.

"Eight years fighting training?" he asked contemptuously. "You couldn't afford the sole of my shoe. You're a street fighter who practices by jumping people. I've been Greenhill's under sixteen Spar Champ for three years; let me show you how civilised people do it."

For a moment I was stunned anyone with enough brains to get into Sythe School would be suicidal enough to goad me like that. Then he came at me with both fists. I caught bruising blows on both forearms and kicked him back.

"Rarkin!" the Trainer protested.

Chareck roared and lunged. I sidestepped, blocked a punch with my right and sunk my left into his stomach, then danced aside.

"Chareck!"

He was turning, both fists flying at me again. He was big, strong and intended to pound me until he won. Good luck.

I ducked a high blow and danced back from a low blow aimed at my retreat. Miona stepped beside me, fists casually raised, shooting Chareck a warning glare.

"Need a *woman* to defend you Rarkin?" he mocked. "A he-she at that! A samer! What's *wrong* with this place?"

He was a true 'me and my way are right and everyone else is wrong' kind of bastard. I wanted to pound him into the ground, but Miona reacted faster.

"Is Sythe School more than your tiny mind can handle?" she asked him bitingly.

My heart skipped a surprised beat. Chareck flushed and his eyes blazed, but the Trainer reached us before he could reply.

"Enough," she said firmly, stepping beside us. "Chareck; you are until further notice banned from my classes. I have no tolerance for blatant discrimination. Leave your gloves behind you and make your way to Headmaster Zatrack's office, where you can make your case for continuing to study at Sythe School."

"*I* have to make *my* case?" he practically shouted, his voice cutting through an otherwise silent room, in which everyone stood frozen, staring at him.

"Sythe does not foster bullying, hostility, prejudice or discrimination of any kind. We exist to oppose them; to enforce *universal respect*. Which means your personal beliefs are in direct contradiction of our mandate and you currently have no place in our ranks. Consider that before your first words to Headmaster Zatrack prompt your immediate expulsion."

"I'm *not* putting up with this!" Chareck roared.

He flung his gloves and vest on the floor and stomped out.

How did a prejudiced prick who threw toddler tantrums get into Sythe School? His friends seemed taken aback, averting their eyes as he stormed past. The blond even eyed us guiltily...

My awareness switched to Miona's solid presence. This was the first time someone had stood beside me while someone else attacked me. Somehow, it was more reassuring than Trent chasing my father out...because we faced Chareck *together*.

"Thanks," I said.

She eyed me curiously, then smiled.

"Sorry," I added. "He had no right to speak to you like that."

I looked down, unable to even look at her as I spoke, because she'd copped that abuse because she defended *me*.

"Do you think I haven't heard those comments before?" she asked, and I looked up again. "I was nine the first time someone called me a he-she at my sparring club and it wasn't just boys; sometimes it was their fathers. Dad told me some men can't handle women being better or good at things some people expect men to be better at. Couple that with the fact I date girls instead of boys...

"Dad said it bruised fragile egos at my sparring club and that men with fragile egos tend to lash out in misguided, futile attempts to protect their egos, but not to let that hold me back. Mum told me that the boys or fathers who made nastier comments might struggle to accept that I'm a skilled fighter *and* more intelligent than they are; which is certainly Chareck's problem."

I eyed her with wonder. Chareck's comments didn't wound or make her angry. She didn't hold the fact he was an arrogant, prejudiced, tiny-minded bastard against him, she just accepted he had issues; whereas I wondered how many blows without padded gloves were necessary to knock sense into him...

"You don't mind having a girl come to your aid?" she asked.

I thought about it. "The boys might tease me. ...I could always... ask you to get them to lay off?"

I smiled, meeting her gaze, while she laughed.

"You don't mind that I'm... more skilled than you are?" she pressed.

"Honestly," I replied, "I think *everyone* should be able to hold their own because *anyone* can become a victim."

I paused, seeing Trainer Sirona walking towards us.

"You realise you used excessive aggression as well Rarkin?" she asked.

I blinked, then shrugged. "There wasn't much point facing him with anything less."

"You could have walked away."

"And turn my back on a gorilla throwing a temper tantrum?" I asked.

"Were you angry at him?"

"After what he *said*? Furious."

"Yet you didn't lash out?"

"I fight them when they come at me. I stand my ground. I'm not a piece of scum like him," or my father, not that I was telling her that.

"Headmaster Zatrack wishes to speak to you," the Trainer added, cutting into my thoughts. "With Chareck's behaviour as appalling as it was, and your attacks being only defensive in nature, you may have evaded serious disciplinary action, but your aggression may have consequences."

I frowned. My actions were appropriate and necessary but *not* ok? Did Sythe take their principles *that* seriously?

"The Head's offices are directly above the main office on this floor," the Trainer continued. "The headmaster is still speaking to Chareck, but his secretary will tell you where to wait."

I nodded and strode out, stuffing nerves down and approaching a directory on the corridor wall. It displayed four Heads offices two corridors down.

I walked quickly, trying to stuff down thoughts of how serious being sent to a Head was, until I turned into a quiet corridor with secretaries sitting behind desks on both sides. A young male secretary motioned me to a seat beside his desk, which had an entrance labelled *Zatrack Adorphis*; *Head of Sytheren and Syther Students,* behind it.

I sat, and it became a slump. I was too tired to worry about what Zatrack wanted. They couldn't kick me out for defending myself and if they wanted to throw me in detention or whatever, then whatever.

In my tense, heightened state, I understood the quiet voices drifting through the glass wall at my back.

"An entire syther team? And no one knew they were missing?" a woman's voice asked.

"They were seized at the beginning of their patrol and weren't due to report to Containment Command for another two hours. It was only when their report didn't come in that we knew something was wrong."

"And this is the *only* incident of abduction among Monster Containment?"

I shivered. Someone had abducted a Monster Containment team? How was that even possible? Glenn said sythers could do magic...

"It is the only incident in Bellarian Sythe and the team had no recollection of what happened to them. We think magically induced sleep was involved. Their first awareness something was wrong was when they woke up on a path in the middle of the wrong quadrant of National Park Zone."

"No witnesses?"

"No one. That's what worries Monster Containment most. Mavon is clever enough to be behind this, and they fear this incident is a test of our ability to keep track of our own. They fear Mavon's preparing to hit a new, unknown target."

I shook my head. The abduction sounded pointless. Like this Mavon guy was taunting Sythe. No one did that. No one had the nerve. Was Mavon a powerful crime boss?

Raised voices in the office on my left drowned out the conversation.

"Expelled!? You can't go harbouring thugs and kicking out upstanding city residents like me!"

"If you think this is an environment in which bullying, discrimination and abuse are tolerated, you may have us confused with organised crime," a man's voice replied coolly.

"This is political correctness gone mad!" Chareck accused. "You're just obsessed with Sythe's reputation!"

"Are we, Mr. Greenhill's under sixteen Spar Champ of the past three years? If you wish to buy your way through Sythe School Chareck, the currency you should have used is *respect*. *Money* is only highly valued in the private sector. Good day."

Chareck staggered out of Zatrack's office, looking pale, confused and with both hands balled into fists. All four secretaries paused in their work to eye him distastefully, as he walked past.

"Headmaster Zatrack will see you now Rarkin," Zatrack's secretary called.

I stood to my full height, trying to ignore the lump in my throat and walked past the secretary's desk to an open office door, which the secretary closed behind me. I blinked. The large desk I expected between me and the headmaster was pushed against a wall, with the chair *in front* of it. Where was I supposed to go?

"Hello Rarkin, have a seat."

Headmaster Zatrack sat at a small, low table on the left, on a couch identical to the one opposite, not bigger and more comfortable, as I expected.

I sat and eyed my judge.

"I assume you realise that we take breaches of prohibitions very seriously. Bellarian Sythe exists to protect Bellaria City State, and International Sythe has the same duty to the world. Working for the Syther Force, Military, Monster Containment, Search and Rescue, Healers, Foreign Aid and especially Peacekeeping, involves working under pressure and managing tension and high stress. It requires discipline and control. I am therefore concerned at the levels of aggression and anger you displayed today."

How else was I supposed to react to Chareck?

"I would not expect any fifteen-year-old to keep their temper on the receiving end of Chareck's abuse, but what concerns me is the underlying, deep seated anger Trainer Sirona saw in you today, while your behaviour suggests that aggression is your default response to threatening situations."

"Should I lie down and cop abuse instead?" I asked.

"Not at all," he replied, disregarding my sarcastic tone. "But rarely is pure aggression the most appropriate response for a sytheren city guard or soldier, and beyond that, for any syther in the Field. Most often, sythers solve conflicts through diplomacy or show; not application of force. The aggression you automatically respond to perceived threats with will become inappropriate for you as a sytheren, and especially at syther level."

I suppose magic and tempers at syther level would be a disaster. And let me guess, sythes have god-like temperaments of calm and self-control? But what was he saying? Was there a 'but' coming or was he chucking me out?

"Do you wish to be a sytheren or to reach syther level?"

"A syther," I replied, feeling like I was walking into an ambush.

"In that case, you will need to communicate and cooperate well with your syther team, regardless of which Sythe or government department you work for. Do you feel you can do this?"

I felt hollow. Miona was the only classmate I trusted; the only one I knew. Work closely with a team of strangers? I hadn't thought that far ahead. I had to get through school before that mattered; didn't I? The Head's expression said otherwise, but he didn't press for a verbal response.

"Ideally, Trainer Dorthin will take half your Practical Training Centre lessons next half semester, to teach you marksmanship. Do you think it would be wise to place a stun gun in your hands in a months' time?"

The target I wanted to shoot with a gun was my father. The anger boiling inside me wanted to kill him. I couldn't be trusted with a gun...

"Trainer Sirona was impressed with the restraint you showed today. She said that you didn't press your advantage or try to knock Chareck down. That you used only what force you thought necessary to defend yourself, despite that you appear tired and short-tempered today. Do you agree?"

"I don't wanna get chucked out. I was happy to put a few bruises on him while I beat him off, but even if he's a total prick; I don't wanna knock people down. I just wanna defend myself."

"To use no more force than the situation requires?"

I hate my father. I'll resent him till his dying day. Part of me wanted him dead, and had for a long time. But the rest of me, the part that told me to hold back because I never wanted Mum to look at me with the horror I'd seen on her face when Dad went too far, the part that looked up to Uncle Alan as a syther and Dory and Glenn as good blokes *didn't* want to use more force than I needed to. And the part of me that knew he wasn't all bad would hate the rest of me, if I went too far.

I exhaled deeply and nodded. Headmaster Zatrack smiled. What in Chaos was he smiling for?

"The principle of restraint is a key component of Sythe's mandate. If you are as committed to that as I suspect, and willing to learn to manage your feelings, which will ultimately reduce your aggression, you could make a great syther one day."

I gaped. He points out there are holes in my character big enough to drive an electric-way carriage through, then tells me I can do the job well? What was he playing at?

"Are you prepared to learn to manage your anger, aggression and any other emotions that could jeopardise your career?"

He had the power to chuck me out if I refused... But if Miona hadn't timed her comment so well, I might have been expelled for lashing out at Chareck. I *was* at risk of getting myself chucked out...

"Yeah," I replied. "But what am I supposed to do?"

"Meet with Counsellor Jay. Fortnightly. Until you feel calm, as a minimum requirement."

Calm? I wasn't gonna feel that while my father lived...

"My ultimate goal would be for you to operate within a team in a calm, unguarded fashion."

"That's impossible," I replied automatically.

He smiled and leaned in. "Had anyone told me I would become a Head at Sythe when I was fifteen, I'd have said the same, with the same conviction. Consider it. And make your first appointment with Jay on your way back to class. Or now, if he's available."

I suppressed a shudder at the thought of spending time on the other side of a table with a stranger reading my feelings off my face, let alone having to talk openly and honestly about things that were none of their business. But I'd agreed...

I nodded.

He smiled, nodded back and I walked out, using the directory on the office waiting area wall to find Jay's office.

Trent was my mentor; don't let your guard down, don't tell anyone anything, don't let them in and *do not* make yourself vulnerable to strangers. I couldn't do that *and* achieve Headmaster Zatrack's goals. But if Jay told him I sat silently in our sessions, and we were getting nowhere, Zatrack might chuck me out.

I took a deep breath and knocked on a door labelled; *Jay Laris, Junior Sythe Counsellor*. The door opened. Jay had a sincere, ready smile, contrasting with his ebony skin. He wore smart, new clothes and he looked ten years older than me; some middle-class do-gooder from serene Lakeside, probably.

"Rarkin?" he asked. "Headmaster Zatrack said you might stop by."

I flicked my chin, feeling a surge of adrenaline, because this was our first session. He ushered me to a small table with couches either side and a view across the sports field, and motioned me to a seat.

"What attracted you to Sythe?" he asked, sitting opposite me.

The question caught me off guard. But it seemed harmless, so I answered.

"The chance to work outside the city…to do dangerous work, the kind I might be suited to."

The kind tough guys enjoyed for the thrill of it; stunning and capturing dangerous monsters and relocating them. I didn't usually acknowledge that side of why Monster Containment appealed. It would be too much disappointment, if I didn't manage to follow Uncle Alan's footsteps.

"Anything else?" Jay probed.

Answering that wouldn't make me vulnerable.

"I wanna achieve things. Instead of just seeing everything that's wrong."

"What's wrong for you?" he asked.

That's why he asked harmless-seeming questions; he wanted inroads. Now what did I say? I'd have to give him something, to keep Zatrack off my back.

"My father."

That was all I intended to say. But the next phrase came out of its own accord, "My parents' marriage."

Another thought came; *Mum's parents.* Darkness rose. I tensed and shoved it down.

"And things you'd rather not think about?"

My jaw clenched, and I gazed sightlessly out the window.

He moved on. "What about your father?"

I couldn't help myself. "He's a selfish, drunken prick who never lifts a finger and expects Mum to do everything," I said resentfully. "She's kind, she cares, she tries; he doesn't."

"And where do you come in?"

I shrugged. "I wash the dishes after dinner, make Mum tea and get in the way when he comes home and starts hurling insults. If they aren't directed at me; I bait him to redirect them."

Let him think that was all it had ever been; I didn't want Social Welfare trying to take me away.

Jay blinked and smiled. "You admit things more freely than most guys from the neighbourhood. I haven't had to wrestle you yet."

What? ...guys from *the neighbourhood*... I blinked tiredly. Beyond his new clothes... was the reserved set of his jaw, a familiar look in his eyes and his hunched posture, which made his height less threatening.

"How can *you* be from Brock Heights *and* a counsellor?" I asked. "When every guy from the neighbourhood must be sent to you against their will?"

He smiled, and his dark eyes were pools of warmth in his ebony face. "And I should what, let them drown in anger and aggression and get themselves chucked out? When I *know* it's not easy to get in here, and harder to stay, especially in the first year?"

I sat up straighter. "Why's that?"

"Some things that work for you at home and in the neighbourhood don't work at Sythe. Most government departments refuse to employ hotheads. And the Sythe Base won't consider anyone with a school record of inappropriate aggression. Anger and aggression are probably what's getting you through at home; but the exams alone are hard to pass at syther level, if you rely on either too much.

"Relying on yourself too much is another thing you'll have to change to succeed here. Whether you work as a sytheren, syther or sythe, you'll be part of a team. By syther level your team members will have different strengths. You'll have to start relying on others in their area of strength and trusting them.

"That's where I come in. I'm here to check what you struggle with and what strategies we can give you to make studying and working at Sythe easier and to help you succeed. And I'm not just here for things that impact directly on your studies or your work for Sythe. Sythers and sythes deal with stressful, nasty things sometimes, so Sythe are big on mental and emotional wellbeing, and we can tackle anything else you want."

"What do you tell guys who are too aggressive or angry?" I asked.

"That they need an outlet. A classic mistake is to bottle it all up, because you didn't see how to deal with it from your parents and you don't know what to do with it. My mother turned to drugs and my father was a highly functional alcoholic. I didn't fancy either. Luckily for me people at school suggested I get involved in a sparring club, and I found not just the physical activity, but the discipline they demanded helped. Trainer Sirona runs spear training, which is good for balancing aggression and force with control."

Mum held a knife in her trembling hand and told Dad to stop strangling me.

"I don't wanna use weapons," I replied instinctively.

"If you're worried about hurting people, a punch bag's your best bet," he replied.

The image that prompted was better; a teenage Trent killing a punch bag on Glenn's porch, his shirt sweaty, his face angry and his determined blows ceaseless. If it worked for Trent…

"I know someone who can lend me one," I replied. "But that's not all you and the headmaster are going to ask, is it?"

Jay smiled. "I'd rather nail one thing at a time than get you doing too many things badly or falling in a heap. That's your first goal; make use of the punch bag at home, or in the Solo Room in the Practical Training Centre, which is set up with punch, kick and tackle bags, instead of bottling it up."

"How do you know holding it in's my problem?" I asked.

He smiled and replied, "If you could show restraint against Chareck, that suggests you *never* let it out. It's a good way to avoid seriously hurting anyone, or lashing out at someone you don't wish to hurt, but it's not good for your health."

Nor was my father, but I suppose trying to pour out the anger more, instead of letting it boil might help, *if* I also reserved some for when I needed to hurl it at Dad and shut him up before his words cut too deep. Assuming depriving himself of drink didn't have him coming at me with his fists again…

"We'll talk more next time, see how using a punch bag is working for you and if we think you need another strategy for anything else. For now, I'll let you get some rest."

I considered him. He'd got middle-class looking somewhere along the way, but I could see understanding, care and strength like Des' underneath. This wasn't a middle-class know-nothing fobbed on me from on high; he *was* from my part of town. I didn't know him yet, I didn't trust him, but I was prepared to give working with him a shot.

I stood and let my gaze fall on him. "Thanks."

He nodded. Not a chin flick calculated to get me on side, but a sign of respect. Did I deserve his help?

Chapter 5

Home

I didn't have long to ponder what I deserved. Mum, Uncle Alan and I were in the lounge only long enough to eat a snack that evening before Aunt Lil looked up and frowned. Uncle Alan's expression became dark and closed off. I followed his gaze through the lounge window. Dad was standing on the lawn. He was a big, hulking figure and he stood tall, his hands clenching each other before him.

Mum gasped and walked outside. Uncle Alan glared. Dad tried to avoid looking at him, a sure sign that he feared Uncle Alan.

"He might actually regret what he did this time," said Aunt Lil. "If he braved coming here to apologise."

"He doesn't apologise," I replied, confused.

Uncle Alan opened the window and my father's quiet words drifted up the lawn to us.

"I'm sorry I scared you," Dad forced out, looking pained.

I gaped.

Mum peered at him. His eyes flashed with anger towards me, then to pain again. "I…is the boy ok?"

The boy. Not 'my son'. Not 'our son'. I was *the boy.* Did he mean that question? I thought he hated me?

"Can you…can you try a little more with him?" Mum asked.

Dad's posture tensed, and his mouth hardened in a line. He took a deep breath and said, "Yes."

"I'll get our things," Mum replied.

I watched, open-mouthed. Maybe he was sorry… to have lost her at least. And all he had to do was admit it and then she… My heart turned to lead. He was worming his way back into her life, like he must have done every other time. And she sympathised and forgave him, and they made up, over and over again.

Mum moved through the hallway getting her things. I didn't. Dad's eyes met mine through the window. I glimpsed genuine feeling. I glimpsed a person who gave a damn about me. I saw just enough to believe the slumped, drunken man saying he thought I'd done well the day I passed General School.

Then his face hardened, and he turned away. I wished I hadn't seen. It would be easier if he hated me entirely. Then I could hate him back and fight him and survive. But to know he really did care… How low was I that he could care and still treat me with hatred? I must be nothing; nothing at all.

"You don't have to go with them," said Uncle Alan. "You're old enough to decide to stay here."

But there was so much tension in Dad, so much anger. If I wasn't there for it to come at me …*Mum* was next in line. And from the fact she took him back; she couldn't see her danger. I couldn't leave her.

"I'll go," I replied.

"If he tries anything Rarkin, you call me," Uncle Alan replied firmly, and I frowned.

"You've asked her to leave him," I said, studying his troubled face.

"More than once. I tried to protect my little sister, but I don't know how to protect her from her own choices. The only reason I didn't call the Syther Force about him years ago is because she won't let me."

"She doesn't want him sent to prison," I guessed.

How could she love that monster? Sure, there was a part of him that was human; I'd seen it twice in recent weeks. But its effect on me was that if *I* killed *him*, I'd feel bad about it afterwards. There was so little to love in him…what was *wrong* with her?

Uncle Alan blinked. Then he spoke earnestly. "You have a future at Sythe School, a future as a syther and an employee of Monster Containment. Don't throw that away because of hate. Don't let hatred of your dad make you into him."

How could *that* happen?

"Time to go home," Mum called from the doorway, holding both our satchels.

We were safe, for now. How long would it last this time?

I collected my satchel and walked out grim-faced, letting Mum say goodbye. I walked ahead the whole way, trying to stomp down the resentment with every step I took, as anger at my newfound understanding of their screwed-up relationship churned inside me.

Mum went to the kitchen to cook dinner when we got home, and Dad smiled. It evaporated when he turned to me.

"You study hard and stay out of my way," he snapped, not meeting my eyes. "Or I'll make you and your mother regret it."

He was going to put me in a corner and pretend I didn't exist, because he couldn't stand watching me succeed? He was going to have a good marriage with Mum, his servant who always took him back because she loved the bit of him that was good, and sunk into depression, so the worst of him didn't touch her? Who stayed with him because she thought tolerating his abuse was the only way to get me through Sythe School...because she was helpless?

I wasn't helpless. I was furious. Hatred coursed through me. My body was taut with anger and the magic particles within me hummed with power, making me realise the only way to deal with a controlling, manipulative prick like him; the way Trent had showed me.

"Did you like my fire?" I asked.

He shivered and evaded my gaze.

"If you lay a hand on either of us, you'll feel it again," I said quietly, my eyes likely blazing the anger I didn't dare let flow with my words, in case magic exploded out with them.

He trembled.

He trembled at *my* actions. I was right. The power balance between us had been shifting in recent years. Had I finally got a grip on its upper hand? There was a way to test it.

I did something I've never dared to do before. Keeping my muscles tight and listening intently, I turned my back on him. I walked to my room as if I didn't fear him. As if *he* was nothing. I closed my door and waited.

"I'm going to the pub Elaine. I'll eat when I get home. Bye, love," he said, his voice cracked.

Bye love? He was *never* affectionate...

The front door closed. His footsteps retreated beyond hearing. I'd pushed him back to drinking...

I kicked my clothes box, tearing cardboard and kicked my clothes around the room for good measure. I wanted to rail at him. I wanted to tell him all the things I hated about him, everything he'd ever done to me or Mum that he had no right to do, and the bastard was too weak and had gone crawling back into a bottle.

And I'd just killed the quiet period Mum enjoyed, when he's in a better mood because they've made up and they're pretending they haven't fought, and they appreciate each other, because they notice the things they missed about each other. Which ends with him becoming abusive and ruining it, and periodically getting violent or cruel enough in his words that we go back to Uncle Alan's. That was *all* they had… What was the *point* of it?

I flung myself onto my bed, stuffing my face into my pillow, trying to press away the burning in my eyes. All my life I wondered how it felt to be Trent. To stand tall. To have power. To make a bully back down. It was *so* good not being helpless. But Dad's trembling…

A slap rang through the corridor. My face stung. I was six years old, he'd never done that to me before and it hurt, it really hurt, but I wasn't crying, because I was too busy watching him and worrying he'd do it again. Because that anger burning in his eyes told me he wanted to.

He didn't; not that day. But there were other days. I got older and slaps became punches. And I was scared, and I trembled, until Trent taught me to tense my stomach when the blows came. Until he taught me to hold onto the anger, to use it as a shield.

But I remembered being that helpless little kid shaking with fear and Uncle Alan's words replayed themselves in my mind, "Don't let hatred of your dad make you into him."

I shuddered. I knew where that path began now; with taking control of someone who has it coming and can't take it. Under threat of magic, *he* became the helpless kid shaking in the corridor …and that made me *him*.

Tough guy code for fighting; *never* kick someone when they're down. It's gutless, it shows contempt; it's despicable. It's treating other tough guys the way bastard parents treat you. It's the lowest thing you can do.

Controlling Dad beyond this point was kicking him when he was down. I *wouldn't* become him! But that was the only way to manage him because he'll *never* change. What in Chaos was I supposed to do

Chapter 6

Out

The mood was different in the corridor outside Trainer Lauran's classroom next morning. My classmates talked quietly. When I arrived, the boy with the fine dreadlocks and warm smile, Amon said, "Hey Rarkin. Did they expel Chareck?"

I nodded and was surprised to see relief and smiles on several faces. Had Chareck been bullying people for the past four weeks, and I hadn't noticed it wasn't only me he was a prick too?

Chareck's four friends arrived. They stood on the other side of the classroom door, two avoiding looking in my direction, but the tall blonde turned to me uncertainly, then came over, as Miona arrived.

"I'm from Greenhill too and Chareck doesn't speak for all of us," he said. "I've never seen him behave so badly. I've heard stories about Brock Heights, everyone has, but my cousins are from there and they're good guys. I don't think you've any less right to be here than anyone else."

He held out his hand, his pale face sincere. I had a right to be here did I? That was nice. But I supposed after how

Chareck behaved, he wanted me to know there wasn't animosity between his mates and me. I took a deep breath and did something I never thought I'd do; shook hands with a rich kid from Greenhill.

Rinth smiled, then we let go and he turned to Miona. "Didn't you beat Chareck in a sparring match in Lakeside last year?" he asked.

Miona smiled.

"I don't think he's over it yet," Rinth added, and they both smiled.

Trainer Lauran opened our classroom door, noted Rinth talking to us and eyed him approvingly.

"You've come across them through your sparring club?" I asked Miona, as we walked to our desks.

"Rinth and Ryan are alright," she replied, "but the other two are arrogant."

"Rinth and Ryan are *alright*?" I asked.

"Does everyone in your neighbourhood go around jumping people in broad daylight?" she asked.

I frowned.

"So do you think everyone from the posh suburbs thinks they're infinitely superior to poor people?"

I sighed. I supposed it would be wrong to think *every* rich person is the same; when every poor person isn't. It's just that anyone who ever gave me a hard time in school was from

Greenhill, and if we'd had any kids from City Centre, I'd expected them to be the same.

* * *

Dad kept coming home late, sober, avoiding me entirely and making me edgy about when he'd go back to normal. We did research projects to complete History of War and Sorcery with Trainer Lauran, I did Zushai with Miona, Rinth and Ryan and Trainer Sirona, mostly partnering Miona but I sparred with Rinth once. He was built along the lines of Glenn's mates Wak and Tak, another pair of burly blonds, either one of whom could easily heft me over their shoulder and walk down the street with me. I knew they could, because one day Tak had hefted me, Wak had hefted Cam, and they'd had a race while carrying us.

Rinth was more serious than Wak and Tak. He watched me like a hawk and was skilled but good-natured. And on seeing me not kill Rinth, other classmates agreed to spar with me. First Kay, a tall lanky kid I held back with because he was timid; then Lylez, a girl with an easy smile, whose speed impressed me. And Amon, who attacked me as if he worried he was poking a dog with a stick, yet met my blows with nervous smiles. There was something distracting about him, but I would've had to look into those warm, smiling eyes to figure it out, so I let it go.

My classmates got more comfortable, and people stopped eyeing me carefully when I crossed the room. Surely my last class hadn't taken this long to realise I wouldn't jump them just because they were within my reach? But it felt better having people start to relax around me; made me feel less of a prick.

I saw Jay again and was on edge because Dad had paid off my fees for the semester and was *still* coming home late, sober. Mum and I wondered if by some miracle he was happy, and where he kept going each night, if it wasn't the pub to drink. Jay wondered if Dad was getting better, but I knew my old man too well; something was up.

I found out what on the day we started Monster Studies. Trainer Lauran took us to the Monster Centre, a modern building outside the castle behind the Practical Training Centre. Its roof was several times the height of a normal room and its walls three or four times as thick. The Trainer led us onto an earthen floor corridor between enclosures of thick, transparent glass, which must somehow be shatter-proof, so the monsters didn't escape.

"On my left are the monsters you will begin training with; garls," she said. "Their size isn't a worry, but they will charge if you approach too quickly and seek to impale you with their spikes."

Several people shuddered or wrinkled their noses, but I smiled; that would only happen if you were foolish enough to stare at them instead of hitting them with a stun shot.

"Behind us are tasti, which have barbed wings. The females are poisonous, so you will not be permitted to train against them until much later."

I heard swearing and turned. A panicked, pale blue uniformed syther charged through the upraised glassy door of an enclosure further down. A second syther thumped an ID card onto a reader, but from his swearing, his card wouldn't scan.

A monster scratched the doorframe as it forced its way through, into our corridor. The syther dropped his card and stumbled backwards. He drew his stun gun and took aim, as did the syther who'd fled. An alarm sounded, as I crouched, instinctively ready to meet danger.

The monster was reptilian, with four sturdy legs, a spiked head and large jawed face. Behind it swished a tail with spikes the length of my arm. It was twice my height and long. At the sight of it, my classmates' screams rent the air, catching the creature's attention. It lumbered towards us.

Both sythers shot tranquillisers at it from the sides. They missed.

"Everyone out!" Trainer Lauran ordered.

She stood to one side, firing a stun dart at the monster as our class turned to flee, but Kay stood still. His eyes rolled back. Miona and I seized him by the armpits as he fell. More sythers shot at the monster as it charged, but they hardly slowed it.

I heaved Kay's left arm over my shoulder, Miona grabbed his right and we jogged clumsily away. Heavy footsteps thudded behind us. A shadow loomed. I turned to see its head spikes falling towards me, as the monster collapsed, face first. Pain seared down my left calf.

A syther approached as we slowed, staring intently at Kay, who woke up and stumbled forwards, shocked and confused.

"Your leg's bleeding something shocking," the syther said to me, as Miona explained to Kay that he'd fainted.

I examined my leg. The cut was wider than I expected, blood welling out of it concealing how deep it went and trickling down my calf. The syther grabbed my calf with both hands, holding the split together and Trainer Lauran approached, gazing intently. The bleeding slowed. *Magic*? Was that what woke Kay?

"Sorry man," one of the pale-faced sythers said as he approached. "I couldn't get the door shut; my ID card wouldn't work."

"Take that card straight to the office and get a replacement," Trainer Lauran ordered, and he bowed his head, as his nervous friend approached.

"I'm sorry too," said his friend. "I shouldn't have gone in there; its mating season for Sirlons and I forgot how crazy they get."

I couldn't feel any pain. I was probably in shock.

"You're lucky to get off with just a scar, a good one too," said the syther who'd held my leg, as he stood.

Blood ran down my calf, but the cut had closed; *magic*. I caught the man's gaze and the wild gleam in his eyes. It was the kind of gleam Des got from committing petty theft under people's noses. And this guy had it from after healing my split leg, after someone accidentally set a charging, hormonal monster loose on first year sytheren students.

Was he from my part of town? Surely his attitude was the definition of insanity anywhere else? It was hard to tell, because unlike most guys from the neighbourhood, he seemed beyond the stage where he needed to be tough all the time, at a point where he could enjoy work most people find terrifying. If this guy was from Brock Heights, perhaps Headmaster Zatrack had a point about me being a calm team member one day; because this guy was already there…

They took me to the infirmary to get cleaned up, then Kay's parents came to thank me. They wore expensive suits and grateful smiles.

"Thank you," said the mother. "You could have run and left the sythers to save him, and his height must have slowed you and your friend down."

I blinked. "It didn't occur to me to leave him behind with that thing charging towards us."

The father beamed. "We weren't sure Sythe School was the right place for our Kay, but I'm glad he has classmates like you."

The mother smiled, thanking me again and they moved out, leaving me in stunned silence. I thought Rinth might be the black sheep of Greenhill for offering me the hand of friendship, but Kay later told me his parents live and work in *City Centre*. I couldn't remember the last time any adult but Dory had spoken so warmly to me. And never had a rich adult spoken to me like, an equal... I wasn't worth *that* much.

Mum came to pick me up.

"Your leg!" she said, seeing the scar. "Less than two months in the castle..."

"The boys will love it," I replied.

"Does it hurt?" she asked.

I shook my head.

She met my eyes then, smiling. "I know anyone who joins Sythe needs to be brave," she said. "But this, so soon... I'm so proud of you Rarkin. I know you worry sometimes, but you could do great things in Sythe; this goes to show."

I turned away. I'd forgotten most of the history we'd learnt. If I remembered the notes Miona and I made just as poorly, I could fail the sytheren exams. How could *I* do great things?

"Alan will be proud," she added. "I think I'll invite him and Lil to dinner. He'll want to hear your account."

He probably would. The idea was… awkward, embarrassing. *Me* being fussed over…

She drove me home. I washed and got changed and was leaving the bathroom when the door crashed open. Dad stood there, his bloodshot eyes blazing with anger.

"It's on the news. Escaped monster at Bellaria Sythe School. Rarkin Loreman saves his weakling lover-boy, some rich prick. You give that boy one after you saved him?"

I gaped. I was offended on Tak, Miona, Merin and all samers behalf. Then I realised what he was truly angry about; *I* was a hero. I was doing well at Sythe School, and on track to achieving my dream when *he'd* bombed out. He *was* jealous of me. This was just the excuse he seized to attack me for it. I was having none of it.

"You don't care whether I go for girls, boys or andros," I objected.

"Don't care if you're a man or a cock-sucker?" he replied.

He stumbled forwards. I smiled, ready to put six weeks of Zushai training to the test. I dodged his punch, sunk both fists into his guts then turned to face him, fists up. He glared.

"I should have known," he panted. "You spent too much time clinging to your mother's skirts. If I'd paid attention, I might've been able to beat it out of you. It's still worth a try."

"Are you really that *dense*?" I asked contemptuously. "You think by plunging your fists into people often enough they'll think and feel what you want them to? You think you can force your will on the world?"

"Of course I can. I don't expect some stupid, boy-loving kid to understand. It's a *man's* world! *I* set the tone. *I* make the rules. *I* earn the money. *I* do the work; *she* looks after me and *you* do what you're told. That's how the world works boy."

"You're delusional. *The world* hasn't worked that way for at least four hundred years. It's just you and a few other pricks who think that. My sparring partner, Miona, she could pound your head in. And you know what? So can I. You wanna fight old man? I'm right here!"

"Go stick it up your boyfriend!" he replied, and turned to leave, having failed to land a single punch.

Both my fists clenched, but I hesitated. A motorbike was revving close by. It pulled up in our yard. Dad stared, then straightened, wiping his sweaty face on his hands. The rider got off. She wore a short skirt and had curly red hair under her helmet.

Mum stepped out of her room beside us, looking wrong-footed. "Rarkin, I didn't know you were…"

I sighed. "You didn't miss anything. He's just clutching excuses to rage at me."

On our front lawn, the helmet came off, revealing a face that might have been attractive, if it weren't so heavily made up. The woman strode up the lawn and Dad hurried to open the front door for her. I couldn't believe my eyes.

"Hi Dougie! I just saw the news. I hope Elaine doesn't mind me dropping by."

Mum blinked, bemused at the friendly way the woman I suspected my father was having an affair with smiled at her. Didn't she realise that as far as we knew, mum and dad were still together?

"I wanted to meet Rarkin and congratulate you. It sounds like you're off to a great start in your career in Sythe," the woman said warmly to me.

The layers of makeup looked fake, but her tone sounded genuine. I stared. Dad's girlfriend wanted to congratulate *me*? He was so jealous that he decided I was a samer as an excuse to beat me up, but he chose someone who admired *my* efforts to have an affair with?

"I won't impose. I assume you weren't staying long Dougie? Shall I wait outside?"

She didn't know he still lived here?

"I'll be out soon darlin'," he replied, pecking her cheek, then he pinched her backside as she walked out.

I stared at him as he closed the door and turned to us.

"I was going to say something Elaine. Got together with her the night you betrayed me. She was what I needed.

The thing is, if I stay here, I have to keep seeing boy-lover dreamer and that doesn't work for me. You'll always be mine Elaine, but I'm going to live with Sandy now."

He turned and walked into his room.

Mum had worried how he'd respond to seeing the knife she'd threatened him with. He'd responded by having an affair. But Mum *had* stood up to him with a knife. And with Zushai training, I didn't need magic to beat him. He couldn't control us anymore; couldn't pretend he had anything over us; so he'd found someone else. It still didn't make sense, him holding the door open for her...

He came out with a bag, nodded respectfully to Mum, glared at me, then walked out. Sandy secured his bag to a rack, then he lifted her onto the back of the bike and she giggled at his show of 'playfulness' that was him literally him putting her in her place. Then he climbed onto the front, waved to us with a massive smile, revved the engine and drove off.

Mum was teary-eyed. "I thought he'd forgiven me."

"Did *he* just move out?" I asked. "Did *he* just leave *us*? Why not kick us out and let Sandy move in?"

"It's my house," Mum replied. "This is where I grew up, Rarkin. Don't you remember moving in after your grandmother died?"

A wrinkled, fragile face came to mind and pain rose in me as I forced it and the memory down.

"You were young when we moved in. Your grandad was in prison and I promised him I'd take care of the house, so we moved in. And then he died, and we stayed here."

At several mentions of grandad, a furious face raising a belt flashed in my mind. Terror rose in me. I gasped and forced the memories down. Grandad was worse than Dad. He must have been awful. And Mum had lived here as an adult, where her father had abused her and then her husband had abused her... I felt sick.

"Let's get out of here," I said. "Let's go to Uncle Alan's. Let's *stay* there."

Mum looked worried.

"What?" I asked.

"He can keep pretending to be proud of you to his new woman without paying your school fees. That's why we don't live at Uncle Alan's; I couldn't afford the fees and Alan and Lil have helped so much already. They paid for most of your clothes and bought your bed. I didn't want to ask more of them."

"Do you want to stay here?" I asked. "With all the nasty things that have happened?"

"It's my home. It's always been my home."

"Then make a new home."

"I don't want to impose on Lil. I'm not sure she likes me."

"The fact you stayed with Dad annoyed her. I realised last time we were there. She'll think better of you, if you move out and you and Dad are finished."

"If he stays with Sandy..."

Mum paused for so long that I asked, "What?"

"I could sell the house. I could sell this place; and pay your school fees and use the rest of the money and a loan from money-lenders to buy another home."

"Could you pay off a new house some place nicer?"

She sighed. "If I let Alan help."

"Then do it. Get your own place Mum. Make your own memories. We can live with Uncle Alan and Aunt Lil till then; they won't mind."

I was so shocked to learn this was the house grandad had been a prick in and that I'd somehow forgotten, and keen for Mum to get out of here that the idea Dad was gone and we were leaving had barely sunk in. I picked up my battered clothes box, lifted an image of Uncle Alan, Aunt Lil, Mum and me from my windowsill and chucked it on top, grabbed my school satchel and walked out of my room in a daze.

Mum took longer. She used her bedsheets to tie her clothes into a bundle, packed her bedding, told me to pack mine, then proceeded to load the car with framed images from the walls, her mother's dinning set, a drawer full of cutlery, some books, cleaning products, everything she wanted, while I loaded the motor carriage.

Mum hummed as she drove to Orange Tree Hill. We arrived at Uncle Alan's and Mum explained that Dad had left. Aunt Lil was shocked, and from the fact he didn't comment at all, I suspect Uncle Alan didn't dare to hope.

We unpacked. Uncle Alan cooked dinner. I went to bed, slept, went to school, came back to their place and did it again.

The shock Dad was gone didn't go away. None of us dared believe it was true yet, because it was too good to have false hope. But if I had the thing I wanted most in the world, freedom from my father, then the thing I wanted most now was to do dangerous, thrilling work; to be skilled, accepted, respected and doing something worthwhile.

I'd done something that mattered when I helped Miona pull Kay away from the sirlon. I could make a difference, as a sytheren or a syther. Which could mean disregarding Trent's advice, defying my instincts and opening up to Jay about things I didn't want to think about to succeed...

Chapter 7

Shadows

I felt like I'd moved into some peaceful small screen show. Some dreamy program where everyone felt safe in their house, the weather was always sunny, the local news was always good and it never got cold. I couldn't be living with people who took an interest in me, spent time with me, took me places and made me feel like I mattered.

I still lay awake at night waiting to hear Dad's bedroom door shut. Instead I'd hear the click of Deevey's claws on polished boards, know I was at Uncle Alan's and eventually doze off. My life felt like a children's tale, my road was a rainbow and my feet didn't touch the ground, till I walked to Jay's office for the last time before mid-semester break. This was our last meeting before I potentially trained with a stun gun next semester; *if* he gave me the ok.

I sat tensely opposite Jay. He studied me and said calmly, "If anything stirred your temper in the Shooting Range of the Practical Training Centre, you would have permission to walk out."

I frowned. Permission to make a scene? Wonderful.

"How can I be fit to train if there's any risk of me shooting classmates?" I asked.

"I don't think there is," Jay replied.

I eyed him sternly and he didn't blink.

"I'm concerned about you holding a gun because the idea of holding a weapon makes you uncomfortable."

The knife trembled in Mum's hand as she told Dad to release his double handed grip on my neck. I shivered. He saw it.

"Why does it make you uncomfortable?"

That was the first time he pressed me.

"Do we have to talk about this now?" I asked. "I've never been so happy. Do I have to spoil it by dragging up all the shit that happened earlier?"

"No," Jay replied. "We don't. And you deserve time to enjoy life. But I think we need to have this conversation before your syther exams."

The relief of him not insisting on poking at my barely healed wounds was so great that I took several moments to take in that last bit.

"My *syther* exams?"

"It won't be crucial until then and yes, I think you have every chance of passing your sytheren exams."

That sent shockwaves crashing over me. I couldn't remember half of what I'd studied, I was nervous of holding a gun because of a memory I wanted to *forget*… and because I remembered the power I felt the night I threatened Dad. What if holding a gun gave me the same sense of power?

Jay had a knowing look in his eyes. He knew Brock Heights guys. He *was* one. He had an idea what I felt and its causes, yet he was still confident of me becoming a syther and beginning weapons training. And he was on my side.

I left his office with my head spinning.

***

The mid-semester holidays came and Miona's sixteenth birthday at her home in Lakeside. I met her middle-class friends from General School, rougher friends from her sparring club and hung out with her girlfriend Merin, who, at seventeen, was a mature-age sytheren student. We'd spent some time sparring and talked a bit, but the party was my first proper conversation with Merin and… not exactly comfortable. Not that any conversation with Merin was comfortable.

"You don't fancy anyone, do you?" Merin asked, her slender brown fingers holding a wine glass with a practiced ease mis-matched to someone who was technically underage.

I shrugged. Merin was fun to spar with and witty. But her gaze was too piercing, like a laser that cut through my refusal to look at her face, letting her read me like a book. It was unnerving sometimes.

"It's a shame," she continued. "It would be fun setting you up with someone."

I gaped at her. Those warm brown cheeks were dimpling in a wicked smile, her short black hair curving deceptively sweetly around her face.

"As if I'd trust *you*, with *that*!" I managed to say it firmly, though I couldn't help flushing.

Merin laughed heartily, smiling and winking at Amon across the room, as she happened to catch his eye. There was something in Amon's return gaze, like he was… unhappy about something. I'd have expected him to be happy, a sociable guy like him getting a mischievous smile from Merin. Other guys in the room couldn't take their eyes off her collared, plunging green dress's neck line. But it seemed to be the dark green eye shadow and burgundy lip shade Amon was stuck on. Almost like he was sad. Weird.

Miona smiled as she joined us. "Leave Amon alone," she chided Merin. "He's not mature enough to handle you yet."

"Who's to say *he* would be handling *me*?" Merin retorted.

I flushed and sipped my nonalcoholic drink for an excuse to look away. Miona just smiled, wrapping an arm around Merin, nodding to me, and leading us out of range of Amon's sad smile.

"Tell me you had something other than trying to set Rarkin up with anyone planned for my birthday," said Miona.

Merin smiled and kissed her. I turned away, and might have accidentally wandered away from them, had Merin not taken my hand and led me with them to the back patio. A patio. Chairs with cushions, a waterproof roof, and a garden bed of trees and flowers arching around the garden beyond. It was big and pretty.

Maybe that was why I hadn't pulled my hand out of Merin's. Because I was enjoying the beauty of the place and for once I didn't mind the unexpected touch of someone I didn't know well. Miona just smiled at us. I'd spent the whole semester keeping most of our class except Miona at arm's length, but Merin just walked right in.

"Was she like this with you?" I asked Miona.

Miona smiled. "I was used to being cautious after sparring matches, in case bitter defeated opponents came back for a second round. It was a bitter opponent one day, but Merin responded to him before I could, and sent him rushing from the room, red faced. Then she asked me out, just like that. Next thing I knew, I was walking along the river, eating ice cream, hand in hand with her."

Merin smiled. She was holding Miona's hand too. It was quite a skill; to see people you knew you wanted in your life, walk up to them and just... make them part of it. I could never be like that. So... confident. So... sociable. But maybe I needed more people in my social circle. And few people could just walk into my life the way Miona and Merin had. I'd have to do more about it, somehow.

But the holidays weren't the time for that. They were a rare chance to catch up with my other friends, because Glenn, Wak and Tak, as second year shadower students, had the same holidays as me. We had dinner with Des, Trent and Cam one night and watched a film on the big screen in the Valley about diplomats whose pre-Nuclear War airship crashed in the Miaran Wild, and the magic-wielding monsters they fled to reach the Taron border.

Then the break was over, and too soon I stood with my class watching Trainer Dorthin explain how to turn a gun's safety off, how to stand and how to grip it as you took aim.

"You will practice your grip and posture and I will inspect everyone before you fire a single shot," Trainer Dorthin insisted. "When I give permission to shoot, you are to fire single rubber bullets, checking your accuracy and correcting your aim between shots. I will coach you until each of you can hit the second ring from the bull's eye consistently; which is the accuracy required to pass your sytheren shooting exam. Now; step up to the gun shelf and show me the grip and posture I have modelled."

As we picked up guns from the wooden shelf lining the range, he walked down our line fussing over postures and grips, and eyed me mistrustfully. He continued to stare when he finally said, "Take aim."

Who did he think I was going to take aim at?

My heart sped up as I raised the gun, sighting beyond the wooden gun shelf across painted lines marking distances, to a round target board twenty paces away. Miona raised her gun, squinting as Trainer Dorthin walked back down the line. We waited, continuing to aim, while Dorthin fussed over people's postures, until it became clear he didn't trust us to fire while his back was turned. Guns wavered and my heartbeat increased with anticipation, until he finally turned to face us and said, "Fire!"

Adrenaline sparked, and I fired four rubber bullets in swift succession, before I heard the Trainer shouting and Miona motioned me to stop. What was his problem now?

"Did I not ask you to fire a *single* shot?" Trainer Dorthin demanded.

I rolled my eyes. Did he think we needed babying through every tiny step, or did he just enjoy the sense of power that making us stand like statues gave him?

"How are you to improve your aim with an empty gun?" he demanded, striding towards me.

Did he think the only reason someone wouldn't do what he said was because that person was unintelligent? How daft and arrogant was this prick?

"I asked you a question!" he snapped.

"By reloading; *obviously*," I snapped back.

He glared at me. I glared back.

"If you cannot follow basic instructions, you have no hope of passing this subject," he asserted.

If he thought I was so clueless that that was news to me, how was he intelligent enough to *teach* this subject?

He glared at me. I glared back.

"Go and reload," he snapped.

I stalked towards a rubber bullet box behind us and several people stared when I opened the chamber and reloaded easily. I frowned at them and the Trainer frowned at me.

"It wouldn't have hurt to ask how to reload," Miona told me quietly, as I stepped up beside her. "Everyone's going to assume you've handled guns in Brock Heights."

"You must've handled guns on your farm," I replied.

"I did, but *I* don't scare anyone, and Mr. Fragile Ego isn't threatened by me."

"You think *he* wants a pissing contest with *me*?" I asked.

"You just had one," she replied.

Given how dense he seemed to think I was, I was tempted to shoot Dorthin with my next rubber bullet and pretend I'd mistaken him for the target board.

"One shot at a time," Dorthin said firmly.

My body tensed, as part of me fought the urge to hit him. I pointed my gun vaguely at the target board, brimming with anger and fired. I waited, and waited, then fired again.

"You are *not* aiming!" he objected.

"I wonder what could possibly be distracting me!" I retorted heatedly, and Miona shot me a warning look.

"I am here to *help*," he said in tones of forced calm.

I barely resisted the urge to tell him how woeful his help was. Criticising a teacher –even a terrible one– was probably a good way to get myself kicked out. He didn't press me, finally showing a shred of emotional intelligence. But he watched me from a distance and my anger flared so much that my aim was dreadful. I barely hit the seventh ring from the bull's eye.

* * *

"How was your first shooting lesson?" Jay asked after school.

"Rubbish," I replied.

Jay frowned.

"Trainer Dorthin expects me to learn to shoot with him breathing down my neck and talking down to me as if I've got rocks in my head. How am I supposed to succeed with him around?"

"And you're entirely angry with him?"

Of course I was. He was a control-obsessed prick. What was his problem? Why couldn't he back off and let anyone do anything their way, for five seconds?

…probably for similar reasons dad didn't like letting anyone do anything their way. It was just that Dorthin didn't resort to violence to control everyone. And as exasperating and insulting as Dorthin was and as badly as he did his job, he seemed to genuinely believe he was trying to help. So why had I got so angry with him?

It wasn't how dense Dorthin seemed to think I was. It was having someone who had the power to derail my career obsessing over how I handled a gun, the thing I was most nervous about. It was being stared at by someone who made me uncomfortable, when I hate people looking closely at me. But above everything, it was escaping my control obsessed father only to find I had to pass a subject run by a control-obsessed teacher, when I no longer had any patience for that shit. I didn't truly want to hit Trainer Dorthin, I wanted to pound my father senseless.

"I suggest you take these," Jay said, offering me a pair of gloves and nodding towards a punch bag hanging in the corner.

I stood, muscles taut, heart pounding, adrenaline spiking, my senses hyper aware and hesitated.

"You've never hit a punch bag in complete anger more than a few times? Not truly let loose yet?"

I hadn't. I couldn't. I had to hold on to some of the anger for when... ...but Dad was gone. I didn't need to hold anger in reserve to fight him off anymore. But my instincts yelled at me to keep the anger inside. It was safer to contain it. I wouldn't hurt anyone if I held it in. I wouldn't become *him*.

"What if…what if I start and I *can't* stop?" I asked Jay, carefully not looking at him.

"Your body can't keep punching forever," Jay replied. "And if you keep it up till you need to lie down, and after lying down you need to stand up and keep hitting, you can. You're my last appointment for the day. I can do paperwork in Sarah's office next door, if you'd rather I left."

"No," I replied.

The night I threatened my father was the first time I let out a small chunk of my ever-boiling anger and it didn't just feel good to take control; it felt good to release it. I was scared that that sense of release could become addictive, scared I wouldn't stop because... darkness rose. Grandad's hate-filled eyes and anger-flushed face filled my mind as pain burst over me again and again. He'd been addicted to releasing his anger… *He* hadn't stopped. Grandad had been a monster and he was the one I *truly* feared becoming.

I shivered and pushed the memory fragments down. As long as the fire of anger burned inside me, I was at risk of becoming what I feared and hated. The only way to avoid that was to let it out.

I braced and put the full force of my shoulder into a blow, grunting with the strain. The punchbag jostled. I heard Mum cry out. Saw Dad's blood-stained fist as she fell, and I screamed, "Mummy!"

"Stupid bitch! Now you've upset the kid!"

He kicked her in the stomach. "Useless!"

She hunched into a ball.

My heart hammered against my chest. Where did the anger go? Now there was just the fear of a five-year-old watching his father kick his mother on their kitchen floor.

My fist was flexing. Magic surged within me and I tried not to let it lash out. I roared and dived at the punch bag. I saw the fire in his eyes. I saw the hate. I saw the man who blamed and punished me or Mum for everything. And I sunk my fists into that punch bag until I was drenched in sweat, until my throat was raw from groaning with the effort.

I slumped, panting and the red visor I'd never allowed to descend before rose. I became aware that I was gasping on Jay's office floor, my arm, shoulder and chest muscles seizing up, gasping for air.

It was a while before I caught my breath. Before I took off the gloves, deciding I was too physically tired to strike another blow, despite the fire still burning in my belly.

"Are you alright Rarkin?" Jay asked softly.

I didn't reply. I didn't know what to say.

"Your father's violent?" he asked.

I nodded. I wiped sweat from my face, tensing, trying to compose myself. I'd never let go in front of anyone before. It made me feel threatened.

I straightened, standing, hardening my face and got my guard up before I turned to face him. There were a lot of questions in his eyes, but he didn't press me.

"He's an abusive prick and my grandfather was infinitely worse. But my grandfather's dead and I don't think my father's fool enough to come near me now. I threatened him the last time I spoke to him and I drove him out of the house. He's no threat to me anymore."

"You don't want him to go to prison for what he did?" Jay asked.

"I don't wanna parade my life in front of a bunch of strangers in court," I replied.

I was exhausted. I wanted to stumble home and go to bed. It would be hard enough to face Jay again in two weeks. What if he thinks I'm a monster, now he's glimpsed the anger and violence I'm capable of?

Jay sighed. "I understand your desire to put it behind you. But you have to accept everything that happened first."

That made learning to shoot with Trainer Dorthin talking down to me look like a piece of cake. I thought I was free because Dad was gone, but I was as chained to what he'd already done to me and how I felt about it as ever. My road was still dark in his absence. How long was the tunnel now?

Chapter 8

Field Training

I kept smacking the crap out of a punch bag whenever I thought of things Dad had done that made me angry, how he rarely had anything positive to say, how biology and his presumed right to abuse me were the main meaningful ways he'd acted as my father. I noticed faults I'd overlooked and remembered hurtful things I'd forgotten. I talked to Jay and realised there was great tension in me, but it wasn't just anger. Other emotions lay in the darkness.

I didn't want to think about anything else. Venting my anger took enough out of me. So when I wasn't talking to Jay or pounding the crap out of a punch bag, I pushed away anything that could drag me down.

Miona and I made History of War and Sorcery revision notes for our mid-year exams and I tried to focus on lessons. Our next Monster Studies one was in the Monster Centre, where Trainer Lauran lectured us outside a garl enclosure.

"Small monsters behave like animals. Get too close, make too much noise and you will frighten them, in which case they are as likely to attack as to flee. The best way to understand them is to observe them. You will begin doing so outside their enclosures."

That would get boring quickly… "How soon can we try it from inside, Trainer?" I asked.

She smiled. "When you have demonstrated your ability to keep your calm in their presence and to move around them appropriately."

"As soon as you've got the nerve," Miona translated, her eyes shining, and I smiled back.

The Trainer moved inside the enclosure and her voice was projected through its strange glass walls. She talked too much and I started to zone out. But I zoned back in when she invited me to join her. Everyone stared. Even Amon had nothing to say.

A Monster Centre Trainer swiped an ID card we weren't yet eligible for and smiled at me. I flicked my chin at him as the strange, glassy enclosure door slid upwards. Then I stepped inside.

My heart sped up slightly and my awareness of sights and sounds heightened. I kept my eyes on the long spike covered creature digging a burrow behind shrubs beyond the Trainer. Earth flicked behind it, it grunted, and Trainer Lauran stood so still that it didn't seem to realise she was there.

A twig snapped beneath my feet. I froze. The creature looked up, scanned my end of the enclosure, studied me carefully, then kept digging.

"Their hearing is good," the Trainer said softly, and the creature froze, blinking and listening. "But they are near-sighted. Garls will only identify you as a threat from a distance if they see you moving towards them."

The creature stayed still for several moments, scanned its enclosure and us, then kept digging. It was alert, perceptive, careful... I respected that. Monsters in stories and on film are savage, mindless, destructive forces, but this one was fascinating.

I took a step forward and paused. I took another step and the creature looked up. I froze. It stared at me. Could it tell I was closer?

"Back up slowly Rarkin," the Trainer cautioned. "Any closer and it may charge you."

I sighed, excitement within me deflating as I stepped carefully back to where the Trainer stood. Then I noticed my classmates gawping or smiling at me. The Trainer smiled at my frown.

I wasn't surprised when Miona joined us, moving in a way that made me suspect she'd stalked garls on her farm before telling her parents they needed Monster Containment to pay them a visit.

It was two weeks before our whole class entered the enclosure with the Trainer, and Miona and I started going in without her. Rinth went next, and I respected that against my will. Then Amon went, shaking slightly, and nearly tripped on his second step. I can't decide if he's completely foolish, or a bit brave too.

Four weeks in, the Trainer decided we were ready for field training in the National Park Zone. I was surprised I could go, because my aim with Dorthin breathing down my neck was second worst, and Kay's was so bad I didn't think he was cut out to be a sytheren.

We caught the electric-way north, through the Bellarian National Park Zone and over Gurnya River to Torret, from which a bus drove us to the northern foothills, where we met a syther in a green uniform.

"Today's field training will occur in two groups, led by myself and Ine," Trainer Lauran explained. "Here in the National Park Zone, we may encounter garls that have burrowed under Wild Zone fences, or bizas in caves. If you think you have sighted either, tell your group to stop. Ine or I will stun anything if needed. Don't worry if you stop us and it's only a native animal; we prefer you to be overcautious.

"In accordance with protocol, you will each carry a stun gun loaded with tranquilliser darts, for use in an emergency. Keep it pointed at the ground if you lead your group, or to the side to avoid accidents. You are unlikely to need to shoot anything.

"Today's objective is to navigate your way through frozen tunnels until you reach the central chamber, where lies a yeti in an enchanted sleep. You are to cut off a little of its fur to experience being near a large monster."

Miona and I flashed grins, while our classmates exchanged nervous smiles. We collected our stun guns and the Trainer split us up. Miona was in the other group and I got stuck with Amon, Rinth, Lylez, Ryan and Ine. We started off together on a track through the trees, but it soon forked, and my group turned left onto a lightly treed, boulder scattered hillside.

"Smart," Amon said to Rinth, with that big warm small of his.

Rinth was smiling the first shy smile I'd seen on his face. He was wearing black rimmed glasses, a bit rounded, which made him look smart and a bit posh.

"Do you need them for distance?" Amon asked.

"Yeah," Rinth said. "I'd be wasting stun darts on rocks and tree stumps otherwise."

Ine smiled. "I'm sure Sythe appreciate your thoughtfulness about their resources."

Rinth grinned.

"I dunno," said Ryan. "It's easier to beat him in shooting contests when he's not wearing them."

"And that's your main concern for your brother, when he walks in the National Park Zone and risks bumping into garls?" Amon stirred.

Ryan and Rinth grinned, in a way that made their resemblance more obvious. They had the same long noses and pale complexions, but Ryan was auburn haired like me and freckled, though they had the same blue eyes. How had I not noticed that before?

"You're still happy to navigate?" Ine asked Rinth, who nodded. Ine passed him a compass and they led our group down a narrow trail.

I scanned the undergrowth either side of them for pig-sized creatures with long spikes sniffing for rodent nests. With so many of us, any nearby garl was likely to see and charge us before we stood still. Ine seemed relaxed and he scanned the ground around us, but my group stared at the track twisting and turning ahead, eyeing each bend nervously.

Branches rustled, and Ryan halted us. I glimpsed a bird flying away and Ine smiled and motioned us on. More branches rustled, but it was another bird. Then Lylez stopped us, as something scampered away through the undergrowth.

"That might have been a clever garl," Ine said. "Well spotted."

We rounded a bend and Lylez cried; "Garl!"

Amon stumbled over a rock. Rinth dropped the compass, while Ryan raised his stun gun and shot wildly. I gaped and took aim as the garl lowered its head and Ryan's stun darts rattled through its spikes. The garl charged.

Adrenaline spiked. I fired two shots, aiming at the neck and underbelly. The monster blinked drearily, then fell six paces away. Ine smiled at me, lowering his gun. He hadn't fired a single stun dart…

"I thought *you* were going to stun it?" Amon asked Ine worriedly.

"If Ryan and Rarkin hit it, I would have killed it," Ine replied. "Garls are small and too many stun darts injecting sleep serum into their veins can paralyse their vital organs. We *contain* monsters, we don't kill them unless it's necessary."

I blinked. I'd hit a moving target; twice. But I was rubbish at target practice… Amon gaped at me. Ine frowned.

"I'm not that good in class," I said.

"You have good instincts," Ine replied. "And they kick in when it counts."

Ine removed the darts and pocketed them, leaving the monster to sleep where it lay. Rinth picked up the compass and said, "Anyone else want this thing? I'd rather carry a gun."

Several people laughed and Amon grinned at him. *They'd* both waited for Ine to fire…

"I'll take it," said Lylez and Rinth smiled as he handed it over.

"I also wanted to give you the chance," Ine said quietly to me, as we continued walking. "I mentor trainee sythers and you looked ready as they are."

I blinked. He'd read me better than *I* could read me?

We gave the garl a wide berth, and followed Lylez into the cave, which was dark and made of rock. The back wall sparkled. Walls further in were coated with a thin layer of ice.

"Watch your step, it'll be slippery," Ine warned.

The tunnel wasn't that cold, and I didn't understand how there could be ice. Further in, the ice thickened and developed shades of blue. Daylight shone in through cracks in the roof and made the ice sparkle, and icicles hung from corners.

"This doesn't look like a glacial tunnel," said Amon. "How's it frozen?"

"According to legend," Ine replied, "by the yeti. It came here decades ago and adventurers say the ice appeared and thickened afterwards. The yeti was put to sleep by an unknown traveller and now sythers renew the spell for students to visit."

"And the rest of the time?" I asked.

"Large and dangerous monsters like yetis are territorial, and their territory is usually in the Wild," Ine replied. "We respect their territory, banning human travel through it. It's non-territorial monsters that cause problems, hunting livestock if they escape the Wild and Wildlife Officers patrolling National Park Zones. That's where we come in."

"Why do all the dangerous monsters live in the wild?" Amon asked.

"You know they were bred by sorcerers to fight in the Monster Wars fifteen hundred years ago?" Ine asked, and Amon nodded.

"Hundreds of monsters broke free of the enchantments binding them during battle and retreated into the wilderness, where they bred for years. Eventually, Taros united and pooled resources to expand Farm Zones and protect natural wildlife in National Parks, but by then monsters were so numerous that the most practical option was to contain them in Wild Zones."

Monsters claimed swathes of the continent because short-sighted humans who bred them lost control? *Fools...*

By then, Lylez was guiding us through an icy tunnel, leading us deeper into the hills and downward, to a small, high-roofed chamber. Pillars of ice twisted up in strange curves throughout the chamber and around the walls. At the foot of an outer pillar lay upside down icicles as tall as my forearm. Not icicles; bizas.

Ine motioned us to stop. The bizas moved, revealing pale bluish arms and legs, and walked across our path, while the rest of my group held their breaths and Ryan and Rinth watched with interest. The bizas disappeared through a crack in the wall.

"For those of you who don't remember," said Ine, "Any upside-down icicle-like things here will be bizas. Their venom won't kill you, but it can send you into unconsciousness or a coma. They won't attack unless you get too close and they feel threatened. Don't let that happen."

I shook my head. Class was boring compared to this.

I scanned the ground between the icy pillars as we walked, until I saw piles of snow in the middle of the chamber, with two half oval piles of dirt in front. I smiled; the yeti.

Trainer Lauran's group emerged from a tunnel on our right and Ine halted and asked, "Who's glad it's asleep?"

Ryan swore. The piles of dirt were the soles of the creature's feet. The 'snow' was limbs, a torso and a head, of giant proportions.

Ine led us to the creature's left foot and held up a knife. I took it and trod carefully towards the slumbering giant, watching a mound of fur rise and fall in time to the deep rumbling of breathing. I took hold of fur as long as my forearm and used the knife to gently saw some off, wondering what it would be like to face something this size when it was awake; to contain monsters as a syther.

Chapter 9

Onwards

With more field training, my class became less
awkward about encountering monsters in the open space of the
National Park Zone. But I remained ahead and Ine let me stun
small monsters. I shot more accurately than in class and realised
that without Trainer Dorthin distracting me, I could shoot quite
well.

After weeks of Dad's absence, I stopped listening for
him to come home and slept better at night. I breathed more
freely and worried less about mum, who got a job as a
receptionist and started saving to buy her own home.

I revised everything we studied when I lived with Dad
heavily, but strangely, what I'd learnt since was easier to
remember. Jay said it was because trauma or stress had
hampered my memory and now Dad was gone my memory was
returning to normal. It made me want to kick Dad for every test
I struggled to pass at General School.

My sixteenth birthday crept up on me during revision. I
had a small dinner at Uncle Alan's and I invited Miona and
Merin as well as the boys. Merin flattered Tak with her interest

in his tattoos, or was it his biceps? It was hard to tell. Tak smiled, chatted and seemed oddly captivated by her, given I thought he was a samer. I mean, they're both seventeen, what was I missing?

Miona responded to my frown with a knowing smile, while Uncle Alan chatted to Aunt Lil and mum, pretending not to notice.

Glenn raised his brows at me. Wak frowned with polite confusion.

"She's an aller," Miona answered their unasked questions. "And she loves meeting new people."

"He's uh, not," Wak said unconfidently. "He's always dated guys."

"If any of us was going to be an aller…" Glenn added with a pointed look.

"I… may be the last to know!" Wak replied with a grin.

"I'd expect nothing less of our favourite somer," Glenn said with a smile, while Cam eyed me, and politely said nothing. As if Wak would be last, when I was at sea. Though if Wak is a somer, maybe I'm a noner. All this people having crushes on each other, and flirting and whatever; I wasn't into any of it.

"If he wasn't an aller before," Glenn said, "he might be by the time she's done speaking to him."

Wak raised an eyebrow at Glenn, then eyed Miona.

What in Chaos was this conversation? Why was I in it and why was it happening at *my* birthday?

Miona laughed. "No one's safe, though I can call her off, should any of you feel intimidated."

Glenn smiled. He liked her.

"How about some sparring instead?" Wak offered. "All this who's into who hurts my head."

"And you think sparring with her is going to lessen that sensation?" Glenn asked.

"Of course," Wak said. "We can't leave out birthday boy. Rark and me vs. Glenn and Miona. Cam can referee, or send for back up if we need it."

"He may need to strip naked to get back up's attention," Wak replied doubtfully, eyeing Merin and Tak, who were laughing loudly.

Glenn nearly fell over laughing. Now Miona was raising an eyebrow.

"I'm not the only one here who's not great with people, am I?" I asked quietly.

"You're in good company mate," Glenn said, clapping me and Wak both on the shoulder, as he led us towards the backyard.

"You can do the stripping," Cam piped up to Wak.

"Deal," Wak replied, and he strode into the backyard with such uncaring confidence that Miona and I both raised our brows at each other. Glenn just smiled and shook his head.

"What did I miss?" Des was stepping in through the side gate with a smile, having just finished his shift.

"You tell him," I told Glenn.

Had I made the right choice, mixing my at-school and at-home friends? If I hadn't, apparently it was too late now... Though I hadn't introduced Miona and Merin to Trent yet. He doesn't go in for dinners with family. Another time?

***

Time continued moving too quickly after my party, and the day of our coursework exams arrived. Uncle Alan and Mum drove me to school, dropping me off at the driveway loop outside the office.

"You'll be fine!" Uncle Alan reassured me.

Glenn said the same thing, but he, Wak and Tak had already passed their Shadower Level One coursework exams and were waiting for the opportunity to take their field exam; easy for them to say.

I found two thirds of my class waiting outside our classroom; every sixteen-year-old was present. Miona and I nodded to each other and waited tensely till Trainer Lauran let us in. Our exam papers lay face down on our desks and we sat in silence.

I wished it was over until the clock struck ten. Then Trainer Lauran said, "You may begin."

It wasn't as bad as I feared. Miona's style of note taking with images and words meant some of the History of Sorcery stuck. I remembered we weren't as alone on Taros as General School taught us, and wondered if things aren't as peaceful with our green skinned neighbours the Serenans, or with the human Miarans as this level of our studies claimed. Were Serenans and Miarans who Sythe Peace Keepers worked with? Or did Sythe keep native monsters and magical creatures no longer managed by Miarans in Taros under control? Did sythes patrol the border of the Wild and National Park Zones?

Or did sythes work against people like 'Mavon' from the conversation I'd overheard outside Zatrack's office, about the abduction and relocation of a Monster Containment Team in the National Park Zone? Are the outer zones where all the action is in our era, and where people like Mavon, who apparently have the ability and guts to abduct a syther team, are based?

Despite my wandering thoughts and racing heart, I managed to attempt an answer to every exam question, without running out of time, which was better than any General School test I've ever sat. I had no idea how good my answers were, but there wasn't much time to worry about that, because I needed to prepare and rest up for the practical exams.

* * *

"Attention everyone, the results of your written exams are in."

My class gathered around Trainer Lauran. She read out people's names in alphabetical order from a list and whether they passed or not. Ryan and Amon passed and danced around. Miona passed too.

"Rarkin Lormen, fail."

My heart sank. Everyone was staring at me...

"Check it out. Rarkin's got it right!"

The voice sounded distant. I opened my eyes. I'd been asleep. Our written exam results didn't come out for three more days, and today was the day of the practical exams.

"How ya doin' Rark?"

Wak and Tak were approaching. Wak smiled at me, but Tak turned his grin to Lylez and some girls in our class, who'd paused in their sparring to check out his tall, broad build, and sculpted blond hair. He flicked his chin at Miona, then smiled and blew Amon a kiss. Amon blushed and smiled back.

I shook my head. I couldn't fault Amon for finding Tak attractive. I swear even noners check him out sometimes. But Tak did have a way of disrupting everyone with his presence, in this case distracting them from self-defence practice, or from bandaging each other in the dining hall. Long enough for me to remember that I'd only sat down to put on my gloves, but I'd fallen asleep, so Miona was training with Amon.

"Everyone seems to think exhausting themselves with practice will leave energy for the exam, but you've got it right," Tak said to me with a smile.

I'd been there an hour and most people had been there longer. Chareck's two arrogant mates sat in a corner, red-faced, sweating and panting. Fools.

"You wanna practice with us?" Wak offered.

Wak and Tak are identical twins, aside from Tak's flashy hairstyle. They're both taller than me, two years older and well built. I smiled and nodded, wondering how those two hulking figures wanted to play this and knowing I didn't stand a chance against both of them together, and possibly not even either of them on their own.

Luckily, they decided to go easy on me. Even then, Wak floored me as soon as I warmed up. Tak said he wasn't being fair and dived on him, and the three of us wrestled on padded mats covering the dining hall floor, our laughter hampered by the difficulty squashing each other posed to our ability to breathe.

When Trainer Dorthin called, "You may follow me into the Practical Training Centre, where you will be given instructions," Tak helped me up and straightened my collar, then smiled and pushed me towards my class, while Wak waved. It was the first time I entered an exam room with a smile on my face.

"Unlike your written exams, there will be no time limit," Trainer Dorthin announced to my classmates and the mature age students, including Merin, in an antechamber of the Practical Training Centre. "You will be split into three groups and rotate through three stations. At each station, the Trainer who is your examiner will explain your task and the skills you will be assessed on."

They split us up. I was with Lylez, Miona, Amon, Ryan, Rinth and unfamiliar mature age students. We had self-defence first, in a room with a pile of protective gear and a crash mat at the front.

"For the Self-Defence Exam," said Trainer Sirona, our first examiner, "I will be assessing your ability to make informed defensive decisions while under attack, and your defensive reflexes. You will warm up with a partner, then take it in turns to attack and defend yourself against that partner."

She asked Miona and I to go first. I smiled as I crouched, adrenaline pumping into my veins as we circled each other with calculating looks. I danced beyond reach of Miona's fists, always keeping them in sight, ready to pivot in any direction, and I rarely needed to block. Finally, Miona feinted and got me in the hip, making me stagger. She smiled, and I smiled back.

We swapped. Miona stood her ground, keeping her elbows up, defending with one arm and throwing a punch at the first opportunity with the other. I was calculating, jabbing hard, but I met block after block.

I got into a pattern of multiple jabs to one side, then trying to catch her off guard on the other. She got used to it, defending with her left arm.

By the end of the bout, she got two punches in with her right. We were completely breathless by then and Trainer Sirona asked us to stop, smiling proudly. She met my eyes and I smiled back. I'd passed that exam.

Then she pit Amon against Lylez. Lylez was fast in her attacks, her petite form gliding gracefully around the mat, her long black plait swishing behind her, while Amon flapped his arms like a confused seagull, his neck length dreadlocks flying in all directions, in contrast to their usual neat framing of his head and neck. He finally remembered to crouch and duck his head to shield himself effectively.

I frowned, wondering if he'd done enough to pass, but the Trainer's face gave nothing away. Lylez came at him harder, her gloves thudding loudly into his forearms and he panicked and tripped her. Everyone laughed.

I sighed. Did he take any of this seriously? Did he truly want to be here? I'd worked so hard to get to this point, and here he was giving the impression he'd just blundered through based on charm, good looks and being class clown.

"Criminals rarely fight fair," Trainer Sirona told a sheepish Amon. "There is no such thing as cheating in self-defence. You do whatever you need to."

Amon attacked next and Lylez danced out of his way, graceful as a ballerina. She was the most skilled, until Rinth and Ryan. Both were powerful, their blocked blows landing hard enough to bruise through padded vests and gloves. Both boys grinned fiercely, revelling in the challenge. I shook my head. How could *I* have something in common with *them*?

They were built like Wak and Tak …Rinth had said he had cousins in Brock Heights when we first met. It couldn't be… but Rinth looked like them, and he and Ryan *moved* like Wak and Tak. The four of them must train together… If Rinth and Ryan were my mate's cousins, did that mean I had to *like* them?

I kind of welcomed the dilemma. Because we had our pistol shooting test next and feeling conflicted about Rinth and Ryan was more fun.

Trainer Dorthin's love of talking too much cut through my distraction all too soon.

"The targets for your first round are on human and monster thighs," Trainer Dorthin explained, "because as sytherens, you are most likely to need a gun to stun criminals, or monsters which have strayed into the Farm Zones or rural towns. For the second round, the bull's eyes will be on heads, in the unlikely event that as sytherens, you are required to defend Bellaria or anywhere in Taros during war."

That sent a shiver of nerves through everyone and was typical of Dorthin's tendency to put us off. I grit my teeth, determined to let his words wash over me. We stepped up to the gun shelf, took our guns and ear plugs, then gazed across open space. I noticed slits in the ceiling. What was the prick plotting?

"Each gun is programmed to allow you to fire two darts only. That is the highest average you are likely to get off if a monster attacks you in the field with your current experience. Your shooting will be filmed, and timed. You will be marked on the proximity of your darts to the bull's eyes and on the speed at which you shoot. Defending yourselves and others against monsters requires a balance of speed and accuracy, and that balance is the focus of this exam."

Just stay away from me...

"Your targets will appear in 3, 2, 1. Now!"

As I half-expected, targets dropped from the ceiling before us, at different distances. Mine was a garl a good way off. I sighted, took aim and fired both shots in quick succession. Trainer Dorthin's eyebrows raised, as he stepped into the corner of my vision.

I smiled. Both bullets hit the ring around the bull's eye on the far-left leg, my best shooting in class.

Miona did well on my left, while on my right Amon fired last, at the furthest target, putting one bullet in the ring round the bull's eye and the second *in* the bull's eye.

"Bloody hell!" Ryan exclaimed, as Trainer Dorthin smiled at Amon.

Miona smiled, and I shook my head. Amon and I were the only ones doing better in the shooting exam than during class. Since when was Amon a good shot?

"Your second and final targets will appear in 3, 2, 1. Now!" Trainer Dorthin cried.

Targets dropped. Mine was so close I put two bullets in the bull's eye before I realised this one was shaped like a human, and the bulls' eye was on the head. I shivered, wondering if I'd do the same if Dad entered the room when I had a gun in hand.

"You're a natural at responding to danger," Miona said with a smile.

She'd taken her time, while I just raised my gun and fired. That was no surprise, I had years as a kid where I couldn't waste a second when Dad came home sober. Hesitation meant pain.

First aid was up next, and it was a joke, bandaging cuts, knowing that if someone gets impaled by a knife or glass you don't pull it out in case they bleed to death, so you bandage around it etc. The role plays about finding someone injured in the field were just as easy. Then we were free till Mijoraday, first of the next working week, when we would collect our results from our classroom.

* * *

I was tense on Mijoraday. Even if Miona and I aced Self-Defence and my memory was better, I've never been confident about tests.

"If you fail, you can re-sit the exams at year's end," Trainer Lauran reminded us from the front of our classroom. "If you no longer wish to be a sytheren, consider this a learning experience. You will receive your envelope in roll order with your results and a comment from each Trainer who assessed you."

Kay got his envelope first and bit his lip.

"You still applying to be a Wildlife Officer?" Amon asked him, and he nodded. "Then don't worry about it," Amon said, clapping him on the shoulder.

I stamped on the tingle of nerves that hearing a classmate was already having to leave Sythe School triggered in me.

Lylez smiled and her dark eyes flashed as she read her letter, while Amon grinned and waved his in the air, dancing gracefully back to his seat with an overly serious smile that had Ryan and other kids clapping and calling out encouragement. What was wrong with his fingernails? Were they blue? He shifted his letter so it obscured his fingers, shooting me a nervous smile.

I turned away. I didn't need reminding of how easy he'd had it while I sat here stewing about whether I'd passed.

"Rarkin Lormen," said Trainer Lauran.

I hardly dared to breathe as I strode forwards, only realising I'd lapsed into a tough strut when Lylez shied back. The Trainer ignored my posture as she handed me my envelope, with a small smile. The first page read:

Congratulations, you have successfully passed your sytheren exams!

Time stopped. I couldn't take in the rest of the letter. I'd passed my sytheren exams… There was just one problem; family were invited to the Sytheren Ceremony. What if Dad decided he wanted to know me again? His girlfriend would want to congratulate me…but what if he turned up late, and he lost it and started hurling insults in public?

I almost didn't notice my classmates gathering around a table in the Food Court, as I crossed the open space, seeking the nearest exit and fresh air.

"You all right Rarkin?" Amon asked. Amon, of *all* people.

"You wouldn't understand," I replied, trying to brush him off.

He followed where my gaze was frozen on the congratulation letter, the part about family.

"I suppose it's about parents? Well yeah, I *wouldn't* understand…"

I frowned at him. He teared up and rushed off. How could Amon have family issues? The guy who can't stop smiling?

I took a deep breath and strode after him. I hate apologising. It's admitting you were wrong, which is showing weakness. But it was the decent thing to do when you upset someone unintentionally.

"I'm sorry," I said, when I found him sitting on the edge of a raised garden bed on the edge of the sports field.

"I grew up in an orphanage," Amon replied.

I gaped. He was *far* too happy for that…

"I was there ten years and it was one carer each day between fifteen kids. They tried to spend time with us and give us attention and everything. And I got more than most coz I'm loud. I got adopted by this old couple when I was ten, who've been really good to me. But I've seen other families… it's different."

Why tell me when for all he knew I could use it against him?

"No one knows who my real parents are. I don't know if they abandoned me, if they're dead, if they're looking for me. I was found by an old lady outside a shoe shop on Blossom Hill, and that's all I know. And at the Sytheren Ceremony, everyone will be there with their parents. They'll have what I don't."

Fair enough.

It was none of Amon's business, but if he wanted to share, it was only fair to tell him something. "I'll have half," I replied. "My Dad's a drunk and a prick. He thinks I'm a failure. Every word I've written, every action I've learnt has been hard, trying to pass while being related to him. What if he shows up? He'd come late and make a scene."

Amon seemed surprised, but not shocked.

"That's awful. I guess I've always thought of fathers in a positive light. But they'll have syther guards at the entrance. They'll chuck him out, if he doesn't behave."

I blinked. How could Amon just accept, and see a solution so quickly?

"I didn't think of that," I replied. "Anyway, I don't think he'll come. He hates me for doing well, when he failed to become a syther."

"What a prick," Amon replied, and I smiled at hearing a kid I'd assumed was soft, middle class and well-raised calling my father that. Maybe I was too hard on Amon. Maybe he was alright. I should say more, but what else did I say?

"I never guessed..." I cut off. How did I finish that sentence? "You're always so happy..."

Amon sighed. "Did you think you were the only one with issues?"

How could the feeling of cold water down your back sting like that? But his expression was open, considering. He meant that as an honest question. Did I not see that other people might be struggling too? No. I hadn't. My gaze fell.

"What does a guy have to do, to get your approval?" Amon asked. "Does he have to be big and strong? To be a good fighter?"

I frowned. Cam wasn't like that at all. We'd always been good mates. And it was Glenn's earnestness, his honesty and brains that I liked.

"No," I replied. "He has to know I'm shit with people."

Did I just say that? To *Amon*? I mean, Glenn knows full well I'm shit with people and Cam gets it too but... There was something about the light in Amon's warm brown eyes. The smile playing around those lips. I was laughing. Why was I laughing? Amon was laughing too. There were tears in his eyes. What were we even talking about? How in Chaos was *I* making a fool of myself in front of *Amon?!*

Amon wiped a tear from his cheek, then eyed me self-consciously. His index fingernail was painted lavender, instead of blue, like the rest. It was kind of pretty.

"Why don't you paint all of them that colour?" I asked.

Amon's smile broadened and he looked me right in the eyes. Why was he so happy? A dude wanted to paint his nails, why would that be a problem? I maybe, kind of liked him, but he was definitely confusing.

"I'd better go," Amon said. "My grandparents –the couple who adopted me– came to pick me up so I can tell them my results."

"You call them 'grandparents'?" I asked.

"It saves questions. You'll see what I mean when you see how old they are. See you at the ceremony."

Those eyes were too warm, too happy and too free. Was that what made me uneasy about him? Was it that every time I looked at that smile, at how openly his feelings played across his face, I wondered if I could *ever* be like that? Like the kid who never felt the need to hide anything from anyone, because he trusted everyone and he felt *safe*?

"Bye," I said, happy, confused and lost by the conversation.

* * *

The Sytheren Ceremony was held in a posh hotel in Bellaria, with a large balcony and veranda, yellow lights glowing warmly in its windows and two big guards flanking the doors. A sytheren stood beside them, checking off names, identifying sytherens by the new, smart navy-blue uniforms we were wearing. I glanced around uneasily, but there was no sign of my father. Mum had called to tell him about tonight and Sandy had called out congratulations from the background, but he hadn't said much. He was probably out somewhere with Sandy, distracting himself from me achieving what he hadn't.

Uncle Alan and Aunt Lil accompanied Mum and I, in a suit and gowns. We got our names ticked off and walked into a richly furnished room, with a man in a smart black uniform on our right.

"Sytheren Ceremony?" he asked.

Aunt Lil nodded, and he replied, "On my right and up the stairs."

We walked along a carpeted, chandelier-lit hallway to a grand staircase with wooden statues of guards saluting at both ends of its railing. It was the most richly furnished place I've ever been. I felt like an imposter climbing those stairs.

At the top was a large ballroom with chairs before a stage on our right and a crowded dance floor ahead. Miona was introducing her parents to Trainer Lauran. When she finished, I introduced Uncle Alan, Aunt Lil and Mum to Miona's parents, who thankfully didn't comment on Dad's absence. Merin and her parents joined us. Amon smiled at me from beside two elderly people across the room. He waved, with a hand of all lavender painted nails. Part of my face tried to smile back, but my jaw locked up, at how much I'd let my guard down the last time.

I straightened and nodded stiffly. It only softened his smile.

"Wait a minute, I thought you said you weren't-" Merin cut off.

Miona was eyeing her sternly. "What did you two talk about the other day?" she asked me.

Amon's voice echoed in my head, "Did you think you were the only one with issues?"

I hunched over in shame. "Kid has his issues," I replied evasively. "I shouldn't be so hard on him."

Merin smiled. "We'll teach you social skills yet."

Miona grinned at her and Merin's smile broadened as she met Miona's eyes.

I shivered. Coming from Merin, that sounded like a threat. She smiled, linking arms with both of us and led us towards our seats. She was linking arms with me... in public. Part of me was panicking. Miona was eyeing me questioningly. She wasn't affectionate much, that was more Merin's thing. But linking arms wasn't as intimate as holding hands. Other people were doing it around the room. I supposed it wasn't a target on my back...

Catching Miona's look, Merin eyed me too. I shook my head. "You're going to be the death of me."

She smiled sweetly. Despite the blend of emotions twisting my gut, I couldn't help but smile back. Merin was bold. She made me nervous, and she was too clever and perceptive, but under the playfulness, she *cared*. I suddenly understood why she and Tak had hit it off so well. He was exactly the same. Just as cheeky. Just as forward with his affections. They had the same heart, and it was seeing in her what I trusted in him that made me trust her too.

There was no more time for her to wind me up though, as everyone was taking their seats. I sat with my family beside Miona, Merin and their families. Then a speech from on stage cut into my thoughts.

"Welcome," said a man's voice. "I am Trainer Marn Kovik of our mature age sytherens. We are here tonight to award sytheren certificates to some of our finest students."

It was a boring, standard special occasion speech which did nothing to abate the fireflies Amon, Merin and the prospect of having to step onto that stage in front of everyone had set flying riotously through my guts. Then the certificates were presented, and my chest tightened, as my classmates walked across the stage and everyone clapped.

"Rarkin Lormen."

My heart drummed in my chest. I stood, taking a deep breath and tried to shrug off polite applause as I walked towards Trainer Lauran. I bowed my head as I shook her hand and received my certificate, trying to ignore the scorching discomfort of so many gazes on me. No-one in the audience would smile that way if they met me on the street. It was because I looked like some well-behaved middle-class do-gooder in my sytheren uniform that I got approving smiles. It made me feel fake.

I was grateful to get out of the spotlight and join Miona and Merin at the finger food.

"Rarkin," Merin said, in a tone that did nothing to settle my nerves. "For such a good-looking guy, why do you hate being the centre of attention?"

My mouth hung open. Tak was good looking. Chaos, he was *gorgeous*. Glenn was good looking too. They were both confident and kind and… chaos, Amon was good looking too. It helped A LOT that he smiled a thousand times more often than I did. But me, this awkward piece of flesh being good looking?

Miona shook her head. "Of course you're an innermind! I should have figured it out ages ago. You don't like talking to strangers, you don't like being the centre of attention, you often don't know what to say. You're yourself in private. It's not just that you're Brock Heights 'don't let anyone know me,' it's more than that. Why weren't you diagnosed at General School?"

I snorted. "*Me*, let someone diagnose me? I mean, sure, if I was bleeding to death I'd let some diagnose and treat my wounds but…"

It had *never* occurred to me. I was always quiet and reserved because I didn't trust strangers and I didn't let my guard down and… and that masked my awkwardness around people. Like I'd flat out told Amon, I'm shit with people. Innerminds are… well, not necessarily shit with people. But awkward. My levels of awkward. But the idea that a bunch of things that made me *me* had a name... having to share deeply personal traits that made my life harder with *other* people, total random strangers... I hated the idea. I'd rather be me and... and alone and misunderstood?

I was glaring so hard at the floor that I didn't snap out of it until Merin took my hand. "You don't have to get a diagnosis. But can I please teach you some social skills? You can only get so far as 'brooding tough guy'. We're going to have to get jobs next semester, and that will mean speaking to strangers. And the way you avoid eye contact, and glare at people and are utterly unreadable, is going to scare some of them halfway to Siro."

There was no chance in hell I'd become smiley, everyone's-friend Amon. But I supposed I could try to be less grumpy...

"Are you considering my offer?"

There was no mistaking Merin was pleased, from the glow in her eye and the curve of her lips.

"Maybe," I replied sternly.

Miona smiled. "I'm sorry Rarkin," she said. "For bringing Merin into your life. You never stood a chance."

She was biting down a smile.

"We can't *both* be sensible and reasonable all the time," Merin replied, her eyes gleaming wickedly.

I shook my head. "I have never met two people so opposite, yet who like each other so much. You two don't make any sense at all, and yet you make all the sense there is."

Merin smiled at Miona. Miona beamed and kissed her. Merin wrapped her arms around Miona.

Rinth was eyeing us across the room, dumbfounded. I laughed then. How on earth had *I* come to be friends with these girls? Why did *they* want to be friends with *me*? It was funny and ridiculous and whatever the answer, I was glad they had.

There was dancing after that. I tried telling them I didn't dance, but Miona ignored my protests and Merin toed me to the dance floor. They both took me by the hand and Merin led us in a three-partner dance of sways and turns, surprising me with her grace. It turned out dancing was easy. It wasn't so different from Zushai, constant athleticism and balance to the rhythm of a beat.

Rinth was eyeing us again, confused.

"I think we may have given Rinth the impression it's the three of us," said Miona, following my gaze.

Merin smiled, eyeing him appraisingly. "Tak's cousin? How do you think *he'd* feel about the four of us?"

I flushed.

Miona glared at Merin, who burst out laughing. She was joking. I kind of knew that. But… I swear that girl will be the death of me!

A jazz number started. Miona's mother wheeled herself onto the dance floor. The way Miona's father spun her chair around brought the dance floor to a halt, as everyone stared in wonder. Some audience members looked worried her father would stack the chair, but her mother showed no concern for the angles she was tilted or spun around at. She smiled the whole time. Could I trust someone else that much one day? Could I enjoy myself that much if I did?

Chapter 10

Sytherens

My new syther studies class chatted enthusiastically outside our new classroom at the start of second semester, as did Miona, Merin and the mature age sytherens. I still felt as if I didn't have my exam results yet. Like I was stressed about whether I'd passed.

Our new Trainer invited us in and told us to choose desks. Our new desks were metal and glass, with screens with the Sythe School 'S' logo on them. I've heard people in posh suburbs still have access to this kind of tech, but I'd never seen it. It'd been too far outside our price range in Brock Heights since the Nuclear War, and the nearest General School could only afford it for kids taking advanced subjects. I sat on the edge of my expensive leather chair at a desk beside Merin and Miona's, feeling like I didn't belong.

"I am aware that you haven't used screens yet, but I will explain them later," said our new Trainer. "For now, I am Trainer Morea, and this is Trainer Lauran, who is learning to instruct syther students. Today is an introduction to where continued study can lead and the jobs you are qualified to do as sytherens. Those of you still studying will continue Monster Studies, Marksmanship, Self-Defence and Zushai. You will also complete a basic but comprehensive study of Introductory Taron Law and its enforcement. This is compulsory, because in times of crisis all sythers may be called upon to support the Syther Force.

"Your coursework next year will depend on the government department you wish to work in as a syther; Syther Force, Monster Containment, Search and Rescue, or Field Assignments appointed at government request. To gain syther rank, you need to complete a minimum amount of coursework and exams in the Practical Training Centre, but also a Field Exam. This will be a real situation, a criminal arrest or capturing a stray monster in the Farm Zone. It will test your capacity to follow orders, to work effectively as part of a team, and to work well under pressure, in dangerous situations."

I sighed. We had to get good at taking orders and teamwork already?

"When I believe you are ready, you will be promoted to the position of Trainee Syther and be assigned to an experienced syther team. They will mentor you and decide when you are ready to sit your Field Exam. If you pass, you will be able to apply for work in the department of your choice as a syther. If you fail, you will reflect with your team on where you went wrong, have additional mentoring and complete a second Field Exam."

He talked about jobs we could do as sytherens, but driving sythers to field work or working permanently for City Guard didn't appeal to me. Nor did being a sytheren taking orders in the army, but everyone boarded a bus to Bellaria Army Base for an introduction before we made decisions.

Once we were sitting in the army hall, a Field Captain came in and yelled and snapped at us. When people yell at me, I yell back to say I'm not taking their crap. But the captain didn't seem to know how to talk normally. And when he talked about being a soldier, my doubts were confirmed.

"If you desire to become a soldier in our ranks, you will be required to live on these premises. We have a shuttle bus that runs to Sythe School if you wish to attend it. Apart from your hours at Sythe School, you will be expected to follow our timetable."

That timetable started with getting up at 6am for exercise every morning and had an activity for every minute of the day. I can't understand why anyone would volunteer to stick to a rigid timetable; it'd drive me insane.

Then he talked about how we would be required to follow orders to the letter, whether we were helping with humanitarian crises or fighting wars. No allowances made for dim-witted commanders, prejudiced ones, corrupt ones, or pricks. Just unquestioning obedience. I've seen enough fools in authority to reserve the right to judge, ignore and disobey them. If my commander told me to do something questionable, or that

I thought was unnecessary, I'd tell him where to get off. The military was no place for me.

But the afternoon provided a chance for the job I had once wanted as part of my plan to escape Dad. It wouldn't serve that purpose now, but it could go towards buying a home; mine and Mum's. That meeting was with the guy in charge of employing city guards and it was on the sports field, back at school.

"Welcome kids, my name's Garry and I'm from Bellaria City Guard. If you work for us, you'll start at city exits, then move on to patrolling the shopping district, areas with a reputation for crime, big events in town or guarding City Government buildings. Your duties will include breaking up fights, arresting thieves and drunks, searching all vehicles entering the city for drugs or other illegal items, supporting Syther Force Sythers who request aid and occasionally containing monsters.

"While you're new, you'll have at least two experienced guards working with you each shift. They'll arrest people if needed. You can't make arrests till you've been on the job for at least six months and got your permit from the Syther Station. When you're working, the most experienced guard will be in charge, and any sythers who need your help will give you orders.

"If everyone can line up in front of my chair, I'll interview you one by one and at the end of your interview, you can take on Toron or Sinia."

He gestured to the young man and woman standing either side of him. They were of medium height and had great builds for their genders. There wasn't much chance of us having to fight built, well-trained people on the job. What was he really testing?

We lined up and Garry asked questions; how long we've been at Sythe School, situations we've worked in teams etc. He was unsure of me, but I was unsure of him... Then I was wearing padded gloves and facing off with Toron, who flicked his chin at me. Of course he was from Brock Heights. I returned the gesture, dodged him and struck his lower back as I ducked past. Then I pivoted to face him.

Garry laughed. "That's enough lad. I can see you'd face down a herd of hundaira. There's no need to tear strips off him."

I blinked, confused and watched Miona and Sinia smile at each other, then dance back and forth, attacking or blocking. Garry was too surprised to call them off and eventually shook his head in wonder. Sinia backed up.

"If you ever want an experienced sparring partner," Sinia offered, and Miona smiled.

"He's testing our nerve, whether we stand our ground in stressful situations and whether you keep your cool and don't rip heads off," Miona said when she joined me.

I frowned at her and she grinned. She was teasing me.

Lylez went next. She didn't attack Sinia, but she dodged and held her off until Garry said, "I think you'd have no trouble in real life, you'd have her unconscious with your baton by now."

Amon panicked when it was his turn, leapt aside from Toron's charge and somehow ended up on Toron's back. Rinth did well, dodging and striking and Merin was excellent, but our classmates were cautious.

Most of us got the job and we spent the second day of Week's End each week doing training at the Guards Office on how to search luggage and motor carriages effectively. We also practiced dealing with drunks —regular, sad figures— with the help of experienced guards. Then our training month was over, and we got at least three hours work a week, around our studies at Sythe School.

Me and Merin worked at South Gate on Esladay evenings, standing just outside the walls, under a vast blue or cloudy grey sky. It seemed somehow more enormous, without the multi colour sheen of the shield rising up from the city walls between us and it, the filter through which I'd viewed the sky for the first years of my life, before starting to take the Electric Way out of the City and studying at Sythe School.

The vast open space before me made the lights of small towns in a narrow strip of darkness before us seem vulnerable, exposed to the world, while the city behind us was shielded from monsters. Stranger still was the space beyond, Farm Zone cut short by National Park Zone marshland, vaster than the farmland between the city and Sythe Castle. On a clear day, we could see the sea beyond, a pale blue line spanning the horizon, making me feel like the world was far larger than I had any inkling of.

We stood at different booths, one for pedestrians and several for motor carriages and we inspected farmers selling or buying at the market, and occasionally merchants with truckloads of clothing and household goods manufactured far away, distant Naydah.

I soon noticed which sections of shaded wall to expect bedding along, and which street corners to expect a humble, downcast beggar with a cardboard sign asking for help to sit at. There was a homeless woman by the city wall every Esladay evening, in the shadow of glass and steel monoliths of City Centre, homes of the wealthy and head offices of corporations, giving way in the east to multi-storey apartments in Greenhill, with lush rooftop gardens. So much wealth, so close to this woman, yet most people ignored her, staring past as if she didn't exist. The contrast and injustice made me burn with anger.

I learnt that her name was Molly. She had no family, except her abusive husband and sons. When her sons started treating her with contempt too, she walked out, with only the clothes on her back, her husband having charmed her friends to the point they claimed she must have 'fallen down' and accused her of lying when she showed them bruises. If I ever met the prick...

A charity got Molly a job helping run a market stall, but she didn't earn enough to afford food, clothing *and* accommodation for all six days of the week, so three nights a week, she slept rough.

"Don't City Government do something to help homeless people?" Merin asked Azar, one of the experienced guards, after we learnt Molly's story.

"There's public housing and women's shelters for women, andros and children, and separate shelters for men fleeing domestic violence, but there's never enough," he replied. "We're asked to make sure they don't obstruct doorways or loading bays, but most rough sleepers sleep wherever it's warm and dry because they've got no other choice."

"Can't charities help?" Merin asked.

"They do," Azar replied. "Some provide waterproof bedding, tents for families, or run kitchens to provide a healthy meal each day. But no-one wants to ask why people aren't welcome, safe and happy in their homes, or why they aren't earning enough to put a roof over their heads. Family violence, toxic masculinity, mental health, disability support, poverty and addiction aren't easy to manage, or cheap to improve. People who aren't affected by them don't like to think about them."

Was this another reason Mum feared leaving Dad? Because she didn't want us living on the streets, like Trent had done? Things had been bad with Dad, I'd struggled to sleep at night and to get through school, but we'd always had Uncle Alan as a backup. These people had no one…

I ground my teeth as I watched people walking past those humble figures, pretending they didn't exist. Did rough sleepers make passers-by uncomfortable? Did the sight upset their cushy little lives?

Merin gripped my arm to urge restraint when we overheard loud comments about 'bums who sat around all day,' and 'what an easy life it must be.' Contemptuous, ignorant, small-minded fools. They weren't there when drunks came running because arrogant bastards decided to 'clean up the streets' by driving rough sleepers away with violence, or because some heavy decided to recruit homeless women to work in brothels.

Most people didn't see rough sleepers brushing their teeth at drinking taps, struggling to find somewhere to shower or suffering from common colds for weeks on end, because their immune systems were weak, and they couldn't afford medicine. But I did. The injustice made me want to punch heads in. I knew who and what was behind this; arseholes like my father, like Trent's. Mental illness and disability. Pathetic addictions like Cam's dad's drinking and gambling. The constant stress of poverty breathing down the necks of everything else. People who couldn't do enough to help themselves and whom no one else helped.

Azar saw my mounting fury and tried to head it off.

"We run our own charity," he said. "The City Guard's Council donate a percentage of the company's profit to a fund that buys land in cheap suburbs near Brock Heights, and builders and suppliers we've met on duty donate materials or their time to construct housing for the homeless, and some merchants donate some furniture they import. We can also donate a portion of our pay. And sometimes City Government gives our charity grants to help. Some of us get it Rarkin. Some of us are doing something about it."

"Where do I sign up to donate?" I asked.

I wanted to help Mum put our own roof over our heads, but we had Uncle Alan's roof, and these people needed some of my pay more than I did. Every Esladay, I looked at Molly sitting in the shadows of grand buildings and people of great wealth, and one-night Merin and I spotted, through the multi colour sheen of shield overheard, what we thought was a shooting star and Azar said was once an international void station that was now space junk. I didn't understand how our world had become advanced enough to send people to the void, and bring them, back alive, yet we were incapable of making sure everyone had somewhere safe to sleep at night.

Chapter 11

Stress from the Amygdala

I spent lots of time at a punchbag after I started working as a City Guard. Jay was concerned about how much the injustice of homelessness angered me and suggested I resign, but I was having none of it. Jay and Headmaster Zatrack said I needed to get better at working with other people and working as a city guard was practice I did not want to pass up. The only team I trusted was Glenn, Wak, Tak, Cam, Des and Trent. And now, maybe team Miona, Merin and me, which was too small and not flexible enough for the syther team I wanted to be on one day.

I didn't tell Jay all of that, but he still questioned my choice. So I blurted out something I didn't intend, but not the worst thing I was holding back on. "Miona thinks I'm an innermind. And Merin thinks I need better social skills."

Jay frowned. I suspected the quick movement of his lips suppressed a smile.

"What do you think?" he asked.

I sighed, deliberately not looking at him. "Merin's right. I *don't* like talking to strangers. For all kinds of reasons. But I need to get used to speaking to them, to be a syther and I dunno, better at being human."

Jay didn't say anything. I think I actually managed to surprise him. I didn't confide much in Miona or Merin either, and I hadn't intended to confide in Amon, but I'd talked to all three of them more than Jay about this. Maybe my progress caught him by surprise.

I looked out the window, so I didn't have to see his reaction. "Merin says I can't get by as a grumpy, brooding guy my whole life and she's got a point. Guard duty is practice, isn't it?"

Jay's face split in a grin. "I have to admit, never in the last five years as a councillor have I seen a guy from Brock Heights sit where you sit, and stubbornly tell me why he needs to do something he'd rather not."

I frowned.

"You're thinking about things I want you to think about, and asking questions I want you to ask, without me saying a thing," he added. "The very stubbornness that could have isolated you and exacerbated everything you struggle with, you're wielding it to make the case that guard duty is the best way for you to break out of social isolation and to develop skills you currently lack."

I had trouble processing that, because he wasn't saying anything I anticipated. But I got there in the end. "You think I'm right? Or, doing this bit well, or something?"

Jay's smile was pained. "I think you are achieving the absolute maximum that is possible for someone under your circumstances. There are things you do *well* Rarkin. In this case you're doing well against your instincts, listening to the kind of logic even adults prefer to ignore, because it makes them uncomfortable. You are right, under circumstances it must be difficult to be right in."

He wasn't just saying that I could keep being a guard, was he? He agreed with all of it. I had a point. For the first time ever, I'd come to see him and I was a step ahead. Who would have thought that could be possible?

"You need to keep managing your anger, and regulating your emotions will become even more important when speaking to strangers. But if you think you can do this, I agree that being a city guard could be very beneficial to you."

Why did getting him to agree make me feel tired? Was it because now he also agreed I should work in situations I sucked at? That I'd have to work hard at? But Jay didn't hold me more accountable than I held myself. He wouldn't push me as far as I pushed me.

Maybe it was because after many sessions, I'd told him what I'd straight up told Amon in our first proper conversation; that I suck with people. And now I'd admitted it to myself *and* him, I kind of had no choice but to work on it.

I was damned lucky the City Guard had paired my shifts with Merin, but we also worked with older, more experienced guards and while Azar was with us at first, sometimes there was a fourth guard and that person was different each week.

My next shift was after my appointment with Jay. When I got to the gate, I stood up straight, arms crossed, trying to look alert. With the right posture, and the loose fitting, high collared grey work suit of a city guard, looking the part was easy enough. It was the rest, the talking to strangers part that I wasn't so fond of.

A motor carriage pulled up before us and I let Merin do the talking.

"Good afternoon. What brings you to Bellaria City?" she asked, smooth and professional, a tone I won't even attempt at this point, because I'd fail miserably and hate how I sounded, at the same time.

"We're visiting my parents," the driver replied, shooting me a glance, then hastily turning back to Merin.

I frowned and studied another man in the passenger seat, who smiled nervously.

"Is it ok if we inspect your trunk?" Merin asked.

"Of course," the driver replied.

Instinct and the passenger's gaze tracking me at the corner of my eye told me to let Merin do it.

"Uncross your arms," Azar whispered in my ear. "It makes you look aggressive and makes people nervous."

I frowned and thrust my thumbs in my front pockets, unsure what to do with my hands. Merin checked the trunk, then waved the motor carriage through the open gates. She walked back to us, and clasped her hands behind her back, relaxing her shoulders and somehow looking casually alert, yet welcoming. I tried to copy her posture. She smiled.

"That makes you loom less. Now we just need to teach you my communication skills, and you could do this job without scaring people into driving back to Terriah."

Azar frowned, but I studied her, then shook my head as she smiled at me. That cheeky movement of her lips lit up her eyes and let you know she liked and was just messing with you. Somehow that let her say shit I wouldn't let anyone else but the boys get away with.

I was fighting down a smile, which only widened hers. "How does Miona suffer you?" I asked.

"It can't be easy being with someone so perfect, but she manages it more gracefully than you," Merin replied with a dazzling smile.

I shook my head and failed to keep a smirk off my face. She and Tak *did* have too much in common. I might need to limit their time together at my next birthday party, so they don't become too much of a bad influence on each other...

"Can you greet the next one Rarkin?" Azar asked.

I suppressed a groan. Merin raised an eyebrow, and I sighed and tried not to peer so seriously at the driver pulling up his motor container.

I nodded to him. "Afternoon. You delivering or picking up?"

"Delivering," he replied. "Timber. The back's open."

I gave him another nod and moved down the side. Motor container drivers were easier. They were regulars who knew the routine. It felt more comfortable being casual with them and they were fine with it.

I peered under an automated, half-folded door at the rear of the container, at long planks of timber stacked along and across the container floor, in rectangular rows. Standard packing, fresh from the port most likely. No hard to see areas, nothing suspicious.

"Thanks," I called to the driver, waving him on.

Merin studied me. It really was unnerving how she looked right at my face all the time, even into my eyes. I swear Miona didn't do that...

"Have you noticed private drivers get nervous when you use short phrases like that? It's like they fill the silence with worrying about how you might be thinking they're doing something sus."

I frowned. Why would anyone use more words than needed? Why not jump straight to the point and get on with things? I already greeted them and made an effort to thank them. Wasn't that enough?

"People seem to assume you're abrupt because you're aggressive, but that's not it, is it?" Merin asked.

"Maybe they have time to stand around talking about fluff all day," I replied. "I've got more important things to do."

Merin smiled. "And the way you look more at vehicles instead of people and rarely look drivers in the eye?"

I frowned and peered away across the road. Who goes around looking into people's eyes, into their souls, all the time? A glance in their direction told them I was listening, or who I was speaking to.

I shrugged. "Aren't people intimidated enough without me doing that?"

I met her eyes when I said it. I guess I wanted to prove a point. I looked away pretty quick. It *was* too intimate. Miona made it comfortable sometimes, but I don't like meeting strangers' gazes. It's invasive. I don't even like looking at them when I'm tired, or in a bad mood, in case they think I'm telling them things I'm not. Why can't we just exist in our spaces, until we're ready to deal with each other? People like Amon go round imposing themselves on others, but I'm not like that.

"It's fine," Azar said. "It won't impact your work."

But it kind of did. Merin could see me too well. Sure, I didn't like people writing me off because they misjudged me and drew superficial conclusions from how I look. But Merin looking at me *too* closely was a different kind of uncomfortable, and there was no chatty Amon, no calmly comfortable Miona to break the awkward silence.

"You're worried it will affect your rep back home, if people realise you're not quite as dangerous as they think, aren't you?" Merin asked, with a mock sympathetic smile.

I smiled, shifting my feet restlessly. Apparently Merin could use humour for anything, having a go at you, having a laugh, putting you at your ease. Her tongue and humour were sharper than Miona's, but I suspected the same good intent lay behind them.

"Will I need to stuff you into the next motor carriage container to stop you telling them?" I asked.

"Not today," she replied. "I already promised today's sparring match to Miona."

I smiled. Merin would be a handful to spar with. Swift, sneaky, probably distracting and doing what I didn't expect. It was just as well; I didn't need that kind of headache today.

The shift ended with things kind of ok between us, but I hoped she'd keep whatever other observations she had to herself next time. I didn't want to know what she saw when she looked at me too closely.

* * *

In my next meeting with Jay, he eyed my crouched, tense posture and said, "How are you feeling?"

I blinked. "Out of place as a city guard. Not quite comfortable with Merin. Uptight. Like I don't belong in a syther classroom. Like there's been a mistake, or the Sytheren Ceremony was just a dream."

"Stressed," Jay replied.

I punched the cushion next to me. "Why would I feel stressed? Dad's gone. I passed the exams. I'm a syther student! It doesn't make any sense! Why can't I just be happy?"

Jay sighed. "You've been through a lot, Rarkin. There's a part of your brain called the amygdala, which prepares your body for a flight or fight response to counter threats. But you grew up with so much danger that your amygdala may be overactive. It may have you suspended in a flight or fight response, cortisol pumping through your system warning of potential danger, keeping you edgy, alert and stressed in reaction to past dangers. You may be experiencing a traumatic-stress disorder."

"Are you telling me I've got brain damage?" I asked.

Jay sighed. "A specific kind caused by trauma, yes."

"So how do I shut down my amygdala? Punch myself in the head?"

"The first step is to recognise that your amygdala predisposes you to be alert, and suspicious of impending threats at all times. And that you feel stressed and threatened when there is no rational reason for it."

"You think I'm becoming irrational?" I accused.

"Because you grew up with your father's violence and instability, your brain has been wired to deal with constant danger. It expects it, anticipates it and works constantly to counter it. You accept rationally that you are safe and have no reason to worry, but you feel the need to counter danger, and your life doesn't feel normal without danger, because your amygdala is damaged."

My jaw locked up. I was a syther student. It *wasn't* a mistake. There was no reason for me to feel insecure or stressed. But I did. I was still uneasy about how quickly Merin spotted traits that helped Miona guess I'm an innermind, and more besides, and now I worried how those traits made it even harder to fit in. Being from Brock Heights was enough on its own.

But it went deeper than that. Part of me was convinced some great threat still loomed and would start trying to destroy me, because that was how my life worked. And no matter how irrational the idea was, I kept looking for a threat.

I noticed how Dorthin provoked me and worried I couldn't shoot well enough to pass my exams. I worried I wouldn't remember enough to pass coursework exams. I worried about dad turning up at the sytheren ceremony. I worried my lack of social skills would impair my work as a city guard. I rationalised my sense of impending threat by thinking I didn't deserve to be a syther student and that I'd be chucked out. I had a looming sense of dread that *was* irrational...

For a moment, I resented Jay for pointing out how screwed up I was, when I'd worked *so* hard on my temper and I hadn't snapped at Dorthin for weeks. But wishing I had less shit to deal with than I did was useless.

"How do you counter irrational fears?" I asked Jay.

"If you need to, ask Trainer Lauran if there was a mistake with you passing your sytheren exams. She will tell you there wasn't. Ask Miona and Merin if they wish to remain friends with you. They'll say yes. Ask your uncle how long you can live with him. I suspect he will reply, 'as long as you need'. Ask how long you can keep seeing me and how long I will be prepared to help you, and the answer will be the same."

I turned away, gripping the couch with white knuckles and blinking back the stinging in my eyes. How did he know I feared those things? Deep down, I stressed and worried, not just because I expected danger, but because the insecurity of my childhood made me insecure about *everything*. Whether friends truly liked me. How long I could keep studying before my results proved me as useless as I sometimes felt. How long I could maintain friendships or acquaintances at Sythe School before they saw how messed up I was and wanted nothing to do with me.

"I mean it, Rarkin," Jay said. "Whoever your friends are, the ones who taught you to be tough and gave you the instinct to hold back from me whenever you can, I think they'll see you through, even if it takes you years to recover. And being as perceptive, smart and determined as you are, I don't think it will take that long. But however long you need, I'll be here, and I suspect others will too."

"I don't deserve that commitment… from anyone," I told the floor.

"Even your mother? Do you really believe that?"

My hands balled into fists and my eyes stung. Receiving so much from friends who owed me nothing, and nothing but abuse from a father who chose not to parent me because he was too busy being jealous of me… how did I reconcile that?

"What your father did to you, testifies only to how messed up *he* is," Jay said quietly. "It doesn't reflect on you or your worth. Your father is neither rational nor stable enough to judge your worth, and I doubt he ever has been. If you feel the opposite is true, then please believe me when I tell you that your feelings on this matter are affected by trauma and are also irrational."

Could I rearrange my father's face now? The Gods know he has it coming! This was a direct result of *his* actions… When would my life be *mine*?

"Everything is easier to accept when it remains true over time, and you've had so much time being abused, and so little time being treated decently by people who are close to you that I don't expect you to find this easy to believe. But you *are* safe. And loved Rarkin. In time, you'll see that."

If I was loved or worthy of love, why was Dad always such an arsehole? Why didn't mum come between us when he got nasty sooner and more often? How could *he* be the whole reason for that? How could it not be because of something wrong with *me*? The boys said it was Dad's fault, so did Uncle Alan and now Jay. But I couldn't reconcile it.

Chapter 12

An Unexpected Journey

My amygdala *was* malfunctioning. I felt prone to stress, worry and like I should keep an eye out for danger. I knew Jay was right, it *was* irrational. So I kept sparring with Miona and sometimes with Merin, which usually cheered me up. Merin didn't ask me anymore probing questions, she just looked at me sometimes, in a way that told me she knew there was more going on with me, but she respected my space. I appreciated it and somehow felt even more comfortable around her than I had been before. I tried to calm down generally too, but a real threat *was* looming.

Seven weeks into the semester, we took Week's End off for a two-day workshop in Torret. We'd get to see monsters from the National Parks of all three cities, participate in activities that replicated each department's work and to ask sythers questions to help us decide which syther electives to study next year. Sytheren and syther students from all three Sythe Schools would attend and I was looking forward to it.

I waited in the Food Court with Merin and Miona on Esladay morning for the announcement about our departure.

Mature age syther students sat at a table beside us, discussing an article in the Taros Times.

"They found gold just before the Nuclear War and sealed the entrance to the mine until they could safely dig it up. It was forgotten until geologists from Trebo studying rock formations found the entrance. The Serenan's didn't come close to exposing all the gold. It's the biggest find since the Taros gold rush!"

A gold rush, in this day and age?

"All syther and sytheren students please report to the hall," a professional voice announced from a speaker in the ceiling.

Merin frowned.

"Do they want to brief us?" Miona asked.

"Why not do that on the bus?" Merin replied.

Miona frowned as we walked to the hall, where Headmaster Zatrack stood on stage before a hundred odd adult and teenage sytherens, in navy uniforms and sytheren students in free dress. Why was a Head briefing *us*?

"We have received intelligence that the electric-way carriages you were to catch have been taken over by a group who intended to capture you," Headmaster Zatrack announced.

He paused for shocked exclamations. My mind raced back to the day I sat outside his office and overheard two people talking about how a Monster Containment team had been magically put to sleep, abducted and dumped in a random section of National Park Zone. They said some guy named Mavon was behind it and that he was preparing for something. Was this it?

"This is not the first time someone has tried to get the Syther Force's attention by such an act," the headmaster asserted, "and we will not allow it to interfere with your training. You will travel on foot until the buses transporting sythers to arrest the criminals return. The buses will then transport you to Torret. Trainer Pershna will lead the way."

"What's the point of leaving on foot?" I asked, as the crowd before us began to follow Trainer Pershna out the hall.

Miona eyed shocked, frightened or worried faces moving past and replied, "They don't want everyone sitting around working themselves into a panic."

We merged with the queue, and I told them what I'd overheard outside Headmaster Zatrack's office last semester.

Merin's dark brows furrowed with concern. "That might be how Sythe identified this plot," she said, as Trainer Pershna led us down a corridor. "If Sythe have been watching Mavon closely since. But that would mean Mavon's been planning this for weeks."

"Abducting Sythe School students is insane," Miona replied. "He'd want to plan it thoroughly."

Anxious conversations buzzed around us, as other students wondered who was behind the abduction plot and why, and asked questions about historic plots. I frowned, as Trainer

Pershna led us down into a concrete tunnel. But Amon's voice, speaking to a group of his friends ahead of us, interrupted my thoughts. "There hasn't been an abduction attempt this size anywhere since warlords tried to build up their armies before the Nuclear Age," he was saying. "No one's had the resources or power since then."

"Then what's changed?" Miona asked his friends and ours.

"You mean why is anyone confident they have the power to attack Sythe now?" I asked.

Miona nodded. I shivered. It *was* insane, a public attack on Sythe...who in their right mind would do that? And *why*?

People speculating around us thought in different directions and we continued to walk down a concrete, dully lit tunnel. We didn't seem to be exiting the castle underground, as I'd assumed. We continued walking down a corridor without windows, only dim lights spaced along where the walls met the ceiling overhead.

Did Sythe fear another attempt to seize us? But if they did, why not cancel the excursion? Surely they were too idealistic to put their reputation of not backing down before *our* safety, to send us on excursion despite an abduction attempt that very day?

I scanned the crowd again. Wrongness jolted through me. Trainer's Lauran and Morea were nowhere in sight. I couldn't see Trainer Sirona either. Chaos, I wouldn't mind spotting Dorthin's infuriating face in this crowd, but it too was nowhere to be seen. Our regular trainers were supposed to come with us, but the only light blue uniform I could see was Trainer Pershna's.

"Can you see the other Trainers?" I asked.

Merin and Miona scanned the crowd. Merin tensed and Miona and shook her head.

We walked in uncomfortable silence. I scanned the crowd for any other wary or suspicious looking students, but it was too hard to tell from the sea of people's backs before me.

Speculation around us gradually ceased and people began to question the point of walking so far. Conveniently, that was when Trainer Pershna raised a device to her ear and listened to a message. She halted in her tracks, frowning and we stopped behind her. Her brows furrowed as she listened, her gaze sharpening.

"Our presumption that the electric-way carriages were seized to capture you is incorrect," she announced. "Force Sythers attempting to apprehend suspects in the carriages have been overrun by a private army. The private army have diverted the train to the Trebo line and are travelling to Trebo to invade."

A random private army had overrun Force Sythers, and stolen electric-way carriages to invade near the Serenan border and the gold rush?

"Our workshops have been cancelled and a state of emergency has been declared. All Sythe and public transport is being used to transport soldiers to Trebo to counter the invasion. But transport back to the castle has been arranged. There is a festival along Gurnya River today, involving private boats and floats travelling downriver to Bellaria. Its intended sytheren guards are now en route to Trebo, so we will replace them.

"The Mayors of Bellaria and Duron are confident that those of you not required as guards will fit below deck. We will follow a passage to Gurnya River, where the water parade departs and return to the castle by boat."

Quiet murmurs followed her announcement, but Amon wasn't good at quiet, so I could hear him from ahead.

"Bomber tunnels! We're in the Bomber Tunnels built at the dawn of the Nuclear War to avoid bomber airship raids!"

That got people's attention and made them suspicious. Good. That would make it easier to convince them the truth and try to get out of here... But before I could find words to explain, I heard movement. A dimly lit concrete tunnel joined ours on the left. As we and a group of mature-age students marched past, military sytherens in black marched out behind them, led by a Field Captain.

"They'd have to be from Bellaria Army Base?" Lylez asked ahead of us, eyeing rows of sytherens marching into our tunnel. "What are *they* doing here?"

"An escort?" Ryan asked beside her.

"When they're supposed to be fighting a war in Trebo?" Merin asked.

Amon shivered on Ryan's other side.

I heard muttering as the Field Captain walked towards Trainer Pershna. She turned with a smile, and called over her shoulder, "Some of Bellaria Army Base's sytherens will escort us to Gurnya River and safely home. Wartime protocol."

How convenient.

"Double bluff," I said quietly, and Amon and his friends slowed to listen to me, Rinth and his arrogant mate who passed the exams, Zan, frowning on their left.

"Tell us there's a plot to abduct us," I continued, "then send us marching off with only one Trainer, defying protocol, in Bomber Tunnels, where even Sythe can't see us. *This* is Mavon's abduction plot. The river parade is how they're going to smuggle us away from Bellaria."

"You think she lied about *everything*?" Rinth asked, turning pale.

"I was looking for Trainer Morea and Trainer Lauran earlier," Amon said hollowly. "They're not here."

He was smarter than I gave him credit for. And perhaps braver, given he was clearly nervous, but still relatively calm.

"You think they snatched us from under the noses of shadower students?" Lylez asked worriedly and I nodded.

"Who are these people?" Amon asked weakly. "What kind of resources do they have?"

"Good ones," I replied.

Ryan stiffened and Amon shivered. I was tense, but not scared. Mavon's people had guts pulling a stunt like this, but that didn't mean adducting us was a good idea. Trent Rule One, don't take shit from anybody. I didn't plan to. Glenn said he thought I'd make a good shadower. I decided to test that idea.

Chapter 13

Swindled

"We need to tell the school where we are," I asserted.

"Only the Trainers will have communicators," Merin replied.

"Then we need a pick pocket," I added with a smile.

She frowned again and this time I looked behind me, where I could see faces better. Three reserved faces among the mature age students caught my eye, faces that didn't look older than Merin. I flicked my chin at them. We slowed, and the tough guys caught us up.

"You lot know what's going on?" I asked.

One shook his head. "Can't deny it now you've picked it too," he replied.

"Know any pick pockets?" I asked.

"What for?" asked the boy in the middle.

"The only way to tell school where we are; nick a Trainer's communicator."

The boy in the middle smiled. "You asked the right person. I learnt a lot more than my parents' thought before they shipped me off to Sythe School. Name's Joe Mentis. My mates

Nick," he nodded to the lanky kid, "and Johnny," the solemn-faced guy who spoke first.

"My girlfriend Miona and our friend Rarkin," Merin replied.

"A double loss for guys," Nick said, with a sad shake of his head.

Joe smiled, and Johnny rolled his eyes.

"Are either of you girls good with communicators?" Joe asked. "You'd be able to hide one under your hair to call school after I nick it."

"I'll do it," Merin replied, letting her hair down.

My gut jolted unpleasantly. I'd have to trust Joe and Merin entirely to pull this off.

Joe flashed a smile. "Excellent. We need to walk separately, so the Trainers and kids behind them don't link us. I'll tell the Captain I'm scared. The Trainer keeps trying to shut him up, which makes me think he's not too bright. I'll swipe the comm, stop to tie my shoelace and Merin can drift towards me with the crowd, take the comm, crouch to pretend to do up her shoelace and make the call."

"The rest of you should split up, so the Trainer doesn't see a bunch of suspicious people behind her," he added.

"And Ryan and Amon pretend they're worried sick about Trebo, because you've overheard everything we've said, and you look nervous," I added, turning to eye Ryan and Amon as they exchanged guilty looks. Rinth's mouth tightened in a line and he gave me a nod.

"You're sure this is the best option?" Lylez asked anxiously.

"How do you think everyone will react if I jump the Sytheren Captain and tell them to run?" I asked.

"If we tell everyone to disobey," Miona added, "people will ask questions or panic, and if the 'military sytherens' are thugs in disguise, they'll side with the Trainer."

My eyes darted to the black uniformed sytherens marching robotically behind us. I prickled with unease. If they *weren't* captured sytherens, we *had* to be careful.

"I suggest you five walk on that side," I told Amon, Ryan, Rinth, Zan and Lylez, gesturing left of us.

Zan frowned at me and might have objected, but Rinth urged him sideways.

"I'll head back," Johnny said, slowing and falling behind.

"Ready Merin?" Joe asked.

"See you soon," she replied with a wink.

Joe moved into the crowd, Merin tailing him slowly on the right, Nick nodding to us and tailing Joe on the left. My shoulders and arms tensed, wanting to fight or at least *act*, not just wander like a mindless robot while someone else saved the day. I'd never watched a friend walk into danger, or take a great risk before. *I* was usually in danger and taking risks to get

184

myself or mum out of it… And while Joe seemed confident, I found it impossible to trust his abilities before I saw what he could do.

Miona eyed Merin nervously. My heart sped up as Joe approached the talkative Field Captain. I couldn't hear their conversation, but Joe looked worried and wide-eyed innocent. The captain replied with a fake smile, then Joe ducked out of sight. I smiled, suspecting his career in thievery had begun well before he started at Sythe School.

When Joe stood among marching sytherens, Merin was behind him. He walked ahead while she dawdled, then ducked out of sight. I waited for her to reappear, having contacted school and abandoned the communicator, but the crowd moved around her, and my heart beat faster when she didn't stand.

Miona sighed. "That field comm might be programmed to contact the rogue Trainers' boss. She'll have to reprogram it."

"How long will that take?" I asked.

"A few minutes, if she has to hack it first."

We'd catch up to Merin soon, then Joe. If she was still trying to reprogram the comm after that, she'd be squatting conspicuously among military sytherens.

Sweat trickled down my back as I walked. I didn't trust the military sytherens and I didn't want Merin near them.

Merin stood and merged with a group of girls from our class. Miona exhaled. Trainer Pershna called, "We're about ten minutes from Gurnya River. I'll give instructions for the parade at the end of the tunnel."

The captain reached into his pocket. "Where is it? Someone took my comm!"

He looked back across the marching crowd at Joe. "It was him!"

"Maybe you dropped it," suggested Nick.

"How can I drop something in my pocket when it's got no hole in it!" he yelled.

Everyone stopped. Trainer Pershna tried to calm the Captain, but he scanned the crowd. He met Amon's frightened gaze over tens of students and yelled, "*You* stole it! Why else would you be so frightened?"

Joe's strained face suggested he wanted to protect Amon, but that would link them. And the fact they stood at opposite ends of the crowd wouldn't convince a paranoid Captain that Joe hadn't passed the stolen communicator to Amon.

"We're all scared Trainer," Nick replied, his face solemn and sad. "Maybe he's got family in Trebo and he's scared about what happened to them."

I smiled, wondering from the way Nick stayed in character and didn't miss a beat, if he was training to be a conman before Sythe School.

The captain frowned, then sighed. A heavy silence fell, in which I wondered where the comm was. Then another girl in our class held her hand in the air and asked, "Is this a comm?" from the back of the group Merin stood with.

"Yes, it is!" The captain replied. He frowned, then asked, "Was it on the ground?"

"Yes," she replied. "It looked like someone dropped it."

I smiled again. Joe Mentis *was* good.

Trainer Pershna spoke quietly, probably saying, "Told you so."

Once the Captain had his comm back, we started walking again and Merin dropped back beside Miona, who squeezed her hand.

"We were lied to," Merin reported. "The tunnel entrance at school was concealed and locked behind us. Shadowers were trying to break it open when I called. School wants us to follow Trainer Pershna to the river and follow her instructions until shadowers intercept us."

"We're playing along?" I asked.

"Protocol is for Sythe to play along with what students believe until they get us to safety. Then they'll debrief everyone."

"There's really a festival on the river?" I asked.

"There is," Miona replied. "I used to go every year, before Mum had her accident and we moved to Bellaria. It's Gotsi Day —the day some fisherman supposedly hooked a sea monster and it toed him the length of Gurnya River trying to escape. There's a noon parade and there'll be crowds and fake sea monsters on boats. But it doesn't sail to Bellaria. It sails northeast, towards Duron and ends in the countryside."

"They're smuggling us to the middle of nowhere?" I asked.

"Past a few towns, to the edge of the Bellarian Farm Zone," Miona replied. "That's how far Gotsi's monster was supposed to have toed him."

"And beyond the perimeter the shadowers are searching, I bet," Merin added.

"There were about forty sytherens on deck last time," Miona added, "but if they hide the sytheren students below deck, no one will realise we're the missing students."

So the parade was an ingenious way to smuggle us beyond Bellaria… And it *happened* to be on the same day as a workshop we expected to travel to.

"What's the date of the festival?" I asked Miona.

"Twelfth of Teliphy, every year."

If the festival date was fixed, were our workshops organised by someone who wanted us to have a reason to leave the castle *and* travel unseen that day? Was whoever set the workshop date working for our abductors? Was there a traitor at our Sythe School?

Chapter 14

Confusion

Trainer Pershna halted us at the tunnel mouth. I gazed out at a pier topped with a building from which boarding ramps extended to two levels of ferry. One boarding ramp was occupied by a spiky fish statue with cheery 'victims' waving from inside its jaws, the second by a rearing sea serpent controlled by puppeteers. The chatter of happy crowds drifted towards us. Did anyone out there have any idea of our situation?

"Some of you will be stationed on boats leading or following the parade or on the mayors' ferries as an honour guard," Trainer Pershna told us. "The remaining sytherens and syther students will travel below deck on the mayor's ferries."

She split sytherens into four small groups and Miona, Merin, Amon and I exited the tunnel with the last mature age sytherens. Crowds lining the riverbank didn't bat an eye as we walked past. People were too busy pointing at costumed figures boarding floats, or else talking, eating or drinking on picnic blankets across the grassy hillside.

Trainer Pershna directed two groups of sytherens along a pier behind people in fish, shark and eel costumes. She sent our group to the top deck of the ferry, where our mayor sat on a fake coral throne holding a harpoon and waving at crowds, who smiled back at her.

We fanned out along the railing of the top deck, and I looked down on women wearing sequined mermaid tails and shell bikinis, sitting on fake corals on the float before us. They were all made up with blue and green eye shadow, eye liner and mascara, making their eyes look exotic and other-worldly. I stared at a broad-shouldered blonde, Glenn's ex-girlfriend Kate, who had graduated as a Level One Shadower last year...

Amon was eyeing the mermaids too. With that same look he'd had on his face when Merin winked at him at Miona's party. A... wistful look? Was that the word?

Amon started, noticing me following his gaze. Then he smiled and asked, "Seen one you like?"

I rolled my eyes. "Seen someone I know." I mouthed her rank.

Amon blinked and turned back to the mermaids. Miona shook her head.

"I know," he said tersely over his shoulder, "they really should have scantily clad boy and andro mermaids down there too, but don't take them being so old fashioned out on me."

Miona's lips quirked. "Is *one* gender not enough for you to admire?"

Amon grinned. "Never!"

A tall tapestry emerged from the tunnel we'd exited, an underwater scene featuring a tentacled monster, which folded back a long way on both sides. I stared, and my heart sped up. That was how they were smuggling students on board in plain sight. The crowd eyed the tapestry and noticed nothing. The mayor waved at the crowds. The atmosphere was so *normal*.

The tapestry moved towards the ferry building, and I guessed forty odd people marched inside it. Merin and Miona eyed it critically, but from the way he eyed the floats manoeuvring ahead of our ferry, Amon didn't notice.

A few mature age sytherens either side of us frowned, but only two commented that something might be wrong. I guess it's easy to believe something's *not* horribly wrong in the face of evidence it *is*, when you're used to life being safe.

A second tapestry followed the first out of the tunnel, then a third and a fourth were carried along another pier behind us, to another building and the mayor of Duron's ferry. Were the military sytherens concealed behind those? Had someone managed to *abduct* tens of sytheren soldiers?

The tapestries disappeared inside the ferry buildings and the high-walled boarding ramps extending from them concealed sytherens and sytheren students from the crowds. But students were boarding from the top deck too and the mayor should see it. I turned. She was distracted by a pretty waitress who'd brought her champagne and was chatting animatedly to her. Had Trainer Pershna paid the waitress to distract the mayor?

The tapestries reappeared, hanging from the first and second story balconies of both ferry buildings. The waitress left, but Trainer Pershna replaced her, shaking hands with the mayor. The mayor was younger than I anticipated, slender and sat leaning back into her chair, her posture relaxed, a glass of wine in her hand. Her jaw wasn't set, and her posture wasn't rigid with tension, like Trainer Pershna's. But she didn't show any sign of being suspicious. Like she had no idea how her ferry was being used...

There was a gentle lurch, as the ferry started moving. Floats set off before us, the second ferry followed us, and a small boat filled with sytherens and the Field Captain brought up the rear. Behind them, boats of varying sizes assembled across the river.

"Welcome to Gotsi Day!" a voice announced loudly. "You have until dusk to do a Gotsi! Accepted fishing gear includes all makes of rods and hooks, industrial netting, harpoons..."

His voice faded as our ferry glided sluggishly past a thinning crowd. Music from two floats ahead became eerie, as people in shark costumes edged from behind fake rocks and chased people in fish costumes. It created a strange tension, the festivity and happy people, clueless they were witnessing a mass abduction, while a few of us wondered when and how we were getting out of this.

The crowd ended, and we sailed past bushland and mountains, then another crowd, another town and more cheering children. By then, so much normality had passed that apart from a hum of anxiety, I felt like we were doing a city guard shift.

Two towns later, the floats dropped off their costumed passengers. Trainer Pershna, some sytherens and the mayor disappeared between small homes of ancient brick and we heard music and cheers from somewhere in town, while we waited.

"There," said Miona.

She pointed at people in navy blue uniforms creeping along the riverbank behind an old building at the far end of town. More sytherens appeared behind them, stepping along the riverbank.

Trainer Lauran accompanied them. I exhaled with relief. When they reached the pier, at least sixty 'sytherens' were in sight.

"What's going on?" a woman on our deck asked.

"Your river journey is over," a new-comer called from the pier. "Your Trainers have come to escort you on buses. It's time to disembark."

The 'sytherens' waited on one side of the pier, while students climbed off the boarding ramps from both ferries. We descended the stairs, and I studied the 'sytherens'. I recognised four faces. When we reached the boarding ramp they stood beside, Glenn leaned forwards and said quietly, "Glad you're ok. This is more typical for a junior agent exam, but since we burst into Trainer Luthez's office and alerted him to Headmaster Zatrack briefing you lot, when Heads only brief Sythes… and we told him they'd marched you off down a tunnel, breaking multiple protocols, and that we'd figured out his phoney conspiracy… only for him to report it to Headmistress Zleena and discover it was real.…"

"He decided it was only fair to let us get involved after that," Tak added.

"And we're his best students," Tran piped in.

"How will you get away with switching places with sytherens in town?" I asked them.

"Trainer Pershna wanted sytherens travelling below deck to relieve the others. We're 'from below deck'. And the Field Captain won't have the guts to tell her he fell asleep on duty."

His smile faded. "It wasn't just lot who went missing today," he whispered to me. "Headmistress Zleena called in a code yellow for you lot. We heard the reply from Bellaria Sythe Base. If you saw military sytherens, Bellaria Army Base is missing a hundred and nine of them. They were on a field run and never came back."

I gaped. From a single Monster Containment team going missing in the Bellarian Wild Zone weeks ago, to a large group of students from *two* Sythe School's *and* an army base. Was this also Mavon? What in Chaos' kind of resources did he, or anyone have, to pull off an operation of this size?

"You're going where we're supposed to go?" Merin asked my friends, and jealousy flashed in her eyes.

"Yep," Tak replied with a teasing smile. "We play along until people in high places confirm they're on the right track about who's behind this, then we arrest those people and haul them in for questioning."

"You get all the fun?" I asked.

"Are you lot sure you chose the right career?" Tak replied with a grin.

They smiled, then turned to board the ferry with their comrades, while Miona, Merin, Amon and I followed students along the riverbank and around large hills, which screened four buses from town. Trainer Lauran waved us onto a bus, marking our names off on a screen as we boarded.

We took our seats, then the engine rumbled to life and we drove off, but not very far. There were murmurs when we parked outside a large motel amidst a vineyard. Beyond it lay a small city and mountains; Torret. We were still well north of Bellaria City.

"We are not returning to school," Trainer Lauran informed us. "We will stop here for a debriefing with the other

Bellarian students, while the military sytherens are debriefed on their buses."

How in Chaos had they abducted so many soldiers? The military were supposed to *protect* Bellaria City State —not be a liability! If Mavon was an organised crime boss, what was he playing at?

We crowded through the motel reception into a ballroom lined with chairs and I sat next to Miona and Merin. Joe, Nick and Johnny flicked their chins at me further back and I smiled and returned the gesture. Trainer Morea nodded to us and Trainer Lauran, Trainer Dorthin and other Trainers took their places. That caused a low murmur and speculation, until Trainer Morea stepped forwards and everyone fell silent.

"We have brought you here to tell you the truth about what happened today," he began. "Trebo was not attacked. Your Way carriages to Torret were not controlled by a private army. Had that happened, your excursion would have been cancelled and all Trainers would have been present when Headmaster Zatrack announced it. You would not have departed without us, in an out-of-sight tunnel, nor would Sythe send you anywhere on foot.

"The reason many of you exited the tunnel hiding behind a tapestry and boarded the ferries below deck was to conceal your numbers. The 'sytherens' who replaced you were shadowers, impersonating you to arrest whomever they are led to."

"If we were abducted, why did we just walk openly onto buses?" Zan demanded from beside a pale faced Rinth.

"You did not," Trainer Morea replied calmly. "The shadowers passage' to and your passage from the pier were disguised by illusion magic. But after the lies you have been told, I do not expect you to take my words at face value. That is why there is a large screen behind me."

Low murmurs faded, as Trainers parted and everyone stared at the screen, or eyed the Trainers suspiciously, chewing lips, fidgeting, or sitting with fists clenched. There was a fuzzing sound and colour spread outwards across the screen. It showed a roadside with a sign saying *Welcome to Trebo*. A man beside the sign said, "Hello. My name's Ree and I'm a reporter in Trebo. I'll give you a look at our town, so you know everything's ok."

He turned and walked into town, where he knocked on doors and asked people about their day. Some people replied rudely, others told him to go away because it was lunch time, but some chatted and asked why he was interviewing them. There were too many people behaving too naturally. After a while, cynical murmurs around us died down, Trainer Morea thanked Reg and the screen went blank.

"What kind of sicko tells us there's a war on when there isn't?" Johnny asked aggressively.

"I believe you have answered your own question," Trainer Morea replied.

"Was the war in Trebo lie an excuse to justify us walking to the river in bomber tunnels and boarding the parade ships behind banners?" Merin asked.

"We believe so," Trainer Morea replied.

"Where were you when we were led out of school by imposters?" Zan demanded, and the accusation in his tone cut the air like a knife.

Trainer Morea sighed. "We were distracted by an incident that is now under investigation, which shadowers believe was intended to delay us until after your departure."

So not only had someone perhaps impersonated Headmaster Zatrack, and Trainer Pershna, someone else had infiltrated Sythe to conceal our abduction from our Trainers? What sort of distraction would delay them, when surely they must have heard the announcement calling us to assemble and been on their way to investigate it? Had someone paged them privately to a bogus briefing too? Something didn't add up there.

"Where's Headmaster Zatrack?" Joe asked.

People shifted in their seats or tensed in anticipation.

"Headmaster Zatrack has been suspended, pending a full investigation."

Joe and I exchanged significant looks and Merin's face darkened. Sythe thought Zatrack was guilty…they must have taken him into custody. Unless he *was* guilty, in which case he'd have done a runner.

The crowd broke into tense murmurs, but no one pressed Trainer Morea and he took the next question.

"What about Trainer Pershna?" Miona asked.

"Trainer Pershna is undoubtedly a traitor. She will be arrested along with her accomplices, as soon as they deliver their pretend sytheren captives."

"But there weren't as many shadowers as captives," I protested.

"There doesn't need to be," Trainer Morea replied. "Illusion magic will make up the extra numbers."

I tingled all over. Glenn said it was appropriate for a junior agent exam… were there *agents* wielding concealment magic among the shadowers?

"What do we do now?" Lylez asked.

"When our debriefing is complete, we will proceed to Torret and begin our workshops later this afternoon."

There was more discussion, the Trainers gave us time to accept, then they got us back onto the buses and to our workshops. My group did team building exercises like those used by Search and Rescue, then role-played as Force Sythers, trying to catch out *real* Force Sythers who'd volunteered to role-play as criminals, so we could interview them. It was interesting, and we were too busy discussing it afterwards to realise they'd kept us in our school groups the whole time. So I didn't realise the true extent of the security breaches, or the abductions, until Glenn broke protocol and told me about it later.

Chapter 15

On Standby

I slept lightly that night, waking at every unfamiliar sound. Our abduction was over, but we were staying in an unfamiliar hotel and I wouldn't feel safe until we returned to Bellaria City. When someone knocked on my door the next morning, I sat bolt upright.

"Trainer Lauran wants everyone in the Breakfast Room in five," Merin's voice said. "We're to have a briefing."

Another briefing? What else had happened?

I jumped out of bed, washed my face then hurried to the Breakfast Room. My classmates and other syther or sytheren students gathered around me, in rumpled uniforms. Our Trainers sat waiting and when most of us had gathered, Trainer Morea addressed us.

"The shadowers made arrests last night," he informed us. "Traitor and imposter Trainers were captured, but some thugs escaped. Being unwelcome in any human city, they fled to Serena, which is problematic for reasons our studies of Taron history didn't mention. After Tarons drove the Serenans off their land and enslaved others, and after the Nuclear War fragmented international relations, the Serenans started killing Taron trespassers. It remains their best defence against slavery and was the most likely way they would respond to the escaped criminals entering their land.

"So the criminals lied. You may have heard about a gold discovery on the Taros-Serena border. The criminals claimed to be approaching Serena to warn them that Bellaria planned to invade Serena to seize the gold, which is what we would have done historically. The Serenans sent out spies late last night. The spies saw our shadowers in sytheren uniforms, assembled to return to Bellaria Castle. They believed it was an invasion force.

"The Serenan chief refused to believe our sytherens had been abducted. He thought it was another Taron lie to conceal a Taron attempt to exploit his people. He said they would not tolerate such an attack and cut communication.

"Our spies report that the Serenan army is mobilising. We believe the criminals have goaded them to fight the battle on Taron soil, to minimise Serenan collateral damage."

Those lying scum had started a *real* war to ensure they were welcomed in Serena?

"But they'll turn back?" Amon asked, his voice cracking. "If they don't have the same intelligence as us, they couldn't have the same weapons or tech. They wouldn't stand a chance against us in open warfare!"

"Nor will the military wish to crush them when they march because *we* failed to arrest *our* criminals," Trainer Morea replied. "But it is likely to come to a military standoff. A state of emergency has been declared and the Bellarian Army, Syther Force and City Guard are mobilising. They will move into position to defend the city and seek to display our strength to deter an attack. Attempts at diplomacy will continue, and we hope that travel time will reduce Serenan anger.

"For now, we are treating this as an invasion. A transport will fly us home in half an hour. Those of you who work for the City Guard or the Military will be required to report to them when we return. Any unemployed sytherens will report to the City Guard. You will most likely be given guns and positioned on rooftops, to display our numbers. Sytheren students, we will return you to the castle once we have dropped off the sytherens."

"We heard about an invasion yesterday," Miona said critically but quietly to me and Merin.

"The criminals sold the Serenans the same story," Merin replied. "To us they claimed a private army was invading Serena to seize the gold. To the Serenans, they claimed *Bellaria* was invading for the gold. They used a familiar lie to save their worthless backsides when the abduction went badly for them."

Self-centred opportunists, the definition of career criminals…

And Bellaria City *was* at war... ...and as City Guard, Miona, Merin and I would help defend it.

I straightened, my face and muscles hardening, my jaw locking in place. We chose a table and I was careful not to break porcelain or glassware as I forced down what breakfast I could, then hurried outside. On the verandah across the front of the building, people whispered nervously, fidgeted or shuffled. Merin and Miona held hands tightly. Ryan and Lylez did the same. Nick paced the veranda, Rinth and Zan mock sparred, and Joe watched Johnny fiddle with a knife that wasn't standard issue.

Short, sharp breathing rasped in my ears, but my breathing was steady. I ignored the dread and darkness inside me, and focused on my alertness, tight muscles and readiness for action.

Soon, a huge navy blue, ovoid airship glided towards us, propelled by rockets on its sides and underneath. It didn't look like Nuclear Age Tech. It was more Void Age. But the Void Age hadn't come, the Nuclear Holocaust saw to that. This ship was a thing of Science Fiction.

"I thought no one used those since the Nuclear Holocaust?" Amon asked quietly, as everyone stared at the sleek leviathan, slowing as it neared our motel.

"Sythe Schools have lots of secrets," Merin replied. "We're not high enough in rank to know them yet."

The airship hovered above the road and vineyard, stairs folded down, and the Trainers led us towards them. I looked up as we climbed the steps, muscles still tight, wondering how the strange metal transport could take our weight *and* rise into the sky. There were aisles along both interior walls, and rows of leather chairs down the middle. How much did this thing weigh? How could it possibly *fly*?

I sat on the end of a row beside Miona, buckled on my seatbelt and gazed at the wall, then blinked at heavily tinted glass spanning from floor to ceiling, giving me a view across the vineyard, motel and the mountains rising beyond. I could see for leagues. The sides of the airship must be made of special strength glass, like the Monster Centre enclosures.

The floor vibrated. A humming sound made me grip the armrest in discomfort. I didn't like sitting in the bowels of this strange machine with no clue how it worked. Then the vineyards dropped away, a faint whirring sound rose from the floor and the countryside below us and mountains on my right streaked into blurs.

I gaped. Everyone did. If we were moving fast enough for scenery to blur, we should be pinned to our seats by g-force, but I felt only slight pressure. The blur of scenery felt like fictional entertainment on a screen.

People around us whispered nervously, worrying about Bellaria, but I wondered why I'd never seen anything like this airship in the sky before. Where had this machine been hiding?

I watched the scenery carefully. When it became less blurred, I assumed the airship was slowing as we neared Bellaria. My heart rate sped up, my adrenaline spiked, and my joints relaxed, ready to confront a frightening reality, because a well-told lie had escalated Serena from peace to war like flipping a switch. I hoped Sythe was hunting the scum responsible.

Hollowness tinged with fear grew inside me, as the walls of Bellaria City came into sight. I wasn't ready to work in a team. I trusted no-one here but Merin and Miona to have my back. The Trainers too, but they were probably needed elsewhere. How was I supposed to help the City Guard in this emergency?

Sytherens had set up a barricade of armoured vehicles in front of the city gates, which were chained shut. Gunners shifted on the battlements. Navy blue and black uniformed sytherens and light blue and brown uniformed sythers were positioned on apartment rooftops and balconies beyond the walls. The calm city I'd spent six weeks guarding the gates of, was now crowded with rigid postured, armed figures poised for battle.

Sharp intakes of breath silenced murmured conversations around me. Eyes widened and people pointed at signs their home city was preparing for war.

My classmates weren't ready. They had no idea what it was like to watch every direction at once for physical danger.

Or to poise to flee, fight or hide at any moment. Dad had just come home, on a city-wide scale. Could *I* handle this?

Our airship touched down outside the heavily guarded walls. The downward folding stairs revealed a sergeant waiting for military sytherens, while Toron waited for city guards. My muscles tightened, as I noted a vehicle loaded with guns parked behind him.

I walked towards Toron, leading a hesitant crowd off the airship.

"Don't worry," Toron told frightened faces warmly. "The military are defending the city walls and the gates. Our guards are stationed at the mayor's residence and the town hall in City Centre, where civilians are taking refuge. Your objective is to be part of a grand display of force making the cost of fighting clear to the Serenans, *if* negotiations fail."

"And if the Serenans attack?" Johnny asked.

"They have little hope of overcoming the military and getting beyond the city walls," Toron replied. "If they found a way of entering the city without going through the gates, the military and Syther Force have gunners and sharp shooters stationed atop buildings throughout the city. Walking the city streets will be as dangerous as climbing the walls, and we doubt the Serenans will attempt it."

"But if they do?" I asked grimly.

Hope shone in many eyes around me, but hoping for the best was dangerous. You *had* to know what the worst was, to be prepared to counter it. It was the only way to survive.

"Then your orders are not to open fire unless the building you defend is attacked, or every building around you is under attack. We don't want this war, so we'll give the enemy the chance to ceasefire and withdraw, whenever they realise they can't win. Collect your guns and follow me."

I slung my stun gun strap over my shoulder and held it by the grip, ready to raise and fire. Miona and Merin drew nervous breaths and nodded as they fell in beside me. We followed Toron, leading the other sytherens towards the city walls.

Every face on my right was pale and hands or knees trembled as we crossed a grassy paddock. I was aware of everything, armed sytherens marching around me, sheep hiding under trees on my far left, a ladder against the stone walls ahead of us, armed sytherens moving atop the walls.

The climb up the ladder was unlike any training exercise, and from the way Ryan had to encourage Amon behind me, the height must have made Amon nervous. I focused on hand and foot holds, uncomfortably aware of open air at my back, until I climbed onto the wall top and looked around. Hundreds of sytherens and sythers spread across stone battlements left and right, holding long range guns, or erecting powerful, automatic weapons on stands between crenelations in the wall. Any Serenans who marched too close would do so through a hail of bullets. Surely they'd turn back when they saw this…

We climbed down a ladder against the inside wall, then boarded a bus. The drive down a main road past small houses was tense, my classmates holding their breaths and clutching guns tightly. The streets were deserted, aside from an armoured military truck driving towards the walls.

Everyone must have been told to stay inside when news of the Serenan army's approach spread. I hoped Mum was with Uncle Alan and Aunt Lil. They'd keep her calm. Des would stand in for his useless father and help Ma Tully watch over Cam. Most people I knew were probably trembling in their homes, except Trent, who was probably impersonating a sytheren somewhere he could tell the Serenans they were barking up the wrong tree. The thought made me smile.

We drove through nicer suburbs nearer City Centre and they were just as quiet, aside from private security guards, or their motor carriages patrolling mansions and estates in Greenhill. Then the glass, steel and wood blended buildings of City Centre rose around us beside deserted footpaths. The only traffic was sythers and sytherens on foot or in vehicles. All were heavily armed. It was like a scene from Big Screen fiction.

The bus drove us up the central hill of City Centre, stopping in the motor carriage bay beside the cylindrical town hall. Toron led us round the back and had us spread out along the back wall. That was a nuisance, we couldn't see much of the city or its walls, only the greenery of public gardens, and brick, concrete, or steel and glass mansions rising above the gardens at the back end of City Centre.

I strained my ears for sounds of attack, but heard only quiet talk from sythers stationed on the roof above us. I crouched instinctively, but Merin shook her head. She was right; I'd tire too quickly in that posture. I straightened, eyeing Toron, who carried a long-range gun and a comm in a pouch at his waist. He'd give us orders or tell us what was going on. Until then, we had to wait quietly.

Chapter 16

The Attack

I hate waiting. My senses are excellent at the first sign of danger, but you can't stay on high alert forever. Gradually, your heart beat and breathing slow down, your muscles relax and the adrenaline fades. I kept my breathing quick, trying to counter the temptation to relax. How close was the Serenan army? Could they see our defences yet? How fared the negotiations? Were Mum, Uncle Alan, Aunt Lil and the boys ok?

My mind leapt from one concern to the next, until I heard a flap overhead. I gazed up at a furry, four-legged creature flying over buildings on my left. A tarth, a large mammal with sharp teeth and menacing red eyes. It carried a large rider whose only weapon was a spear, in a holder on his saddle. Was he insane?

Johnny tracked the rider with his gun.

"Steady!" Toron warned. "He's not attacking us, so we don't attack him."

The Serenan's skin was olive green, and his long-braided beard and hair were black. He scanned buildings and gunners below him fearlessly, as his tarth's scaled wings flapped, and it hovered.

I stared while the Serenan assessed our numbers, from *within* range of our guns. Sythe must want him to report our numbers accurately and that attacking the city was futile.

The creature flew away.

A cry cut the air over rooftops on my left. I crouched and raised my gun instinctively. I couldn't see the city walls, but a distant, dark object rose above rectangular rooftops on the left, then dove down. Distant shouts rose.

"Was that a serpent?" Merin asked.

The air rang with gunshots. Distant automatic weapon fire hummed. Shouts and gunfire continued, and I glimpsed more large shapes looming above rooftops, then descending to the city wall.

Serpents attacking sythers? I couldn't think of anything else that matched the distant movements... what in Chaos were the Serenans thinking?

I inhaled heavily, gripped my gun tightly and wished I could take out whatever was causing those screams.

Merin pointed to two spherical airships in the distance. The roar of automatic weapons doubled.

"General! Serpents are in the sewers! Repeat, serpents have infiltrated sewers and entered the city!"

We turned to Toron, who frowned worriedly. Several tense moments passed, then heavy footsteps thudded towards us; Trainer Morea walking uphill.

"Rarkin! Amon! With me!" he ordered.

Miona gave me a tense nod, Merin squeezed my upper arm and I nodded back, then jogged down the steps. Amon caught me up, his warm brown face multiple shades lighter than usual, his dark eyes wide, his mouth slack with fear and bewilderment. I actually felt bad for the kid, because he'd never known fear or uncertainty like this and this was a brutal way to learn it.

We ran down stone steps, alongside the high metal fence and greenery of public gardens. Then down a street past grand multi-story homes, with balconies and large front yards.

"Where are we going?" I asked the trainer.

"To the nearest sewer running out of the city walls," Trainer Morea replied. "A place that's otherwise of no strategic importance, so it's undermanned."

"Why us?" Amon asked faintly.

To my surprise, Trainer Morea grinned. "You'll show yourself soon."

My lips twitched. We'd both done well in our shooting exam... *better* under pressure. Trainer Dorthin must have told him.

Adrenaline mixed with my anticipation. I hadn't stunned anything larger than a garl, but the chance to fight serpents was insane; and *brilliant*. Beneath my tension and nerves, a thrill rose within me, as the grand homes around us shrank and we ran through deserted streets, passing the occasional cat fleeing across front yards.

Footsteps thudded. A pair of sythers sprinted out of a side street, heading our way. I tightened my grip on my gun, as my hands became slick with sweat. We rounded a corner and my adrenaline spiked. A dead serpent lay along the road, the length of *five* parked motor carriages.

Shouts rose and gun shots echoed further down. Two sythers raised their guns and shot at a dark scaled head rising from a damaged storm water drain. The reptilian mouth opened, revealing foot-long fangs.

Amon stared and slowed.

"Keep moving!" I yelled, shoving him with my left hand.

He was easily distracted; I'd need to keep an eye on him.

Trainer Lauran knelt on our left, beside a soldier with a bleeding chest and a pale, grey face. Bitten. Poisoned. I grit my teeth and we ran on.

One set of gunfire ahead of us paused. Three sythers leapt aside, dodging a serpent's lunging head, while the other pair provided cover fire. The three hit the ground and rolled aside.

I fired at the serpent but didn't do much damage. Trainer Morea and Amon opened fire. Amon's fingernails on his gun grip were orange. The colour of fire. It seemed fitting. What was wrong with my brain, that I was noticing *that*, now?

There was a small explosion. Two sythers on our left paused and the woman yelled, "Down!"

Amon stared, as a second serpent smashed its way out of the drain, sending asphalt chunks of road and gutter flying. I seized him round the waist and dived, pulling us to the ground. I landed heavily on my shoulder and rolled to lessen the impact. Small rocks rained down around us, and larger chunks of asphalt flew overhead. Amon grunted in surprise.

For a moment I worried I'd hurt him. Then it sunk in. I'd stopped him from getting hit in the head by large chunks of rubble. There were worse things to worry about.

I let him go and sat up, raising my gun, peering ahead. The second serpent slithered up from the crumbling road edge. The first serpent lunged at the three sythers fleeing on foot, as it emerged from the drain.

I growled; not confident I could hit that serpent instead of the three sythers. But Amon raised his gun, his eyes wide with fear and jaw clenched, his hands steady. He fired three shots. All three struck the serpent's head. It collapsed.

The second serpent turned away from the two sythers, towards us. I stood hurriedly, pulling Amon to his feet with my free hand so we could run if we had to. The serpent lunged. Amon just stood there. I shoved him to the right and the serpent came at me.

Trainer Morea pulled me aside. Amon was firing repeatedly.

The Trainer and I turned with guns raised. The two sythers leapt back as the serpent thrashed. It was dying. It collapsed across the road. Amon stared in shock.

"Everyone back!" the woman syther commanded. "Explosives in five!"

I stepped forwards, grabbing Amon's arm and pulling him back. We ran, ignoring the roar of automatic weapons behind us, the thud of footsteps and hissing of serpents.

Trainer Lauran had moved to a front yard. I leapt the picket fence between us and crouched under a nearby tree. Amon and Trainer Morea ran through the gate, as Trainer Lauran tried to stop the wounded man's bleeding and a third syther used a comm to call for help.

Explosives cracked and rumbled down the road and the earth swayed beneath us. I stumbled, as a woman in a white dress stepped around the corner. She knelt, placing her hands on the man's wound and closed her eyes. The man's head flopped, and she lifted her hands, revealing healthy skin on his chest and bloodstains on his torn shirt. There was no sign of the wound.

Trainer Lauran thanked her, but I stared. She *wasn't* a syther.

A voice sounded through the comm. "We need a healer! Corner of Padson and Davison roads. Poison's killing Trama!"

The woman in white vanished. Trainer Lauran blinked, and exchanged a look with the third syther, then they turned back to the wounded man. If they hadn't done that, I might have thought I'd imagined a vanishing woman. But I hadn't. I'd just seen a sorcerer…

The background noise of gunfire and distant shouts faded, until it gave way to silence. Was the first phase of the Serenan attack defeated? Would diplomacy have a chance now, or would the Serenans start phase two?

Trainer Lauran turned up the volume on her comm as a report came through.

"Ma'am, we've sighted men driving from Trebo towards Serena. They're heavily armed and have drilling equipment and digging tools in the back of their four-wheeler."

Did those fuckers start a war to give themselves a clear shot at the gold?

"We think your city is in danger!" a man's voice yelled through the comm. "We did not intend to rob you, but someone did. They accused us to remove your army from their path. If you do not believe me, look at this."

"The ambassador is talking to a Serenan messenger," Trainer Lauran reported. "But the messenger looks sceptical. They are distracted. There are smoke signals on the southern horizon. Serena is signalling an attack. A Serenan is shouting at the messenger in their own language."

"If you are not in league with these thieves, will you lend us your weapons to slay them?" a deep voice asked, the challenge in it clear.

I turned to Trainer Morea.

"That would be murder, under our laws," he clarified. "The Serenans won't just fight to defend themselves from thieves, they'll kill them all. But if we refuse the Serenans weapons, they'll think we've been lying all along."

I shrugged. "The crims started a war, then set out to murder their way to a fortune. They *should* be executed."

"We've not had the death penalty in Taros for centuries," Trainer Morea replied.

"Do the Serenans?" I asked.

"For humans who cheat and murder them? Always. But it would be a shame to buy peace with blood."

"How else do you buy peace?" I asked.

"This time?" Trainer Morea asked. "We wouldn't."

There was a pause, in which it was obvious that my attitude bothered him and gave Amon pause. But these pricks had started a war so they could commit theft in Serena, and if the Serenans had the death penalty for that, good for them.

We waited tensely to hear the Serenan chief's decision. Finally, Trainer Lauran exhaled. "The General is landing an airship to transport the Serenan vanguard home. She is giving them automatic weapons. She is also sending one team of Force Sythers with long range stun guns to capture criminals for questioning. The Chief is suspicious of the sythers intentions, but the Serenans are departing. The invasion is over."

My muscles relaxed, and my heart beat gradually slowed.

Trainers Lauran and Morea led Amon and me back up the road towards the town hall. Amon eyed me sheepishly as we walked.

"Sorry I kept shoving you around," I said without thinking. "I didn't want you getting killed and you were too slow to move out of harm's way."

Amon slowly smiled. "I think I'm ok with you wanting me to live."

His smile was so big and so sincere that I couldn't help looking at his face. And smiling back, as I processed my own words. We'd just run a gauntlet with Chaos himself. It had been insane. And I'd been so quick to keep Amon safe that Trainer Morea hadn't had to do much. I hadn't realised my instincts for safety could keep other people as safe in immediate danger as they did me.

"You could uh, balance it out with a hug?" Amon added uncertainly.

What? He… "I, don't really go in for those," I replied awkwardly, turning away. What was it with this guy?

"I know," he said, with another of those smiles, warm brown eyes through dark, long lashes. No one should have eyes that pretty, or that warm. It was distracting.

"Do you think you might?" he asked. "One day?"

I shivered, then sighed. 'One day' seemed a world away. Jay kept telling me I needed to change things to succeed at Sythe. But me, being someone who goes around *hugging* people?

He was *still* smiling. Whatever my face was telling him surely wasn't the answer he was looking for, yet he was *still* happy. I swear I'll never understand him!

Though, maybe the world needs people who don't stop smiling. They kind of balance out people who rarely smile, like me. Maybe Sythe School needs both of us...

We met our class beside the town hall soon after that conversation. Miona surprised me with a hug. I froze for a moment, like I always do, on the rare occasions people spring that sudden closeness on me and I feel wooden and don't know how to position myself.

But this was Miona. I trusted her and it wasn't complicated. Though it was still several moments before I awkwardly placed my hands on her back, not sure whether to hold her gently or firmly or what. I stood up straight, taller than her, kind of aloof. Was that not how it should be? How on Mijora's green Earth would I know?

I saw Amon's raised eyebrow at the edge of my vision and pretended not to.

Then Merin distracted me by pecking me on the cheek, making me blush. She smiled wickedly, and Miona rolled her eyes.

Ryan and Lylez hugged Amon. Johnny, Nick and Joe flicked their chins at me and I returned the gesture, much more at ease with it. Rinth nodded to me and I nodded back.

Trainer Lauran led us onto the bus and Miona said quietly, "You're the only ones who fought."

Great. I hate people making a fuss, but somehow I doubted we could avoid that.

I sat in front of her and Merin as we drove past people coming out of houses calling to each other, kissing and hugging. It seemed over the top. We hadn't been in *that* much danger. Still, they cheered and waved at our bus, even though most sytherens hadn't done anything.

"Why did you pick us?" I asked Trainer Morea, who sat diagonally opposite me.

"Trainer Lauran said you can keep your head in any situation, and we suspected Amon would be a crack shot. He has the makings of a great shooter, but it took that kind of pressure to prove it. He achieved it because you kept him alive."

"But you had his back, if I didn't," I said uncertainly.

"I didn't expect you to protect him. I expected you to focus on fighting. Instead, you demonstrated teamwork of the kind I hadn't thought you ready for. Teamwork is essential to sythers. Whether syther teams work for the military, the Syther Force or other departments, the skills and strengths each person brings make a team a strong, clever, capable unit. I suspect you will find yourself on a syther team earlier than you anticipate."

He was wrong. I'd spotted danger, Amon hadn't so I protected him. Sure, I had his back, but I didn't trust him to have mine... I'd fired at both serpents he helped kill, for all the good *my* shooting did.

Amon was talking to Ryan on my left and most of the bus was listening. "We helped the sythers fight serpents bursting out of storm water drains," he said faintly, as if he didn't believe it. "I helped bring them down and Rarkin stopped me from getting bit or killed by flying asphalt in the process."

They plied him with questions, but he shook his head and said nothing. Maybe he had aftershock.

"Is he telling the truth?" Ryan asked me.

All eyes on the bus turned tentatively towards me. I gazed out the window, trying to ignore the blazing discomfort of all their gazes.

"Yeah," I replied. "He gave three sythers cover fire so they could move to safety, then helped two sythers kill a second serpent."

"And *you* stopped him from getting *bitten*?" Ryan asked, his mouth opening in wonder.

I shrugged. "He looks better without fang shaped holes in him."

Amon smiled nervously, probably at the image I'd put in his mind, and then they were eyeing both of us with awe. Great, I'd just made us even *more* the centre of attention. Amon didn't seem to mind it normally, but the way he'd gone quiet, this seemed too much even for him.

I was glad when the bus drove around the loop outside the Sythe Castle, and everyone flocked off it and through a side gate to Central Courtyard, where a crowd of parents turned towards us eagerly. I walked slowly, letting everyone else get ahead.

"Rarkin!"

I turned to the sound of my mother's voice.

"I'm so proud!"

Uncle Alan and Aunt Lil stepped out from the familial crowd on my left, following my mother.

"Trainer Morea tells us you saved a classmate's life today," Uncle Alan said with a smile.

I shrugged it off. "Amon's alright. I didn't fancy a serpent eating him."

Mum paled, and I kicked myself mentally. I should have left that comment for when she wasn't there, but Aunt Lil and Uncle Alan smiled.

Amon rushed past us, hugging his grandparents. Everyone was hugging and talking excitedly or exhaling with relief. I suppose we'd technically been invaded, for the first time in centuries. Maybe coming out so well as a city was something to celebrate.

Chapter 17

Traversing the Dark Tunnel

A serpent surged towards Amon. He didn't see it. He was aiming at another. I ran towards him, but I didn't have a clear shot. The serpent opened its fangs to bite him. I opened my mouth to shout a warning, but my jaw was locked shut and I couldn't speak. The serpent's jaws closed around Amon's torso. He didn't make a sound.

Pain struck my back. I was bitten from behind. My back burned. I screamed. The serpent bit me again. I couldn't move. Something was holding me in place, other than the pain... Why was it going so wrong? I looked around, hoping Trent would come, but he didn't. I didn't know him yet. What in Chaos was this?

"I'll teach you," said Dad's voice.

That made no sense at all. But he was walking towards me. I punched him in the face and woke up in tangled, sweaty sheets, panting. I was lying in bed in my dark room at Uncle Alan's. All of my muscles tensed, and my heart was racing.

Everything had gone so badly wrong. My dream version of the serpent battle was so different from reality. Yet, the helplessness I'd felt as Amon got bit was so real, as was the pain on my back and the feeling of being held in place.

My eyes adjusted to the morning light as I climbed out of bed and straightened the covers. The dream faded, but I was still short of breath as I pulled clothes out of a drawer and put them on. Movement didn't relax my tension. My breathing didn't slow. I had to resist the urge to peer nervously over my shoulder. There was *no* threat. But my hands still balled into fists and the knowledge did nothing to calm instincts that shouted at me to *watch* my *back*.

It didn't help that classes were cancelled for the next week and mid-semester break started early, because families were shaken up by the serpent attacks. I didn't like the change in routine. It took away the comfort of friends' company and the distraction of study to occupy my days. It made me uneasy, restless and left me in my room alone, with troubled thoughts.

Jay called, wanting me to see him and I was almost glad of the excuse. I hated not understanding what was going on in my own mind.

"I hear you did very well yesterday," Jay said that afternoon. "How are you feeling?"

I sat tensely on the couch opposite him. My posture said it all.

"You told me I have traumatic-stress," I said. "I'm getting the anger out and accepting shit my father did, but I've done nothing about trauma. I think yesterday made it worse."

226

Jay sighed. "No one could have foreseen the attack. It even shocked the staff, Rarkin. That said, Trainer Morea walked a fine line taking you and Amon to fight serpents. He's facing an inquiry."

"Why did he pull us into the fight?" I asked.

"It should have occurred to Sythe that the ancient sewers were a weak point, but it's been so many centuries since the city was attacked that we overlooked it. Too few sythers were near that breach."

The admission gave me chills.

"They didn't just need just extra gunners," Jay continued. "Amon's accuracy killed the second serpent and helped kill the first and you saved Amon's life at least once. The sythers are sure some of them would have died if you hadn't been there and Trainer Morea took you both because he foresaw that. But he exposed you to greater danger than you are qualified to meet."

Trainer Morea had tried to correct Sythe's mistake of not guarding the sewers properly by choosing two sytherens he thought were up to the task...he thought highly of us.

"Yesterday made your trauma worse?" Jay asked.

Instinct and Trent's teachings made me want to flinch away from that admission, but the feelings in my dreams were so out of line with how the serpent battle had unfolded. And feelings from dreams shouldn't stalk you after you wake up.

"Bad dreams," I admitted. "In the dreams, I watched while the serpent bit Amon and another bit me. I couldn't warn or help him. Something physically restrained me."

How was the pain from that dream familiar? I'd never been bitten by anything.

"Were you scared in your dreams?"

My mouth firmed, and my hands balled into fists. Never admit to weakness. Don't be vulnerable in front of others. But Jay might figure it out and I couldn't do that on my own.

"It wasn't just about yesterday," I realised.

The helplessness, fear and pain rose strongly in me and I tried to push them away. "I don't wanna deal with that yet," I said determinedly. "I wanna learn to stop hating someone who isn't here anymore, before I take on something else."

Jay sighed. "That's wise, but hitting a punch bag only achieves so much. As long as you keep revisiting things your father did to hurt you or your mother, each revisit will make you angry again."

"I'm supposed to just accept that he ruined my life? To stop fighting it? That's why I'm still sane! Because I fight everything that can hurt or destroy me!"

"Do you realise how much that fight takes out of you? How it makes you restless and makes it hard for you to rest or relax properly?"

I frowned. "How do you know so much?"

"I see it in your posture. I see it on your face whenever topics you don't want to discuss come up. It takes a lot of energy to constantly resist things that are part of you."

"I don't *want* them to be part of me! I don't want these memories!"

Jay sighed. "They *are* part of you. And you have them."

"Then I'll push them down!" I declared angrily, leaping to my feet. "I'll shove them aside. I *won't* let them hurt me!"

I blanched. Was that the thing that *truly* angered me? Was that what I was running from? Pain? Did I *fear* pain? How weak did that make me? How was Trent not disgusted by the sight of me?

"You avoid pain for the same reason as other guys in the neighbourhood," Jay said. "You think it makes you weak. But avoiding it for days, weeks, months on end, that wears you down. It makes you tired and short-tempered, less able to deal with anything and ultimately, weak."

"You're saying I can be weak, or I can be weak?"

"What's so bad about being hurt now?" Jay asked. "Who's going to kick you after you fall Rarkin?"

I tensed. He knew too bloody much. That *was* why I hated being weak or vulnerable, because my old man had been a rampaging bull who'd take me out regardless of the state I was in, and if I was feeling hurt at the time, that could result in emotional agony or actual death.

But Dad wasn't here. But letting myself feel pain went against all my instincts, and how I'd lived my *entire* life. It didn't matter that I couldn't point to someone who'd destroy me if I let myself remember and feel the pain, I felt the threat and I did *not* want to expose myself to it!

"I can't do this now," I said, shaking my head. "It's too soon."

Jay didn't say anything, and it was a while before I turned to look at him.

"Your sytheren abduction was like nothing Bellarian Sythe has ever seen," he said patiently. "At no point in history has anyone achieved such a feat against Sythe. I think we know who's behind it, but that's no guarantee that Sythe can stop them soon, or that they won't try something else.

"This is a dangerous time to be a sytheren or a syther. It's an extremely difficult time to juggle other challenges. I worry that other stressful events may soon unfold. I wouldn't normally rush anyone Rarkin, but with a powerful enemy on the loose, you may not have time to meet personal challenges before your work life becomes too much to deal with on top of them."

I could see concern in his eyes. He believed what he said.

"I need time to think," I replied. "It's all crashing around in my head."

"Think on it," Jay said. "Take what time you need. But if something on the scale of the city's attack arises soon, I don't want you participating."

I hated being less capable than my classmates. I'd been fine with serpents. …But if things got worse and I cracked up on a field assignment…my nightmares of Amon being bit by a serpent weren't far-fetched.

"Do you think Trainer Morea *will* be suspended?" I asked.

"Given the circumstances, his reasons and the results, I don't think so. Please don't let him know you know about the inquiry or tell anyone else. I follow unique protocols which allow me to reveal things that help people work through their situations, but in this case that information is classified by normal protocol."

I flicked my chin. I was uncomfortable knowing something about Trainer Morea that I shouldn't. But if him leading us to fight serpents faced an inquiry, had he breached protocol? Had he asked more of both of us than Sythe thought he had a right to expect? And I *had* stopped Amon from being killed. How could I be weak *and* functional enough to save someone's life at the same time? I didn't get it. But I did get that Sythe was becoming a very dangerous organisation to work for and that I needed to get my shit together.

Chapter 18

Surprise

After my conversation with Jay, I felt wrong-footed when Trainer Morea called and asked me to come to school five days after the attack, to room four hundred and seven. The door was open when I got there, and Amon sat confusedly at a table, his fine dreadlocks sculpted into a braid that looked like a short ponytail. It was kind of feminine. It looked good though. Everything looked good on him.

A smiling Trainer Morea and Lauran sat opposite Amon. They welcomed me to a fourth seat.

"I reported your deeds of last week to Headmistress Rinas, who has taken over from Headmaster Zatrack," Trainer Morea explained. "She was impressed with your efforts and she agrees with me that although you have only just begun syther studies, you are ready to become Trainee Sythers."

We were being assigned to an experienced syther team to help with Field Assignments *already*?

"I believe you have met Ine, whose team you'll be training with, in the field of Monster Containment. Congratulations."

I sat with my mouth hanging open, like a fool. I'd never anticipated making Trainee so soon. Had they decided we were exceptional and to promote us, rather than to demote Trainer Morea for breaching protocol?

I turned to Amon, but his features were blank. He must underestimate how good a gunner he is.

"I suggest you both resign from the city guard," Trainer Morea continued, "As you need to be available for Field Assignments at Week's End, as well as during the week. But as Trainee Sythers, you will be paid similar rates to guard duty, probably more."

He thought we could do this, and the new Head agreed. I wouldn't be held back by my classmate's hesitancy in field training anymore. And we'd be paid as Trainee Sythers…

Half a bell later, Des gave me a lift to his place and I rang Glenn. He wasn't home, but Dory congratulated me on my position. Then I joined Des, Cam, Wak and Tak in the lounge.

"It was easy," Tak was saying confidently. "With a little help. Once we knew who to watch, and the fool forgot to burn his supplier-bosses' hard copy instructions and we nicked them. We set up sythers to arrest the supplier and dealer."

"Our first assignment," Wak explained, as I sat on the end of the couch.

"I told them where to find their dealer," Des admitted.

I blinked. "Isn't that risky?"

"Not in this case," Trent replied, as he walked through the front door. "These suppliers sell dodgy stuff that's put a few kids in hospital and killed a couple more, school kids, who think drugs might be a fun way to party. And this dealer's a crooked pimp. He's too well connected for anyone I know to take out, so I got Des to sell him out to sythers. Once he's in prison, his boss will take him out to ensure he doesn't name names."

I sighed inwardly. Trent ran away from home when he was eleven. His father had killed his mother. Trent hadn't been strong enough to stop him. He spent two years on the street, doing jobs for petty criminals because he was too young to get a legal job, until he was asked to nick something from Dory's forge.

Dory took him in. He ran off twice, but came back both times. Dory got through to Trent. I think that's why he ran away. He'd had no one for three years and he didn't want to stay with a potential father in case it turned to shit. I understood. Part of me hadn't wanted to get used to Dad being gone, because how would I cope when he came back and ruined everything?

But Trent stayed with Dory and Glenn till he was sixteen. That's how he met us and got his first honest job, and his crummy, one room apartment. But he knows people from his time on the streets, every crim in town I suspect. The problem is, they know him. If anyone from his meaner circles realised his mates Wak and Tak are shadowers and put two and two together, they'd come after him.

The front door swung open again. Glenn and Tran had entered the room. They both smiled, but a hint of their previous expressions lingered. Something was bothering them.

"You *did* pass your exam, didn't you?" Des said, teasingly. "Or were Wak and Tak winding me up?"

"Said we couldn't have done better," Tran replied, as he and Glenn flopped onto a pair of beanbags beside the couch I was sitting on.

"Then what's wrong?" Cam asked.

"The most important part was a massive arrest," Glenn explained. "They said little about the results, but we know some important people got away."

"You're not blaming yourselves for the invasion?" asked Des.

Tak sighed and Wak flexed his fists.

"It sucks," Tran replied and that was the end of the conversation.

***

I saw Glenn the next day. We got milkshakes from Zargo's and sat on a bench in an overgrown park nearby. Glenn looked serious and deep in thought.

"How much do you know about the people who abducted you guys?" he asked.

"Just that a Trainer from school and a Captain from the military were leading us and military sytherens somewhere in secret. And that what Headmaster Zatrack told us was a load of crap."

That weighed on me. The Head who'd let me stay in school, but expelled Chareck. The one who'd made me meet Jay, and said I could do well, a traitor.

Glenn sighed. "Your school and Bellaria's Army Base?"

I blinked. Why was he was repeating what I said?

"Did they hit another school?" I asked.

Glenn sighed deeply, staring into the distance, grappling with something.

"Not all three?"

Glenn shivered. He couldn't say anything without breaching secrecy protocols. But I could tell from his silence that I was either right or it was two schools.

"They didn't want us to know?" I asked. "At the workshops, they kept us in our school groups. They had each school stay at a different motel. They didn't give us the chance to speak to each other. But why cover it up?"

"Because of what we're doing right now," Glenn replied.

"Talking and spreading the news?" I asked. "They didn't tell us because they didn't want the continent to know?"

"It wasn't in the news either."

"Then how do you know?"

"When Trainer Luthez went to tell Headmistress Zleena about you lot being missing, another code yellow came through her system first, an audible one. It was Azmalah Sythe School. Eighty of their students who were supposed to be at the workshops went missing. We had to sign paperwork swearing we wouldn't speak of it. I only mentioned the Bellaria Army base sytherens because I was sure you'd clock who they were from how they move, if you saw them at the Gotsi Day Parade."

"But why the cover up?" I asked.

"Why are they afraid of exposing a high-level breach of security in our defence forces and education system?" he replied. "Can you guess how we felt hearing those breaches as they were reported? My heart was pounding the whole time. If we hadn't done our Shadower Exam, I wouldn't have slept that night. Sythe hasn't been this vulnerable to outsiders, or faced this kind of determined, successful opposition for centuries, if ever."

Jay had said the same.

"I suppose that'd cause panic," I replied. "Trainer Morea said our Trainers were distracted in some likely deliberate way, so they didn't intercept us as we were marched out."

Glenn inhaled swiftly.

"What really happened to Headmaster Zatrack? Other than him being suspended as a Head?"

"I think he's on the run," said Glenn. "Got himself out before we came for him. He'll have agents after him now."

"You think he's a traitor?"

"I think if someone put him out of the way while they abducted a large percentage of students he's responsible for, he would have turned up by now. From things I've overheard, I suspect that's what happened to the Azmalahn Head of sytheren and sythe students. But I don't think it's what happened to Headmaster Zatrack."

So Mavon had managed to recruit a Sythe School Headmaster, and possibly others. Or to infiltrate two or three sythe schools and military bases, simultaneously, and successfully abduct hundreds of students and soldiers. How well-resourced was he? How powerful? And what in the name of Chaos did he want?

"Why take us?" I asked. "Was Mavon trying to expose every city's vulnerabilities and frighten everyone? Was this an act of terror aimed at each city? Or did he actually hope to achieve something?"

"You've heard of Mavon?" Glenn asked, and I explained the conversation I'd overheard outside Headmaster Zatrack's office the day Chareck got expelled.

Glenn nodded then asked, "If they gave you orders, or field assignments, would you have completed them?"

"Without our Trainers present?" I asked. "When we were supposed to be going to workshops or home? No. Some students would have been too scared to follow orders from strange Trainers, and if they'd given me a stun gun and told me to threaten or harm anyone, I would've taken pot shots at them. All the tough kids would've. They would've risked a mass uprising if they tried to get us to do anything other than docilely follow where they led."

"That's what I thought," Glenn replied. "They've demonstrated that we're vulnerable, but if they knew we were *that* vulnerable and they have an agenda, why didn't they follow up? Why didn't they use our vulnerabilities to gain something? People smart enough to pull off that abduction wouldn't be silly enough to think they could put guns in your hands and have you obey them."

"The military sytherens were armed," I remembered.

Glenn grunted. "Their guns aren't fitted with tracking devices. Did your abductors know that? Someone high up in Sythe Schools must be allied with them."

"And you have no idea what they were trying to achieve by taking us?"

"After lying awake at night trying to puzzle it out, no. Nothing that matches how clever and well-resourced Mavon is. Nothing that makes sense."

As unnerving as it was to have an outside force march into our Sythe School and abduct us, it was almost more frightening not knowing why. Because if we didn't know what they wanted, how could anyone know what they would do next? Let alone catch them…

Chapter 19

Our First Assignment

I was uneasy about our abduction and the invasion. Tense after that conversation with Glenn, as I waited for Mavon to hit us in another unexpected way. I had more nightmares about mishaps with serpents, but they stopped after a while. Jay said it was probably bits of unpleasant memory I'd repressed, jumbled up with recent memory. There were things lurking in dark corners of my mind, but I didn't want to touch them. Having Mavon looming over us was bad enough.

I sparred with Miona or Merin at lunch or after school and stalked monsters in the Monster Centre as often as Trainer Lauran let us. The physical activity helped me feel less stressed, but it did nothing to ease my worry.

"About you being an innermind," Miona said in the Training Centre one day.

I started, having drifted off into space, despite that we stood opposite each other, gloves on, poised to spar in a small room. It was second break and quiet, which was probably why I'd zoned out, without background noise pulling me into the present.

"Is that what's worrying you?" she asked. "It was kind of hard to tell, given our abduction and the invasion and everything."

I clenched my jaw. Jay had said I should confide in her more. Here was my chance. But she'd asked in the sparring ring, the space we felt like equals, where I wouldn't any longer, if I had this conversation. Or I could tell her about my traumatic stress and how I'm obligated to see the school councillor regularly. How would *that* go for us being on an equal footing?

I chanced a glance at her face. She was smiling.

"You tend to miss a lot, because you don't look at people's faces. I know, it can be off putting and distracting, seeing what they're feeling. Makes it hard to keep track of your thoughts. But it does mean you have a better idea of what's going on. That's why I try to look at people's faces when I talk to them. Have you ever noticed I don't look you in the eye? That's not just for your comfort; it's for both our comfort."

My mouth dropped open in wonder. "*You're* an innermind?! But... you can speak to people! You can follow and join in with group conversations. You know what to say!"

"Haven't you ever noticed I rarely speak first?" she asked.

I thought about it. She'd talked a bit at my birthday, with my mates. But she was always replying to them. And Merin usually started the conversation when it was the three of us. And often it was me when it was the two of us. Besides, conversation with two people is loads easier than with three or more.

I looked thoughtfully at her face.

"It's easier to… to listen to the others and think about what they're saying," she said. "To know what they're talking about and have time to think. Then add something to the conversation."

"You like thinking before you speak, too?" I asked. "You like knowing what you're going to say?"

She nodded.

That was something else I envied Amon for. Not just the way he smiled, the way he just opened his mouth and words that made people smile and like him poured out. If I did that, I was too blunt, and I could sound aggressive, or people just didn't know what I was talking about. I needed time to think and plan my words first. That was what made seeing Jay so hard, I didn't get much time to think what to say to him. I had to think fast, then speak. I kept going off script with him.

I guess… I guess that was why I didn't like talking to lots of people. Too many eyes, too many feelings. Their thoughts and ideas distracting me. I couldn't think straight, most of the time when everyone was looking at me. That's one of the reasons I hate it so much, not just because I hate them staring. It's like the stares scramble my brain and I can't think, and I worry I'll say something stupid or not make any sense, and they'll misunderstand me all the more.

"So we're… I'm shit at something you're also not great at?"

Miona laughed. "You're too hard on yourself. The specialists picked up on me being an innermind when they diagnosed my trouble with reading and writing. But you've been so busy dealing with other things that you didn't properly notice, did you?"

I thought about it. Traumatic stress had loomed much larger. Even though the way I'm an innermind makes speaking to people and being in social situations such a nuisance, *all* the time. It was a stumbling block right in front of my feet, and I hadn't even seen it.

"How do you manage it?" I asked. "Talking to people, I mean."

"I let them speak first, like you often do. Then I just… have a go. Say what I think. Take a risk they won't get me or they won't think what I mean as a joke is funny."

Give my tongue permission to shoot itself off, even for a fraction of the extent Amon did. The way I'd done that around him unnerved me. Maybe that was loosening my tongue too much. But given how frustrating I found being around and speaking to people I hardly know sometimes, maybe I should talk more. Let myself go a bit in conversations. I suppose that was one way to get to know people better. To test if it was safe to relax, and let my guard down round them a little more, like I did with Miona.

And I hadn't worked this out, about her. She'd chosen to tell me. I looked at her face again. "Thanks. For telling me. I wasn't keen on the idea, but if you're an innermind, I guess it can't be that bad."

She smiled. For a moment, I almost wanted to hug her. I never hug people. Ever. I don't like being touched, most of the time. But maybe it wasn't so bad, with people you liked and trusted. When you wanted it, and it wasn't the normal invasion of my space. Was I really a none-er? Or was I just nervous of trusting another person to share my personal space? There was no chance in hell I wanted to get naked with anyone, but that didn't appeal because it was like literally dropping your guard. I'd been too quick to assume I was a noner...

"We should head back to class," she prompted and I nodded.

But I didn't have long to think about the things she'd made me think about, because our first field assignment distracted me completely.

Our Field Captain, Zagoni, was of medium height, with a long black braid, and she walked with casual confidence, as she led Amon and I out of school, speaking with a calm, quiet authority that was easy to respect.

"We will take a motor carriage to the Outer Ring of the Farm Zone," she told us. "One of my teams is setting out to capture a mother garl and her litter, which have taken up residence in a field. The syther team will approach in a semicircle formation, sythers on the left attacking garls on the left, sythers on the right taking garls on the right. You will walk in the middle, and fire darts after the experienced syther beside you has done so, unless every garl has been stunned."

We climbed into a green motor carriage on the driveway loop, with the large MC on a fence painted on its doors, the Monster Containment logo. The motor carriage drove us through the gates and into the Outer Farm Zone, west of Bellaria City.

"The shooting order ensures no more than two people shoot at a time, which reduces the risk of hitting a creature with multiple darts and potentially killing it with an overdose," Captain Zagoni continued. "We may call them monsters, but in Monster Containment; we try to avoid unnecessary cruelty. We also take care to avoid stunning native animals or farm animals, which can get in our way.

"You may not need to shoot today, but I want you to take note of how the syther team functions. Who do you see doing what, when, why do you think they did it and how well did it work? I will ask you about this on our way back to school."

To my surprise, the mini lecture made my world feel more normal, after our abduction and the invasion, and I appreciated it, instead of worrying about important details slipping through my head.

The motor carriage took us to a hilly farm, down a gravel driveway between barley fields. The farmer met us on his driveway, waving and directing the driver down a laneway behind the farmhouse. Curious young children peered through the front window as we drove past. The driver stopped the motor carriage before a trail of fresh droppings across the lane.

We waited until a green van rumbled along the gravel behind us, painted with the MC logo on its sides. Everyone climbed out and Ine nodded in greeting, passing Amon and I stun guns. Was that a purple dreadlock in Amon's braid?

He noticed me noticing and smiled shyly.

"You'll be in the middle with me," Ine told us, as his team, two women and another man, quietly formed a line across the lane. "This is Gorn," he said, nodding to the man, "Team Leader Tali and Comor," he nodded to the other two and we said hi.

Then I moved to the middle of their line, between Ine and Amon. The others raised their guns and I did the same. The captain stood back. She was there to keep an eye on Amon and me, because these adults worked independently. Today, so would we.

I liked moving towards the field, watching the experienced sythers. Gorn motioned to Tali on the left end of our line. She sighted down her stun gun and fired. I saw no sign of a garl. Not until shoots rustled as it fell. Then I glimpsed fur and spikes between green leaves and barley clusters.

My senses sharpened. This time, I heard a faint rustle before Gorn took a shot. Another rustle and Ine fired. I tensed; it was my turn. Barley clusters wobbled, and I took a shot, aiming just above the ground. More barley stalks rustled, but Amon hesitated. We glimpsed a small, spiky section of torso before he put a stun dart in it.

Tali stepped onto dirt between two rows of grain, Comor following, and they fired two more shots. A rustle on my right. Gorn fired.

"Clear," said Comor.

"All clear," Ine called, and everyone lowered their weapons.

Amon's mouth hung open. They were so professional. So confident and efficient. They moved like a single unit, each person aware of and able to stun the creatures by sound. And they moved so quietly, communicating without a word, so they could hear the slightest sound from garls. They were a world away from our class blundering into small monsters and fumbling to stun them in field training.

"Take the women's weapons," Ine instructed Amon and I. We did so, while he took Gorn's gun and led us back to the van.

"We're going to pick those things up and transport them to the National Park Zone, aren't we?" I asked.

Amon's face went slack with uncertainty, but Ine smiled. "They're harmless enough in National Parks. They eat insects and small rodents, but fruit too, so they don't hunt too many native animals. But farmers find them annoying. They're nocturnal, so they burrow under fences of National Parks and into the outskirts of the Farm Zone at night, digging up crops.

"Farmers own stun guns and will capture one or two, then call us to transport them, but they have to call Monster Containment for three or more garls, in case it gets nasty. Farmers avoid litters completely. The mother garl grows a horn when she falls pregnant, and gores humans who get too near her young."

The captain was consulting a portable screen, and she paid us no attention as we loaded the guns in the van, and helped Ine pull a large wheeled crate of protective leather gloves back to his team. We left the crate on the gravel lane, and everyone put their gloves on, pulling them up past elbows. Then Ine motioned us to hang back.

Tali and Comor moved among the grain shoots, in which I glimpsed bits of spike or brown fur. I supposed that when removing monsters from fields or orchards with poor visibility, sound was the most important thing.

"Garl young travel in creches," Ine explained to Amon and me. "Sometimes with multiple females, but males are normally a threat, and that applies to humans. Garl mothers tell gender by pheromones, so Tali and Comor will pass us the young and carry the mother garl out at the end. We'll move back for that, as even sedated, they can get restless if they smell male pheromones."

I watched how the women moved as they reached into the grain shoots. They lifted the baby garls by wrapping one arm around their front legs, and one around the back legs, holding the creature's weight on their forearms by the soft underbellies.

I've never seen Amon as quiet as when he took his first garl from Tali. He reached hesitantly under its belly, and she had to prompt him so it didn't slip over his arm to the ground. I could tell, when my gloves brushed against my own baby garl, that its back spikes were rigid, though they flexed a bit, presumably so they didn't break off if the creatures got tangled in trees. The thing snuffled as I carried it towards the crate, and its warmth radiated through the gloves.

When I lay it on the dried grass the crate was packed with, it curled into a ball. They were kind of cute, when not trying to impale humans.

There were eight young, and Amon and I got to carry two before moving well back. Then Tali and Comor carried the horned mother upright, holding the base of her legs where they met soft underbelly. The women lowered her into the middle of the crate, Comor dropped some apples in, then they sealed the crate and wheeled it back to the van. We kept well back until Tali and Comor had used a lift on the back of the van to load the crate.

"And that's all there is to it," said Gorn.

"You mostly capture garls, don't you?" I asked.

"Mostly, yeah," Gorn replied. "But after today, Captain, I think our Trainee's will be up to helping us, or at least watching us contain anything more interesting, if it gets out."

The captain eyed us appraisingly. We said goodbye to the team, who returned to their van, and Captain Zagoni quizzed us in the motor carriage.

I could tell from his silence and intense concentration that Amon hadn't been analysing anything, he'd just watched and helped capture the creatures. So I stated everything I'd observed, and Captain Zagoni seemed pleased.

"Trainer Morea was quite right to promote you," she said. "You've a good eye and a sharp mind."

I blinked. I guess I was good at watching and remembered what I saw better than what I'd read... But Merin had the sharp mind, she never missed a thing.

The captain turned to Amon, who looked sheepish. "I expected you to need to think before answering me," she said. "I don't expect Trainees to make notes in their head during an assignment; your friend has rare skills there. You can answer my questions next time."

Amon swallowed, nodding and looking relieved I'd said everything there was to say. Apparently I was good at learning on the job.

Chapter 20

A First Encounter

Time passed. We studied protocol for bodily restraint during arrests and acceptable use of stun guns on criminals in Introductory Taron Law. We reviewed monsters in the Taron Wild and which ones were sold on the Black Market for illegal monster fights, or kept as pets by weirdos. Trainer Dorthin finally backed off in Marksmanship, where we shot at robotic moving targets. Amon and I learnt to track monsters by sound and plant movement on field assignments, and Miona got promoted to Trainee in our team.

"Welcome to the team!" Amon said enthusiastically, when she told us after class.

She smiled, but it was somehow restrained.

"Something wrong?" I asked.

"Merin's almost ready to be promoted too, but they told us we can't be on the same team."

"Why not?" Amon asked.

"Sythe don't like couples being in the same team. They told me permanent teams can become like family, but if two people are very close before they get to know the others, it can mean you're more likely to take risks for that person, or to not follow orders out of concern for that person. It puts you in a harder position emotionally and ethically than if you're just friends."

"You agree?" I asked.

She nodded. "I'm just a bit sad because we'll see less of each other, if I'm off training with you two and Merin's training with another team."

"But I'm sure you two will have her back," Merin said, as she walked up to us down the corridor, eyeing Amon and I sternly.

"I'm pretty sure she'll have ours," Amon replied, and both of them and Miona laughed.

I shook my head. Amon had been promoted first. Clearly Sythe thought he was up to being trainee, yet he seemed to think she was more capable. I got his point though. Miona said she often spoke second in conversations because it gave her processing time. But it also meant she presented as calm, collected and responsible. She probably presented as a better trainee syther than me *and* Amon.

And Merin wasn't far behind her. It was only two weeks later that Merin approached us in that same corridor, eyes gleaming, a big smile on her face.

"Which syther team?" Miona asked.

Merin's smile broadened. "I think Rarkin will approve. It's Joe and Johnny's."

I smiled. It was a good choice, and Joe and Merin's confidence and competence made them a good match.

"How do you think you're doing, as a student?" Jay asked in our next session.

I shrugged. "Alright."

"That's your response to being one of only four trainee sythers in your class?"

I frowned. "Trainer Morea gave us a chance to prove ourselves. That's the only reason Amon and I made Trainee so early."

"Would everyone else have done so, with that opportunity?"

"No."

"Yet you have trouble accepting that you're good at Sythe School. What do you think of yourself, Rarkin?"

Maybe it was time to spit it out. Time to defy Trent's teachings and push recklessly forwards, like my career was progressing, and see what happened.

"That I'm less aggressive and less like Trent than I used to be. That I don't know who I am now, or how I do things, or what I'm becoming. And I don't like it."

I sat with my arms crossed, staring into the distance. That was my go-to with him now, when I got frustrated or angry. Whatever I was unhappy about wasn't Jay's fault. He encouraged me to talk about it but he didn't cause any of it. So I was determined to never take it out on him, like Dad always did with us. I shot my angry looks at the walls, because the walls couldn't hurt.

Jay's eyes widened and my jaw clenched. I *didn't* like myself. I knew that. I just didn't want to tell him. Didn't want to make myself weaker by admitting it.

"What do you think Miona thinks of you? Or Merin?" Jay asked.

I shrugged. "They like me."

"How much do you confide in them?"

I shrugged again. "I told Miona about my dad's nature and how dysfunctional my parents' marriage was before Dad left."

"Have you told her anything since?"

Of course I hadn't. Ok, so she was an inner mind too. But she didn't have any of my messed-up-ness from a fucked-up family life. And I was still determined not to touch any relationship that resembled the power imbalance of my parent's marriage.

"You won't be able to stand alone as a syther, Rarkin."

I wasn't a syther yet. Jay had done nothing but support me for months, but I was barely beginning to peel the bandages off for him to see what lay underneath. I wasn't tearing them completely off for anyone.

But I was starting to need to trust. I saw it in my next field assignment.

"Amon, Miona, Rarkin, you've a Wild Assignment," Trainer Sirona told us during Zushai.

Miona and I exchanged enthusiastic smiles. Merin shook her head in mock disapproval of our recklessness. My heart sped up as I stood, seizing the comm Trainer Sirona handed me and my stun gun from a table near the door. Miona towed Amon past surprised, awed, or admiring classmates. I blinked them away, unable to take in their reactions.

Then we jogged out of the Practical Training Centre and down the corridor. I played the briefing message on the comm. "Two torian birds have been sighted flying over the Outer Farm Zone north-west of Bellaria," Captain Zagoni's voice reported.

My smile widened. Full grown torian birds have a wing span of twelve paces, and are more reptilian than feathered, with razor sharp teeth. And these ones were fast, to breach the Wild Zone and fly over the National Park Zone before Monster Containment caught them up.

"Proceed to the Landing Site, behind the sports field. We will travel by airship at speed. See you in five," Captain Zagoni added.

"Torian birds wouldn't attack farmers, would they?" Amon asked worriedly, as we rushed through the Food Court.

I sighed. "Only a serious problem like food shortage would drive them so far south. They might take what they can get."

"That quadrant of Farm Zone will be in Lockdown," Miona added, when Amon paled. "No one will be allowed outside until Monster Containment give them the all clear."

I shoved the external doors open and sprinted across the sports field towards a huge asphalt square with markings for airships to land on. I loved the rushing, the excitement, the thrill of challenge, the danger and freedom of becoming a syther. I almost felt like I belonged to it.

We paused at the edge of the Landing Site, behind a fence marking the passenger waiting area. Miona pointed to a blue blur ahead. Watching how an airship moved from outside was worse than travelling in one. How was I supposed to trust that contraption after seeing it shoot through the sky like a bullet, with no idea what stopped it from plummeting to the ground like a stone?

The airship paused over the Landing Site, a navy-blue metallic sphere, like fiction or forgotten history. It touched down so swiftly that I winced, instinct telling me its engines had cut out. Its stair hatch folded down and I jogged upstairs. The cabin was small and circular, with Ine's syther team and Captain Zagoni seated around its walls. I flung myself into a seat at the back, beside Ine and Miona and Amon sat between me and Gorn.

The door closed as we buckled on similar harnesses to the ones firmly holding the others in their seats. I eyed the windows circling the cabin and gaped at blue sky and blurred dots that might have been birds. I'd felt nothing. How were we airborne?

"These are the good ships," said Gorn. "This is what people were getting around in, in sky lanes, while scientists and engineers were trying to develop travel to the far side of the void."

I stared at him. What on Unmarinaris was he talking about?

"I can't believe everyone walked away from all this," Amon replied with an eager smile.

"Sythe didn't," said Tali. "I suspect they didn't walk from anything, just stockpiled the best tech where rogue governments, dictators, terrorists and militants couldn't get hold of it."

Miona gave me a meaningful look and I remembered what Merin had said about Sythe keeping secrets. But I was distracted by something else.

"Who makes sure no one corrupt in Sythe gets hold of it?" I asked.

"What do you think agents are for?" Comor replied. "Shadowers investigate organised crime, but I suspect Junior Agents keep an eye on shadowers and Force Sythers. And that Sythe Agents watch Sythe Bases, governments and Sythe Schools. From what little I've gleaned over the years, agents and sythes are trained, based at and work outside of the publicly known Sythe buildings and command structures."

"Where do they service and repair this kind of tech?" Amon asked.

"Sythe Bases," Tali replied. "Officially, their job is Foreign Aid and International Peace Keeping, but I've known some damned clever people from General School to work there. I suspect that's where engineers, scientists and technicians maintain and develop the best tech on the continent.

"We get to borrow their airships and pilots occasionally, for Wild Assignments. They loan tech to Search and Rescue in National Parks sometimes too, when half-mad adventurers blunder into the Wild. But we can only guess what else Sythe Bases get up to."

"Last leg," the pilot informed Captain Zagoni.

She nodded to Ine and Gorn, who hefted their guns and nodded. Light chinked in, as Ine and Gorn's seats rotated to face outside the cabin, either side of the airship. From the fact the wind didn't blow their limbs off, we must have slowed down.

Tali smiled opposite me. "The real sight's behind me."

She sat before the broad fore-screen, the pilot sitting further right. Beyond the screen, a monstrous scaled hang glider wider than the ship swerved. It came right at us. I stared, and my heart raced with excitement as its beak opened, revealing double rows of dirty teeth.

Ine and Gorn opened fire. The torian bird screeched and veered above us.

"Damn crazy birds," muttered the pilot.

"Missed," said Gorn.

"I scored a hit," said Ine, "But one won't be enough. It's flying back towards its mate."

"Are we hunting them by air?" Miona asked.

The captain shook her head. "We're landing now. The first Terriahn team is waiting for us in their four-wheeler. We'll take our own four-wheeler and tandem hunt them from the ground."

Amon blanched.

"I thought you were getting bored of garls too?" I asked him with a frown.

"He is," Miona replied, smiling. "Just not this bored."

The stair flap lowered. Miona and I exchanged grins. Amon eyed us as if we were mad. I leapt from the cabin to ground, Miona at my heels. We climbed up into the rear tray of the four-wheeler side by side. Tali and Gorn helped us into harnesses attached to a bar running across the tray behind us. Then I leant back, resting my gun against the bar and gazed over the rear of the tray, across grassy hills and open skies behind us. The engine roared to life and the landscape before me retreated.

"Can anyone see them?" Tali asked.

"They disappeared over the hills on the right," a voice yelled from the second four-wheeler, on my left and behind me.

I tensed at whatever danger we were driving towards being at my back. But Tali, Comor and Gorn were covering that direction. Ine, Miona and I had to watch anything sneaking up behind the vehicle.

"Watch out for the other two," the man's voice added. "There're two males pursuing the female in a mated couple, too aggressively for the mated pair to fight off. They'll be wild as they come."

"Mating Season's dangerous in our field," Ine explained. "The males probably chased the female from the Wild. If it was just one, the female and her mate would kill it, but two torian males are too much for them and hard work for us."

"Duron's containment team is on their way," Tali reported. "The Azmalahn teams are too far away, but Torret's sending four-wheelers."

"Aren't there more Bellarian Containment teams?" I asked.

"We have six teams rostered on, for seven days and nights a week during Mating Season," Ine replied. "Two teams are trying to track the males while we track the couple."

Were torian birds that dangerous? Or were Monster Containment being cautious, because the birds had entered a human inhabited zone?

Gunfire cracked over the hill on my left, single shots.

"Take cover Artoo!" Gorn yelled.

I craned my neck as an ear-splitting screech cut the air. A torian bird wheeled ahead, swooping a sprinting farmer carrying a shot gun. The woman's hat blew off as she dived behind a hillside.

"Fire all!" someone yelled.

I looked up and tried to take aim. For its size, the reptilian bird was damned fast. I missed it, twice. Beside me, Amon waited till it reached the low point of its dive, cresting the hill the farmer hid behind. It slowed. My third shot missed. Its talons extended. Amon fired, striking a wing, as did Ine.

The farmer cried out, as the bird crashed into the ground before her, lashing her with its tail.

"Stay inside next time Artoo!" someone yelled.

"Mummy!"

Someone swore.

We drove past the Terriahn four-wheeler, as a child crawled out from under a bush and ran towards the farmer. A Terriahn syther unclipped her harness from the frame, leapt the side of the vehicle and sprinted for the child.

The second torian bird screeched and glided towards us from my left. It turned slightly, angling for the child. My heart leapt into my mouth and my whole body tensed. But my hands were steady as I focused.

The bird's narrow torso was exposed as wings rose. They fell and blocked it. They rose, and I fired, missing. Darts hit wings, at bad angles, not enough to inject stun serum.

Amon's shots hit dead on. Two more struck the torso and it screeched.

The syther seized the child and dived. The farmer screamed. The torian bird clipped the farmer's shoulder, throwing her down. Dust rose as the bird crash-landed before farmer, syther and child. It lay in a heap, unmoving.

The syther stood and the little girl ran to her mother, who sat up, moving her injured arm awkwardly.

I exhaled and tried to catch my breath. I managed a smile at the sight of the child safe in her mother's arm, but watching a torian bird swoop her had been more terrifying than having a serpent try to bite me... because I could dodge serpents, but I hadn't been sure we'd save that kid.

"Think I'll work on my shooting when we get back," said Miona. "The next time I see a monster threaten a little kid, I want to be a better shot."

Amon stared wordlessly, as the farmer cried, hugging her little girl with her good arm, while the Terriahn sythers attended to her.

I couldn't imagine being a parent out here, where your kid wandering off could get them *and* you killed. I assumed that's what had happened.

"Lock Down is signalled by a central alarm system that can be activated by any Monster Containment comm," Ine said, leaning against the back of the driver's seat. "Farmers on this side get unwanted visitors during Mating Season, and they don't let their kids wander off. This was probably a family argument. Don't worry, we get few assignments where kids are in danger."

That was a relief.

"Both targets down," Tali reported into her comm.

"We're heading towards you," came the reply. "They're fighting each other. This shouldn't be too difficult."

We waited, until the syther confirmed that both pursuing males had been stunned.

Moving those birds was no joke. It required large Monster Containment motor containers rigged with cranes and specialised harnesses. We stepped back while the sythers got the harness into position, then helped buckle it to both wings and the torso of the first bird. The crane lifted the bird and manoeuverd it into the container and the other syther team harnessed the second bird to the container's second crane.

By then, the farmer's son had her bandaged and her wife had made lunch. The drivers and half the sythers knew the family, and we helped ourselves to sandwiches and ate standing round the kitchen table. The others seemed at home, but I felt like an intruder.

"That warning we got was from your mob," the farmer's wife said to one of the drivers. "They were in Serena! I heard Bellaria's having dealings with them. Don't know why they'd want to myself, with all them tarths and torian birds about. Then again, you soldierly folk always were strange, running round the country chasing monsters!"

The farmers' kids eyed the sythers with interest or admiration and the parents and labourers laughed as if they thought sythers had strange ways of entertaining themselves.

"Don't they know about the invasion of Bellaria?" Amon asked in soft disbelief.

"They probably don't want to," I replied. "There's a comm on the kitchen bench and a screen behind the table and both are dusty."

"Is this some kind of hermit community?" Amon asked, confused.

"I grew up on a farm," said Miona. "We watched local news about our neighbours, things that affect crops and paid little attention to anything else. Then, when we moved to Bellaria, we listened to urban stories. My father thinks the only reason reporters broadcast city elections is so the mayors and their councillors don't get accused of rigging them. People just pay attention to things they think affect them personally."

"I guess everyone interested in the bigger picture works for Sythe," Amon replied.

I blinked, having never considered it. Then I turned to the farmer's family and the labourers. They trusted Sythe to protect them from danger and seemed to feel safe because they had no idea what was going on in the world. How many people were like that? How many knew nothing and had blind faith in

Sythe? How many thought Sythe was as strong as ever, when Mavon had shown just how vulnerable we were?

Chapter 21

Field Exam

The year was almost over. We had orientation and were advised on which government department to work for, because most classes next year would be qualifications for specific syther departments. Everyone else talked excitedly about which department they wanted to work for, but I felt the usual nerves, stress, uncertainty and doubt. It wasn't as bad as six months ago, when we began syther studies, but I hadn't kicked it yet. So I read silently, overhearing other people's discussions.

"Definitely Field Syther," Amon said confidently from the desk before mine, as we looked at articles, photos and short films on the screens in our desks. Was that a second purple dreadlock in his ponytail?

"Spare parts eh?" Rinth asked from the desk he shared with Zan, on Amon's right.

"Search and Rescue don't go into the Wild much," Amon replied. "It says they mostly cut people from motor carriage collisions and rescue them from natural or man-made disasters. I want adventure and I don't want to arrest petty criminals. Field Sythers get to work with Monster Containment *and* help arrest big time criminals *and* work for the Sythe Base in Foreign Aid. Imagine visiting another country!"

Being a Field Syther wouldn't just be about the thrill of capturing monsters, or crims; it was a chance to escape to faraway places. I liked the sound of that.

"The Sythe Base looks interesting," Miona commented. "Not that the article says much."

"But all we can do there at our level there is Foreign Aid," Rinth replied. "You'd spend heaps of time in an office talking to foreigners on screens. Surely you don't want that?"

Thought of Miona working in an office, even if it *was* at the Sythe Base, was laughable. She'd be bored senseless after a day, two at the most. I'd climb out the window before then.

"If you're interested in politics, international crime, or the monster trade, you might pick up more as a Field Syther," Amon added.

Miona looked thoughtful.

"I'd rather work as a Wild Life Officer," said Merin from beside Miona. "It has monsters, animals, people and the great outdoors. What about you, Rarkin?"

Rinth, Zan, Amon and Miona all turned to me.

"Field Syther," I replied, not feeling like I knew most of them well enough to confide my reasons.

I packed slowly at the end of the lesson. Was it such a big thing, to tell my classmates why I wanted something? Why did it rub me up the wrong way, or leave me feeling edgy?

I started, as something bumped my table. It was just Amon's satchel as he walked past, without appearing to notice he'd inadvertently invaded my space, or, fortunately, that *he* had startled *me*. … My gaze trailed him and his bright peach satchel. The guy's personality was sunny enough. What was with all the colour?

"Hey Amon?" Rinth called softly, stepping after him. "Do you prefer 'he' or 'they'?"

Oh. I'm fucking daft. It was *right* there. Why hadn't I thought to ask- My jaw clenched, as I nearly misgendered Amon again.

"Sometimes 'he'. Maybe, more 'they'?" Amon's voice answered, as they moved out of the room together, while I froze.

I'd spent more time with Amon than Rinth. How many 'they' had I missed? And this was the person who'd asked me if I thought *I* was the only person who had issues. The person who'd prompted me to look at others, not just myself. And I'd somehow managed to overlook *them* constantly. How did I…

I grabbed my bag and trudged off down the hall. It wasn't hard to answer. I remembered my father scoffing at a masculine figure in a dress at the shops one time, and pointedly criticising 'his' poor taste in clothes and telling mum what 'the boy' should be wearing. Dad always encouraged or pushed mum to wear dresses, even choosing the exact one he wanted her to wear, and dainty shoes to go with it. And he complained if she wanted to leave the house without make up on. He had very clear, stereotypical, fictional notions of 'woman' and 'man'. Anyone who tried to explain 'andro' to him would probably break his pathetic brain.

It wasn't easy growing up around someone who had toxic opinions, and who lived and voiced them all the time. Tying to resist the world according to them and to train your brain to think differently took *a lot* of effort, as did being your own person around someone who went out of their way to push their will onto everyone. Usually, I did alright, I think. I suppose because Amon's presentation had been 'typically masculine' when we met, I'd got used to thinking of 'Amon' as 'he'. But Amon didn't just like girls; they liked feminine stuff. I'd seen it, yet missed it completely, the whole time.

I shoved through the school front doors and stalked down the steps towards the Electric Way, feeling disappointed in myself and lousy.

* * *

I still felt bad the next day at class, and Miona noticed, but I didn't want to talk about it. That just made me feel worse. Amon was the same old, still smiling too much, still oddly hesitant at times. They didn't seem to mind. I suppose it wasn't like I used their pronouns in front of them. Maybe they still felt like I saw them as well as, or, given it's me and I'm shit with people, as poorly as I see anyone.

I ended up deciding I should maybe back off myself, seeing as I was taking it worse than Amon, and it was *about*

Amon. It wasn't easy to let go of, but maybe I just needed to pay more attention to my classmates.

When year's End and its three-week holiday arrived, Rinth had also joined a syther team as a trainee. That made five of us who'd progressed that far in our class, more people having managed it in Merin's mature age student syther class. I suspected Lylez, and Zan weren't far behind us. Ryan was getting better at shooting than on our first field assignment, but he wasn't there yet.

Jay tried to argue that so few of us being syther trainees showed how skilled I was at my job, but I still wasn't ready to accept it.

I spent Year's End with the boys, Miona and Merin. Tak challenged Miona and Merin to a sparring match against him and Wak. Glenn frowned at the idea. If I didn't know how ridiculously capable both girls were, I'd have warned them off sparring with that pair of gorillas. But I trusted my friends wouldn't go too hard on them, as they hadn't when they sparred with me before our sytheren practical exams.

Miona straightened with a confident smile as she faced the blond twins, and Merin and Tak grinned at each other. Then Merin danced sideways. Miona ducked low beside her, gut punching a stunned Tak as she rushed past. Tak grinned slowly, as Merin blocked a blow from Wak and danced wide of him. Then Tak straightened, blocking the next blow from Miona, and the next.

"Good thing the girls are into wrist guards," Des muttered quietly, at the smack of guards on guards.

"Tak thinks his wrists look prettier without bruises," Glenn assured him, not lowering his voice.

Tak shot Glenn an aggressive smile and Glenn smiled broadly back.

"Is he angry with you, or trying to seduce you?" Des said quietly. "It's kind of hard to tell."

Cam laughed and Glenn grinned.

Merin was dancing literal circles around a lumbering, smiling Wak. And Tak's smile broadened, as Miona dodged him and landed another blow on his torso. She wasn't too far off him in strength, and she was more agile.

"Remind me never to get into a fight with her," Glenn said quietly in my ear.

"And don't you piss her off either," Des added quietly to me.

Cam just smiled, knowing Miona was no threat to me. Trent didn't do either. He'd nodded in greeting to the girls when I introduced them, and his expression had softened slightly at a few things Merin said. But Miona was quiet around him. Like she didn't know what to say. He didn't seem to know what to say to her either. Then he stood by the edge of us spectators, gaze distant, like he was keeping watch for some distant threat, but Glenn's lawn and the apple tree in the corner were no threat to anyone.

It was only seeing Merin dance below Wak's fist and trip him to sprawl on the ground, with her most beatific smile, and hearing Tak groan, as Miona got a grip on his left arm and he had to surrender to avoid risking dislocating it, that I noticed how withdrawn Trent was. Slouched, kind of hunched in on himself, glaring off into space.

He'd always been like that. It was just… it was much clearer with my smiling new friends in the background. I hadn't told Trent about seeing Jay. I couldn't quite bring myself to tell Glenn either. Des and Cam had promised not to tell and Des approved of me speaking to Jay. But Trent wasn't talking to anyone. Whatever dark thoughts he was having behind that scowl, he kept to himself. It troubled me.

***

When school returned, we continued studies of common and rare monsters across the continent with Trainer Morea, and started Continent Geography with Trainer Faran. It involved study of Farm Zones, National Parks, the Wild and which monsters are drawn to which geographical regions. We continued lessons with Trainers Sirona and Dorthin, and had more field assignments. We mainly supported Ine's team to relocate garls, and once helped Search and Rescue locate some missing hikers in the National Park Zone.

Weeks passed, and there was no sign of mass abductions or anyone starting wars. It helped my nightmares, but my sense of lurking dread didn't end, Headmaster Zatrack didn't turn up and there were no more clues from Glenn's shadower team about what Mavon was up to.

It seemed to me that the parade, and even arrests after the Serenan Invasion, had only captured lower-level members of Mavon's organisation. And Glenn was right; we wouldn't have gone on missions or obeyed orders from Trainer Pershna. Had the double mass abduction of junior students from Bellaria and Azmalah's Sythe Schools and bases been like the abduction of the Monster Containment team I heard about when Headmaster Zatrack didn't expel me? A test, probing Sythe's weaknesses? What was Mavon's organisation truly after, and when would they come for it? But there were no signs, and there was no news.

Merin and Rinth went on missions with their monster containment teams, and Merin started talking about which of us would make Level One Sythers and be promoted to full syther team membership first. The idea made my head spin. Having already started studies for the syther department we wanted to work for was surprising enough. I was *well* ahead of what I'd expected to achieve, perhaps at all, let alone so soon. And I was starting to worry about when my lack of trust for my team would start holding me back. The more dangerous the monsters we worked with got; the more trusting them to have my back mattered, and the more I could jeopardise everyone's safety by not trusting them and wanting to do everything myself. Knowing that didn't make any of it any easier.

Then we got our next Wild Assignment and it became clear my time to learn to trust was running out.

"Rinth, you're to join them," Trainer Morea added to us, when he got the call during Monster Studies.

Trainer Morea didn't say anything more, but from the way his gaze followed us out the classroom, this wasn't an ordinary assignment. Rinth jogged quietly with us down the corridor, flashing me a nervous smile. I played the briefing on our team comm, but it said only, "I'll explain in person. Meet me at the Landing Site."

My frown deepened, as we descended the back stairs. It *couldn't* be a Field Exam. If you had to be sixteen to be a sytheren, surely you had to be at least seventeen or eighteen to become a level one syther? Miona was still a month off that, and she was the oldest of the four of us.

We jogged across the sports field. A spherical, navy-blue airship was waiting for us on the Landing Site, its stair hatch unfolded. We hurried upstairs and took our seats.

"Your Trainers, Rinth's Field Captain and I," said Captain Zagoni, "have called you here today because you have demonstrated your capacity to complete probationary Syther Duties to an independent standard. We wish you to prove this capacity by undertaking your Field Exam, and such an opportunity has arisen in the mountains north of Duron."

Rinth and Miona smiled, but my face went slack. They thought we were *ready*?

"A group of adventurers from Duron has lost contact with Monster Containment near the border of the Wild," the captain explained. "Search and Rescue have sent a syther team to extract them and Tali's Monster Containment team are on their way. You will help Monster Containment defend the Search and Rescue team *and* the adventurers."

Rinth grinned and Miona mirrored his excitement, but I squirmed with nerves. This had to be as dangerous as stunning torian birds, only there were multiple innocent bystanders to protect *and* the pressure of supporting our team effectively enough to pass our Field Exam. Wonderful.

We sped above electric-way tracks that flashed silver in the sunshine below us, towards Duron. The paddocks and fields of Farm Zone became the green of National Park, the dense green of the forested Wild, then phased back to the green and brown patched quilt of Farm Zone paddocks. We flew over the shiny metal glass towers that were the city of Duron, then cycled over farmland to National Park again, as we approached the slopes of Mt Gargass.

I gripped my gun. Sweat trickled down my spine, as we slowed. I tightened my grip as we descended towards a small clearing on a slope, with a cave mouth at one edge and a sheer drop on the other. Tali's team stood at the cave mouth with their gun torches on.

"Get your lights on, we're going straight in," Tali told us. "Search and Rescue are ahead. We'll find them and the adventurers, and they'll need our help getting out safely."

We turned on our gun lights and Captain Zagoni followed us into the cave, and down the tunnel cut into a rocky back wall.

"Why would anyone enter this place?" Amon asked, as narrow torch beams cut through rocky darkness ahead.

"To escape torian birds," Gorn replied. "But they didn't consider what they might encounter in here."

"No more questions," Tali ordered. "We need to listen for danger."

Her team led the way with near silent steps, their guns proceeding them around each bend. They pivoted to face each new section, pausing to scan for danger, then walking on.

I followed, straining to hear footsteps, voices, movement in the darkness beyond our narrow torch beams, but there was only silence.

We turned a bend and I was momentarily blinded.

"Search and Rescue have lit their path," Tali explained.

I stared at a glowing orb of white light hovering beside a rocky wall on my left. Another hovered beyond. Were Search and Rescue maintaining magical lights while they searched? How much skill did that take?

The tunnel soon led us downward, its roof low. Ine, Comor and I ducked as we entered a section of multi-colour, layered rock and the tunnel twisted.

Light flared at floor level. A small lizard breathed fire at Tali. She gazed sternly at it. It opened its mouth, but only a twirl of smoke came out. The creature fled into a crack in the wall.

I flinched at a loud crash. There was a rumble and the floor shook slightly. At last, we heard voices. They were yelling, but I couldn't make out what they were saying.

The syther team rushed forwards. Rinth followed but Miona and I moved more cautiously, and Amon brought up the rear.

We rounded a corner. Six sythers in yellow uniforms stood ahead, with the SR spotlight logo across their backs. They were panting, and Tali was speaking to them in the middle of a cavern.

White light around the cavern walls shone on a segmented creature with many legs, a large horn on its forehead and a half open mouth revealing spiked teeth. It lay on its side, many legs sticking out and smoke drifted from its nostrils. It was at least the length of a motor container.

I took aim at its neck, studying it until I was sure its eyes were closed and it wasn't going to move. What did Captain Zagoni and Trainer Morea think they were playing at, sending us to a place inhabited by these things?

Amon paled at the sight of it and Rinth fumbled with his stun gun. Miona just stared.

"We'll move together now," Tali told us. "The adventurers probably fled deep into the mines to avoid the karon, and Search and Rescue think the best way to get them out is to call them, but that will draw out monsters too, which may keep them back from us. We may have to stun another karon before we reach the adventurers, or to stun monsters in the same tunnels as the adventurers. Trainees, if you're worried you'll hit the wrong target, leave it to us."

I'd rather take any shot I could…but if there was risk of accidentally stunning an adventurer, leaving them vulnerable to monsters, that might mean relying on qualified sythers to protect us. It made me deeply uneasy.

Both syther teams advanced in single file, side by side. We crossed the cavern, passing two tunnel entrances. The Search and Rescue leader seemed to be following tracks I saw no sign of. He led us to the passage at the back.

"This is Search and Rescue!" he called. "We're on your trail. Please wait where you are until we reach you. We'll try to draw out any monsters that threaten you, and neutralise them first."

I strained to hear a reply through the silence, but there wasn't one. We walked on, more magical white orbs flaring into life and hovering beside the walls ahead, as the tunnel moved downward again. My gaze swept the dark tunnel and my ears strained, until the Search and Rescue leader shouted his message again and something heard him.

"Karon!"

"DOWN!"

Heat seared the air. Light flashed as I ducked. The tunnel roof was bathed in flames. I peered up from the ground, at a large figure in the shadows behind the flames, its wide-open mouth omitting them.

Footsteps pounded, as the syther teams split and fanned into the cavern. The fire waned. The karon drew in a breath.

I aimed my gun at a horned face rising from a long torso with tens of thin legs ending in claws. I opened fire. My stun shots caused sparks… my darts were rebounding off carapace as hard as armour. Adrenaline spiked, but I stood still, wondering how in Chaos we were supposed to bring it down.

Pearlescent bubbles appeared over the Search and Rescue team, magical shields. Tali's team opened fire. Fire bathed the shields. Rinth backed up, gun raised, while Miona tried to get a clear shot between Tali's team. The floor sloped upwards; they were in my way.

Amon stepped beside me, their gaze fixed ahead, their face unusually stern and focused. They were aiming between Tali and Comor's heads, at eyes glowing yellow in the darkness beyond the fire. I gaped, but he didn't notice.

They fired a single stun shot. I tensed. The creature roared and thrashed. Tali's team dived aside. The creature surged towards us.

Rinth, Miona and I fired madly. The mouth opened. We dived aside. A single shot rang out as I sailed through the air; Amon's. I hit the ground, rolled and turned back.

Gorn tackled Amon down. Fire flared across the cavern.

More shots fired. There was a crash, and the karon rolled onto its back and lay with its legs in the air.

I stood, panting heavily, dripping with sweat and took longer than I should to raise my gun and scan the room for danger. Tali's team had picked themselves up left of the karon. Search and Rescue had let their shields go.

The karon was unconscious and we were safe.

Rinth stood on my left, eyeing a stun gun that shook with his trembling hands. Miona was swearing with such fluent vocabulary that I cocked an eyebrow in surprise, until she laughed at me, while Gorn helped a pale-faced Amon stand. Amon gaped at how close the karon had collapsed to them.

"Excellent work Amon."

Captain Zagoni stood calmly in the tunnel behind us. At her gesture, a veil I'd barely registered above us vanished. A magical shield? Over Rinth, Miona, Amon and me? I couldn't see a single bead of sweat on her face…

Gorn smiled at us, then said, "The Captain's not just keeping an eye on you lot today. She's our back up. She's a sythe."

I blinked in surprise. What was a *sythe* doing training amateur sythers? Why would she step down to that role?

"Is it safe?" a voice called.

"Where's that thing's mate?" asked another.

"NEST!" a syther yelled.

"Keep back Trainees!" Tali commanded.

Out of the dark of the cavern's far end came the tapping of hundreds of claws on rocky tunnel floor. How many young did karons have?

"Fan out trainees," ordered the captain's voice. "Form the rear line. I'll back you up with magic."

Her tone was calm, confident, expunging any doubts I had about her being a sythe.

I moved to the right with Miona, Rinth stepping further right, Amon coming up on my left and the sythers fanned out right before us.

Someone screamed. The adventurers rushed out of the darkness on our left. They spotted karons charging beside them and screamed again. A small karon, six paces long and three paces high, rushed them.

A pearlescent magical shield walled the creature off. I shot at the karon. Guns fired on our right. At least a dozen young karons attacked the syther lines. A stray karon launched itself at Rinth. He yelped, dropped his gun and seized the head section of carapace. He lifted it with incredible strength, turned it and smashed the head into the tunnel floor. The creature squealed and he lost his grip on it.

"Back up Rinth!" the captain ordered.

Miona dragged Rinth aside, as the middle and hind legs drove the creature forwards, and it tried to gore him with its horn. Then it was before me. I shot into its open mouth and Amon's darts followed mine. The thing slowed, and I leapt back as it collapsed towards me.

"Keep your distance when you can Rarkin," Captain Zagoni advised.

Maybe I should have moved while it charged me, but I wouldn't have been able to stun it while leaping out of its way.

I scanned the cavern. Sythers leapt aside from goring horns, guns fired, and two creatures collapsed on my left, for no apparent reason.

Five karon young blew smoke or fire into magical bubbles ahead, but magic couldn't stop their horns. The adventurers cowered against the wall on my right.

Where was Amon aiming?

Ine leapt aside from a thrusting horn and Amon shot under the face, three times, in quick succession. The creature collapsed paces away and a second approached. I aimed under the face, as did Miona, as she stepped between a monster and the adventurers.

The karon came at Miona, horn lowered. She fired another shot and stepped aside. Rinth charged into my view and smashed a small boulder into its head. The thing spasmed. I kept my gun trained on it until it lay still. He'd killed it. With a rock.

I frowned at Rinth. Miona eyed him quizzically.

"I panicked," he admitted with a shrug and an embarrassed smile.

Perhaps it was the adrenaline and thrill of still being alive that made me smile as I asked, "Is that why you tried to wrestle the first one?"

Rinth blushed. I smiled again and added, "I like your panicking style."

He grinned sheepishly, and Miona beamed at him. Had he panicked because she was in danger?

Two karons breathed fire. Tali and Comor shot one down. Search and Rescue took out the other. There was silence, as everyone panted and struggled to get enough air, in what was now a stuffy, confined space.

Tali's team and I kept our guns pointed into the darkness, but it was silent now.

"So," Rinth said nervously, when it became clear there were no more conscious monsters. "Did we pass?"

I frowned. Miona and Amon laughed. Search and Rescue shook their heads.

"We're not out yet," Tali replied. "Your exam isn't complete until our adventurers are safely onboard a Search and Rescue airship."

"You lot are doing this for an *exam*?" an unfamiliar young voice asked behind us.

I turned. The 'adventurers' had snuck past us during the shooting and were about the same age as us.

"Hey, we're not the ones who fancied a walk in the Wild or who wanted a close up look at a karon nest," Amon retorted.

"We only came this far because that torian bird was trying to *eat* us!" a girl protested.

"The next time you fancy approaching monsters in a National Park," said Ine, "Try doing it on an excursion, as part of your sytheren studies."

"Yes sir!" the first boy replied.

"No more chit chat until our young friends are no longer at risk of becoming anything's lunch," Captain Zagoni ordered.

All five adventurers paled. Her expression was firm, her tone serious, but there was a hint of a sparkle in her eye, and I suspected she was joking.

We repositioned, Tali's team at the rear, me, Miona, Rinth and Amon in the middle, with the fool adventurers and Search and Rescue in the lead. The fools eyed us with admiration, but I ignored them. Only Trent was likely to survive wandering near the border of the National Park and Wild Zones *without* Sythe protecting him. What had they been thinking?

I listened for other unfriendly mine inhabitants as we walked back, but with so many people in the tunnel, it was hard to hear anything but ourselves. The return walk was uneventful, until Amon cried out. Flames glowed near their foot. I kicked the fire breathing lizard instinctively, knocking it away.

"Little bastard!" Amon swore. "Just when I thought we were safe! Thanks Rarkin."

"You're welcome," I replied, a little puzzled to have defended them as instinctively as if they were Cam...

The others scanned the ground carefully after that and I looked out for danger. But I saw nothing, probably because karons ate anything too big to slither away into cracks.

We reached the clearing. Search and Rescue shook hands with us, then herded the grateful adventurers into their airship. Rinth turned inquiringly to Captain Zagoni. She smiled and said nothing.

Chapter 22

Blockade

Rinth *couldn't* have killed a karon with a rock; that was insane. But when I got to class the next morning, Amon was recounting our field exam to Ryan, Zan and Lylez and Rinth joined in. We'd helped stun two karons and their young… *and* helped rescue fools.

Trainer Lauran took us out to her office. She motioned us to sit, and Miona, Rinth and Amon sat on the edge of their seats, with expectant smiles on their faces. I took a deep breath. I wanted to know because I hoped, but I didn't want to know because I doubted. I almost felt sick.

"Captain Zagoni informs me you did very well, and you all passed," Trainer Lauran announced.

I exhaled deeply and managed a smile. Rinth, Amon and Miona exchanged grins.

"You are welcome to continue training with the same Monster Containment Teams until you are fully qualified. From now on, they will mentor and back you up, while you lead stunning and capture attempts."

"When can we sit the full syther exam?" Miona asked.

"At mid-year," the Trainer replied.

A half-semester and a bit away…

"What happens when we're fully qualified?" Rinth asked.

"You could join your team as a qualified syther. But there is only room for one more on Rarkin, Amon and Miona's team, so they may need to join another. Unless Bellarian Monster Containment has room for a new team and two sythers join you, in which case you could form your own Probationary Syther Team and be supervised by a Field Captain."

"I could help you there," Rinth suggested with a smile.

Amon and Miona returned his smile, but I felt dazed by the idea of us setting off on field assignments as a team. How had we come so far so fast?

Having passed our field exam, we got ID cards that let us access monsters in small enclosures in the Monster Centre, outside of Monster Studies and *without* Trainer Lauran or Trainer Morea supervising us. Getting near a monster is called Courting, and we spent most of mid-semester break at it.

When we'd courted enough times, the Monster Centre Trainers updated our ID cards to let us access larger enclosures, where monsters could hide and attack when our backs were turned, like they might on field assignments. We'd have half a semester to court them before the mid-year exams and it should be useful in our work. But our next field assignment was something else altogether.

I got a phone call after dinner one night, and Mum drove me to the Sythe Castle, where I followed lit paths under the pale light of two thin moons to the Landing Site. The waiting area was crowded. Miona, Amon, Rinth and Zan greeted me. John, Joe, Nick, Merin and at least eight other mature age syther trainees stood nearby. What did they need all of us for?

Joe greeted me with a smile. "My bet's a mass arrest," he said. "Johnny thinks monster smuggling. What do you lot reckon?"

He hoped we were going after our abductors…but I knew from Uncle Alan that organised crime smuggled monsters out of the Wild and National Park Zones.

"Monster smuggling," I replied. "My classmates and I are training with Monster Containment, so it's not wildly beyond our abilities."

Johnny smiled. "That's our speciality too."

"Our other classmates are Force Syther trainees," Joe added. "If it *is* monster smuggling, it must be a big operation."

"I'd say so," said Nick, gesturing to an ovoid dark patch in the starry sky moving steadily nearer and getting rapidly bigger. When it landed, the airship was the same size as the one we'd returned to defend Bellaria City from Seranan invasion in. It gave me chills.

The stair hatch lowered, revealing a crowded cabin two-thirds full of Monster Containment in dark green, and one third full of Syther Force Teams in brown uniforms. Miona nodded towards vacant rows at the front and I buckled up between her and Johnny.

"A convoy smuggling monsters has been sighted leaving the Terriahn National Park Zone," Captain Zagoni informed us, projecting her voice loudly throughout the cabin. "We will support Terriahn Sythe with a blockade outside the city to capture the men guarding the convoy and reclaim the monsters. Each syther team will be stationed at a particular vehicle, where you must remain ready to open fire and quietly await further orders."

Was Terriah City under attack? How could anyone be thick enough to drive truckloads of illegally captured monsters to Terriah's walls and *not* expect Sythe to notice?

Force Sythers frowned and muttered amongst themselves. Monster Containment traded concerned looks. But no one questioned the captain.

"Are you alright?" Rinth asked.

On Miona's other side, Amon's usually warm brown skin was turning several shades paler.

"My adoptive brother Nick and my grandparents live in Terriah," they replied. "I wanted to study at Bellaria Sythe Castle to see a new city, so all my friends from General School are in Terriah too."

Rinth sighed. "My Dad lives there too. They'll be ok."

"Sythe's responding in full force," I said. "If they're putting Bellarian *and* Terriahn sythers on the ground, I don't see how anything will get past us."

But I *did* see that Terriah was the city unaffected by our sytheren abduction. Of Taros' three main cities, it would be the least alert just now. What did Mavon want with Terriah?

The flight was filled with people who either sat too still and quietly, or who shifted, fidgeted or talked too much. All gazes were fixed firmly ahead in anticipation, as if people didn't want to miss a thing. It figured that some national emergency would bring me to the second city I've ever seen. The me who lived in a renovated room that used to be a porch, and feared dad coming home each night, would have been thrilled to fly so far from home. Or to even know airships still existed. But the me who'd been abducted and had participated briefly in defending my city from an invasion felt differently. He was uneasy, preoccupied and kept a tight grip on his gun.

I thought I'd be glad to arrive, but I was even less comfortable when we descended into a cow paddock within sight of Terriah's city lights. From the brightly lit sky ahead and shadows below it, I assumed Terriah was ringed with ancient stone walls, just like Bellaria. Though from the way some window lights shone out towards us from above those walls, apparently Terriah's high-rise buildings in the city centre were higher.

Engines roared to life behind us, a small convoy of four-wheelers driving down a ramp from the rear of the airship. Beyond them, spike strips lay across the road, lit by the headlights of four-wheelers parked across closed city gates. Sythers aimed guns across the four-wheeler bonnets, just like they had at the Bellarian invasion. I hoped Sythe was over-prepared this time.

Captain Zagoni handed us stun guns, sent the other trainee's off with Joe's syther team, then led Amon, Miona, Rinth and I down a ramp after Tali's team, towards a pair of four-wheelers in the road blockade. Some four-wheelers were painted with the MC logo, but others had the SF in hand cuff rings of the Syther Force.

Rinth pointed upwards. Six small airships hovered overhead, each with a pair of gunners sitting in external seats on either side. They *were* preparing for an invasion. What in Chaos was Mavon planning this time?

Captain Zagoni indicated our four-wheeler and we strapped ourselves into outward facing seats in its tray, back-to-back with Tali's team. Either side of us, headlights cut through the night towards the approaching convoy and sythers whispered.

A hush fell across the four-wheelers and headlights went out. Soon afterward, two small patches of headlights pierced the night, and distant engines hummed far ahead. The headlights grew gradually bigger, stretching down the road towards us, followed by two more sets of headlights. Were they going to drive into our laps? What was the point of this?

Syther headlights lit up the spike strip across the road. An airship's spotlight beamed down from overhead.

"This is Terriah Syther Force. Pull over!" a voice demanded over a megaphone.

The first motor container veered right to avoid the spikes. The second veered left. Our four-wheeler engine roared to life and we lurched forwards. I gripped my stun gun and bit down on my nerves. Shooting monsters was one thing. The trouble with humans was they might shoot back.

The first motor container's headlights lit up a four-wheeler, parked off-road. Military sytherens standing near the four-wheeler backed up. The motor container turned sharply and fell sideways, with a grinding trail of sparks scrapping across gravel.

Our four-wheeler turned to flank it. Military sytherens moved in. Our four-wheeler stopped, and we undid our seatbelts and leapt to the ground with guns raised.

"Cover the rear doors," Tali ordered us.

Then she motioned Ine and Gorn to the left side of the container and they walked along it with guns pointed at it, while she and Comor walked down the other side. Were they checking for damage the monsters inside could escape through?

Someone groaned. Two men lay on the ground near the container's cabin, at military sytheren gunpoint. One man groaned again, and both raised their hands, but one couldn't get to his knees. I assumed the darker patches on him were blood.

The military sytherens shuffled aside, and a Syther Force team rushed in and cuffed both criminals, leading them away, the injured one groaning again as they lifted him. More Force Sythers approached the cabin and supported a dazed driver out at gunpoint.

"Clear," Gorn called.

"All clear," Tali reported and her team returned to us. "The second motor container's crew have been arrested," she told us, "but the Captain says the third motor container tried to flee cross country and was pursued. We'll wait here till one of our motor containers picks up the cargo in the container."

"How did they get this close to the city?" Rinth asked.

"Their trucks are disguised as furniture delivery trucks," Tali replied.

"Three of them, same as real delivery convoys at Bellaria City," Miona added.

I shook my head. "As if Sythe couldn't detect that there were monsters inside. It's like whoever sent them wanted them captured."

The Monster Containment motor container arrived with a second MC team, who took position beside Tali's, guns pointed at the back doors of the criminal's overturned container.

"Form the back line," Tali ordered us.

We stepped into place, stun guns at the ready. I tensed, suspecting that whatever was inside was nasty. Tali opened the doors. Roars and screeches cut the night. Gun fire sounded. Wolf-like hundaira, with glowing eyes, fell mid-leap. Two karons scuttled along the container floor and flames lashed out towards us.

Many guns fired, including mine. The karons thrashed, wobbled, letting darts enter their mouths, then fell. There was silence.

Everyone else relaxed. I didn't. I was still pointing my gun into the container, scanning and listening for anything that moved. Gorn nodded to me, also keeping an eye and holding his gun at the ready. But it was different. His posture and gun grip were relaxed. He was probably watching in case any of the monsters, especially the karons, started to come around.

I didn't trust we were safe. It had been too fast. We couldn't have neutralised the threat yet. Adrenaline still rushed into my veins, my heart pumped fast and my breathing came quickly. My body and mind did not accept that we were safe. Not yet.

"Stay back with guns ready," Tali ordered us. "While we unload. Ine will back you."

I exhaled and took a few steps back, keeping my gun raised, as the second MC team fetched harnesses, which the sythers fitted to karons. Then the driver activated a mechanism which dragged the karons up a ramp into the MC motor container.

We kept our guns on the monsters, aiming between sythers as they secured harnesses. But Rinth and Miona's muscular arms didn't look as tense as mine. Even Amon was breathing more slowly. I was not ok.

Claws scrapped against metal. I stunned the hundaira before the others even noticed which one had stirred. Amon smiled, impressed. But this wasn't alertness. My arms ached from gripping my gun too tightly. I was fighting my body's urge to breathe as hard as if I was running a race. Like my body was panicking, freaking out.

Only Miona seemed to notice anything was wrong, eyeing me. I shook my head and stared into the container for any sign or sound of danger, as if I anticipated it to reveal itself at any second. What in Chaos was this? I'd faced serpents. I'd faced a whole hoard of karons and not lost it. Why was I cracking up now?

Nothing else stirred. The others gradually lowered their guns, but I kept mine up. My heart rate and breathing were slowing now, but they were still too fast, paced as if we'd stunned the last monster only a moment ago.

"You did well," Captain Zagoni told us as she approached, when the MC container's doors closed, sealing all the monsters from the overturned container inside it.

I lowered my gun slowly, knowing nothing was getting through that door, or wandering the wilderness around me. But I couldn't help turning left and right, straining to hear anything moving in the darkness beyond the beams of four-wheelers around us. I still felt the presence of a threat that didn't seem to bother anyone else. Like the threat of dad coming home, but stronger. And I had no idea why it was bothering me now.

"It's not often that a chance to work under this much pressure comes up and I wanted you to have the experience," Captain Zagoni continued.

They kept pushing me to the brink of what I could do, maybe until I *had* cracked. Yet, no one was eyeing me with worry. Aside from Miona, they didn't seem aware anything was wrong. I must just look like my normal, brooding self. Was I being paranoid?

"Seems a pretty poor operation," said Rinth. "They didn't know we were here and didn't stand a chance."

Which would be a waste of resources, just like our abductors getting captured at the end of the Gotsi Day parade. Surely Mavon knew Sythe's capacity to combat black market monster trade? What was the point of any of this? Unless…

"Captain, was this a diversion?" I asked.

Rinth's mouth dropped open and Amon stared, but Miona eyed the captain sharply.

"That is what I fear," she replied.

A diversion from what?

Chapter 23

Shock

My heart rate got faster, as my body anticipated a trap waiting for us in the darkness. It didn't help at all that Sythe decided not to send us home. That Captain Zagoni was given orders to have us all get back onto the ship, to sleep in our seats. We were to remain outside Terriah's walls, on standby. Because Sythe thought they still needed us.

There was a fair amount of chatter at first, as we settled into our seats. But after over an hour of waiting, Captain Zagoni said, "This could be a long night. I suggest you all get some sleep while you can. I may need to wake you with new orders before morning."

Everyone went quiet after that. The silence and dark of the cabin were worse. It heightened my impending sense of dread, of something creeping up in the dark. That sense could be about the present, but as Amon drifted off, then Rinth, I realised it was the same dread I'd woken up from nightmares of Amon and I getting bitten by serpents with. It was another memory, clawing its way to the surface of my mind, scattering powerful associated feelings ahead of it. Whatever it was, I *couldn't* afford to remember now. I needed sleep. Chaos only knew what we'd wake to.

I lay awake long after the others, my heart beating too fast, my body ready for action, to combat something that had threatened it for a long time, that I must have never truly faced. It would have to wait till I got home.

Eventually, eyes aching from weariness, I drifted off to sleep.

***

"We're too far behind. We can't stop them. You'll have to evacuate the city."

Those words made me start awake with a spike of adrenaline and open my eyes. I was sitting in the airship, surrounded by rows of sleeping sythers. A pitch-black tint over the windows faded, letting early morning sunlight through the cabin's glassy walls.

Captain Zagoni strode down the aisle to the pilots' cabin.

"Any sign of what's up?" Rinth asked.

"I heard a message over a comm," I replied, repeating it. "I'm not sure if it was real or a dream."

Instinct told me it was the latter, but last night's instincts had told me to take cover from impending danger that wasn't there. Did I still trust my instincts?

Lights came on along the cabin ceiling. Captain Zagoni exited the pilot's cabin, her expression stern. Uncertain sythers woke sleeping colleagues and silence fell.

"A Monster Containment Team reported strange movements of monsters on the edge of Torret's Wild yesterday afternoon," she reported. "Similar patterns emerged near Duron last night, at which time we were asked to remain onboard. The same shifting of monsters occurred in the Bellarian Wild before dawn, and has now begun in the Terriahn Wild. Wildlife Officers and Monster Containment agree that the movement indicates wildlife taking cover to avoid something we cannot detect. We believe the threat is flying to Azmalah, or here, to Terriah. From the reports, it can only be dragons."

She paused, leaving stunned silence punctuated by shocked exclamations. Why would a flock of dragons leave the Wild Zone and fly all this way across human inhabited zones? I thought they were smart enough to avoid humans? And why hadn't Sythe intercepted them?

"Six Terriahn ships tried to contain the dragons last night, but two were destroyed. The rest were ordered to withdraw, being insufficient to withstand the heat of the dragons' flames. The dragons are firebombers."

My mouth dropped open.

"What does that mean?" Amon whispered.

"The heat of their flames is as destructive as explosives," Rinth whispered.

Which meant that whoever sent them planned to attack the city...

"Our Sythe Bases have fit powerful water cannons and modified the heat resistance of airship shields throughout the night. They have mobilised Sythe Teams. But the Bellarian ships will not catch up with the dragon fleet until after it reaches Terriah, *if* Terriah is its target. And the modified Terriahn ships are not ready yet.

"The Terriahn comm system is down, but we sent a ship to their Sythe Base and a city-wide evacuation has been ordered and is underway."

Cold flooded my insides. Someone had cut comms and launched an attack from the far side of the continent, with such well-chosen monsters that Sythe wasn't equipped to stop them… even *with* a night's notice? Was I sure I'd woken up? Because this threat level was *far* more consistent with my nightmares than reality.

"If the city is attacked, we will remain here," Captain Zagoni continued.

Several people groaned, but others shook their heads, or punched empty seats in frustration. If *Sythe* ships couldn't withstand these dragons, neither could ours. We were in place to protect the city, but if we tried, Sythe thought we'd be vaporised. So we had to sit here, and do *nothing*.

Rinth punched an armrest. The same frustration at our inactivity and helplessness burned in me too, but not so hot. Sit here, while devastation reigned and the awful happened. More fear and dread rose and I shivered. Why did reality have to so closely parallel my past returning to haunt me?

"When the dust clears," Zagoni continued saying to straight backed, rigid postures across the large cabin, "ships will survey the city. If it is safe to enter on foot, we will help Search and Rescue locate anyone trapped within the ruins, then mark off dangerous areas, before civilians return. If Azmalah City is the target, we are hopeful that our modified ships will be ready to contain the dragons before they attack."

Amon teared up. Merin wrapped an arm around them and they rested their head on her shoulder. They just… let everyone see how they felt. And trusted a classmate to support them. How did they *do* that?

"The Terriahn Mayor is prepared to let the city be attacked without Sythe engaging the dragons?" a woman asked the captain.

"In such an emergency as this, it is for Sythe Bases to determine how they deploy their forces to neutralise the threat. And had they sent ships without modifications, the ships would be destroyed, the sythes on board killed, and the dragons would remain at large."

"When was the last time anyone used dragons to assault a city?" a syther asked.

"On this continent?" the captain replied. "Nine hundred years."

No wonder Sythe Bases didn't have tech to pull out of their storage rooms to confront dragons… I got the eerie feeling whoever planned this attack *knew* that…

"Did the dragons come from Miara?" asked another syther.

"From the Miaran Wild," the captain replied. "The far north and most dangerous region. And yes, powerful concealment magic was used. Wildlife Officers and Monster Containment struggled to accept the logical explanation for erratic animal and monster movements, because their instruments could not detect the presence of Wild monsters."

"They'll be ok," Rinth said through gritted teeth, as a tear trailed down Amon's face on my right.

That jolted me back to the present, because it *bothered* me. Sure, Amon was soft, and they smiled too often, but them upset was *wrong*.

"Do you see how calm the experienced sythers are?" I asked Amon, as sythers talked quietly among themselves. "Monster Containment in particular. Like they're closing in on a karon, about to show it who's boss. Whoever planned this has gone too far, and by the time they attack, Sythe Bases, the Syther Force and Monster Containment from every city will be closing in on them."

"How many buildings could they take out first?" Amon asked softly.

I turned away. How many people were about to lose their homes? I didn't want to imagine.

"This is your captain speaking," a voice said from speakers throughout the cabin. "Please remain seated. Our chameleon skin has been activated. The dragons will fly by three leagues to our northeast, in approximately a sixth of a bell."

Chameleon skin; he was hiding us from the dragons. Were we just going to sit here, watching and waiting, while they attacked?

I didn't realise my hands were balled into fists until Merin gently gripped my forearm and I took a deep breath and tried to relax. She took my hand, and I took another deep breath and let her hold it.

The captain was right; there was no point in anyone martyring themselves playing hero. We were *all* outgunned. All of us were helpless.

Darkness rose, fear raced on its heels and I grit my teeth, my body tensing as I forced memories down again. I would *not* become that. Not while someone else hurt. Never again.

"Six dragons have flown by," the pilot reported. "They are approaching the city walls. They have cleared them. They are firing the city, flying west."

A wave of nausea swept through me and I swallowed awkwardly. Merin bit her lip. Was she squeezing my hand for my sake, or hers? I squeezed it back.

"Bellaria's Sythe ships are approaching," the pilot added, and my heartbeat quickened with hope.

"The modified Sythe ships will reach us in two."

No one moved or dared to breathe.

"The Sythe ships are passing north of us. The dragons are turning at the western end of the city. They are making a bee line for the Sythe ships. We are going to distract them."

I smiled. It was always better to *do* something.

"Seat belts on!" Captain Zagoni called.

Merin and I let go of each other's hands, as seat buckles clipped. I gazed through the glass walls, as the ground dropped away beneath us. Large bat-like figures appeared in the distance. On the right, a fleet of small, bright blue globe-like ships contrasted against dense white clouds, as they closed in on the dragons.

"Our chameleon skin is deactivated," the pilot warned.

Six bat-like figures wheeled in the sky, altering their flight path to make directly for us. My heart rate sped up and I fought down a smile. I'd played chicken with older kids in the neighbourhood on bikes sometimes, letting off steam. Sure, it got the nerves tingling, and could be tense, if you left it to the last moment. But the rush, the thrill of facing danger and dodging it precisely, at the last moment… It made you let everything go. Made you feel alive.

And there we were, being flown by the best of the best, against the greatest threat in the skies. The ultimate test of skilled movement, keeping your nerve and the thrill of getting away with it. 'Chicken' on foot against a bike would never work for me again after this.

The deep red of the dragon's wings became visible. Then the thick, dark collars around their necks. Someone owned and was probably controlling those things through their collars. If I ever got my hands on that person…

The dragons didn't waste fire on the cattle filled meadows between the city walls and our ship. They were saving it. For us.

I couldn't see the Sythe ships. All six dragons were close enough to make out their jaggedly-ridged heads, their gaping mouths…

Two dragons veered diagonally. Water cannons shooting from the sky pushed their wings upwards. Water slammed into three dragons on the left, pushing them sideways. Water shot behind our ship, hitting more dragons head on, slowing and drenching them, from at least ten directions. Was it enough?

Multiple jets of water shot dragons from all sides, causing jets of steam to rise, halting them. The jets ceased. Trailing water arches froze solid. Early morning sunlight shone on branches of frozen water crisscrossing the sky, and ice spreading across dragons' wings and torsos. Did Sythe have sorcerers on those ships?

Almost immediately, cracks raced along the ice. Large cracks shot out from where wings and legs met torso, as the dragon's strained against the magic. Ice exploded outwards from a dragon on my left, shattering ice bridges between it and multiple other dragons.

Jets of water pelted dragons on all sides. Steam rose. Dragons roared and tumbled in the air, crashing into each other. Then jets hit them from above, pressing them down. A herd of cows stampeded in terror below, as water rained heavily into their meadow.

There was a rumble. A first, second and third dragon hit the ground. The fourth closed its eyes and crashed into the first. Torrents of water pressed the last two down, and their large eyes closed.

Cheers filled the cabin, as I resumed breathing. People leapt out of seats, jumping up and down. It was a while since *sythes* had protected anyone, let alone a whole city, so dramatically, armed conflict having been very rare since the Nuclear War. They'd be heroes tonight, but what damage had the dragons done before the sythes arrived?

Chapter 24

The Ruins

"A state of emergency has been declared," the captain updated us, and part of me groaned at the familiar phrase. But, it *had* been nine hundred years since anyone invaded a city with dragons, and four hundred years since the previous armed conflict with Serenans. Taros was becoming less stable, and Jay was right, it *was* a bad time for trauma to hold me tight in its clutches.

"Terriah's Search and Rescue Teams are inspecting damaged areas of the city," Captain Zagoni continued, "and Bellaria and Azmalah's Search and Rescue teams will arrive shortly. Anyone who ignored the evacuation order may be trapped in damaged buildings. Extracting them will be Search and Rescue's top priority, while locating them will be ours. Each of your teams will set out with a comm and be allocated sections of the city to search."

Adrenaline sparked inside me and my body went rigid with tension. I followed Miona towards Captains handing out comms and assigning teams sections of the city, dreading what we might find. Rinth steered Amon after us with a hand on their back. Rinth looked paler than usual but Amon looked sick. It made me feel nauseous.

"Amon and Rinth, you can remain on board if you wish," Captain Zagoni said as we approached. "I know you have family here, and this is a disaster well beyond your training."

"My Dad's house is out there," Rinth said tensely. "I want to go."

The captain studied us. She took in Miona's worry, then eyed me.

"Look out for them, Rarkin," she said. "Bring them back if they need a break."

I sighed. This would be hard enough without leading others through it, but Rinth clutched the stun gun the captain handed him so tightly his knuckles turned white, Miona was oddly silent, and Amon seemed so preoccupied I suspected I'd have to stop them walking into walls. I nodded to the captain and straightened, my face firming as I led my team down the airship's ramp.

I braced myself, taking a deep breath, then walked through open, now abandoned city gates, just like Bellaria's. A three-lane highway stretched before us, deserted. We followed its footpath past a shady suburb of weatherboard cottages built under ancient ever-green trees. On our left ran many side streets with row after row of picket or brick fenced houses, many with motor carriages parked outside or in driveways. That surprised me. I assumed 'evacuated' meant everyone had driven out.

We followed the highway for a while. Aside from occasional Syther Force or Search and Rescue vehicles, it remained quiet. Other teams branched off to search suburbs, looking for smoke columns.

We cleared a hill and I peered down a smoke column to a property nearby. I jogged towards the smoke, which billowed above the imposing brick outer walls of a large estate. Over solid gates rose the top storey of a white-washed mansion, glowing and crackling with flames. There were plenty of untouched normal homes near here, but the dragons had gone for the rich people. Interesting.

If that house had as many servants, gardeners and whatever other jobs spoilt, rich people paid other people for as its sizes suggested, that meant a lot of people who potentially ignored the evac order.

I shoved instinctively at the gate, but it was heavy, probably remote controlled. How were we supposed to get close enough to hear anyone calling for help over the roar of the flames?

"Hello!" Rinth's deep voice boomed behind me. "This is Sythe! Is anyone in there?"

I moved around the fence, searching for trees with branches overhanging the walls. No luck in front, so I jogged down the side fence. Something was thumping. I stopped and strained my ears. Repeated thumping against wood. Was someone trapped?

Finally, I saw the tree I needed, with a nice heavy branch overhanging the wall. Adrenaline powered me as I grabbed it with both hands, walked my legs up to the lowest branch, then climbed branches till I reached the one overhanging the wall.

Someone screamed. I took a deep breath, spread my arms out for balance and walked along the branch. It forked over the wall. I crossed the wall, squatted, got my hands and wrists around one fork and hung from them, then dropped into the mansion grounds.

Someone was shouting but I didn't understand the language. Fire from the house was licking its way across timber stables. The thumping continued, and the wooden stable doors moved. They pressed against heavy bars of wood suspended across the outside of the doors. Who the fuck trapped people in a burning building?

Rage surged in me. I sprinted to the stables and heaved at the beam. I lifted one end off, but the strain was too much and I dropped it. It ploughed into the ground. I was damned lucky it didn't break my feet. The other end groaned, weighing down with so much pressure that it snapped its bracket and fell too.

People groaned, more shouts rose, then both doors slowly opened, shoving the fallen bar forwards across the ground. Smoke curled out of the door. Dark young men and women emerged, coughing. The crackle of flames was loud, but not enough to drown out panicked tones from inside, as a small crowd rushed past me. I pushed through them, surveying the room.

Two men led sooty-faced children to the exit. A woman helped an elderly man. Near the back, people stumbled and coughed in dense smoke flowing ahead of the flames. I squinted through it. Were those bodies on the ground?

A woman bent over and reached for one of them. I sprinted forwards, ignoring the sting of smoke in my eyes and forcing a throat that wanted to cough to breathe normally. A second woman bent down and the two lifted an unconscious girl to carry her out, one calling for help.

I rushed forwards, heaving the second unconscious girl over my shoulder. My respiratory system betrayed me and tried to hack up a lung as I lumbered forwards, bent double against the weight and trying to keep my head below the densest smoke.

It was getting darker, but anxious voices ahead told me which way to stumble. I blundered through smoke and open doors into a bright, dirty yard of people speaking in panicked voices, in a language I didn't understand. Why wasn't anyone speaking Siroan, or at least its Taron dialect?

I groaned, trying to lower the girl carefully to the ground.

"Whose kid is this?" I called over the din of anxious voices. "She's breathing ok, but she needs looking after."

The two men holding children's hands near me backed away, towing their kids with them. An old lady shouted and pointed at me, as if she was worried I'd toss her back in the burning stables.

Where was Miona? Rinth? Chaos, *Amon* could talk their way through this confusion better than I could. But Miona was still climbing through the branches of my tree behind the panicked crowd and I couldn't see the other two yet.

"Please, no jail," a man said imploringly as he approached, both hands held palms facing outwards. "No prison."

I gaped. "We know you didn't start the fires," I said wrong-footedly. "It was dragons. Sythe will be hunting whoever collared them and sent them flying this way."

A woman spoke hastily to the man in that strange language. Was that *Miaran*? Terriah *was* the closest city to the Miaran border, to where the Siroans had herded the Miarans when they stole land to found Taros, several centuries ago. But wouldn't the Miarans have stayed in their own country, when Taros broke up into inward looking city-states, during and since the Nuclear War?

What were a group of Miarans doing on a Terriahn manor's grounds? And why had someone locked them in its burning stables? None of it made sense.

"You no take us away?" the man asked.

"Only out of the burning building, to safety," I replied. "Sythers are roaming the city to help anyone who didn't evacuate."

The man frowned. "Boss no say evacuate. He say siren mean get in stables."

I gaped. "Your *boss* locked you in there? He tried to get you…"

"Rarkin!" Miona cautioned.

She was walking towards us, eyeing the two dads holding their kids protectively. In my shock, I was probably scaring the kids. Dammit, I didn't like working near kids! First I'd worried I couldn't save one, now I was scaring them!

"You care about that?" a young woman asked. "About us?"

"About a bunch of people I just had to save from their boss's attempt to mass murder them? You bet I care!"

"We're here to help," Miona added diplomatically.

How was she *so* calm?

She eyed the kids. A few sooty faces cringed away from me. Right. Some piece of shit had just tried to kill this lot and me getting furious at him wasn't helping them feel safe.

"We can do so by telling the Syther Force of your boss deceiving you and locking you up while the building burned," Miona added.

"Is ok," said the first man. "Nobody hurt. You save us."

I frowned. Why would he *not* want us to tell the Syther Force?

Rinth swore, as he landed heavily below the branch and wandered over.

"I'm guessing they don't have visas," he called, and the nervous man flinched.

"You think Sythe would give a shit about that when their boss tried to kill them?" I asked him incredulously.

"No," Rinth said, "but *they're* scared the Syther Force will care."

"What happens to children, if we go prison?" one of the fathers asked.

"Your boss is the one going to prison," I replied, "if I have *anything* to say about it."

"How did you come to work here, without visas?" Miona asked the Miarans.

"They said we could be seamstresses," the young woman with good Siroan replied. "Or labourers. They offered us better wages than we can get in Miara, enough to help several villages whose harvests have been poor. But the contracts they had the others sign were for indentured service. Only I could read Siroan well enough to spot it. And when I protested, they abducted me and took us all as slave labour."

I gasped. *Slavery*? In *this* day and age? And I thought homelessness was bad, but at least that was just societal failure and neglect. *Slavery* was some people actively harming others. How had Sythe not stopped this?

Everything within me wanted to scream *how can slavery still exist*? But around me were hunched postures, older men and women standing protectively around young ones. Heads were bowed and eyes were wide with fear or flicking nervously between me and Miona.

It wasn't just me that made them nervous. I'd opened the door to freedom for these people. There were more of them than us. And most of those blokes looked big and strong enough to take me and Rinth out between them. Yet they were scared of four teenagers, even though Amon was only belatedly trotting to join us.

"Sythe will want to help you," Miona assured the young woman. "You haven't committed any crimes. It's your boss they'll want to arrest."

Adults exchanged nervous looks and a few swift exchanges in Miaran, while the two kids and the first of the unconscious girls, now stirring, eyed us nervously.

"You tell Sythe," the first man said, then bit his lip.

It was like he barely dared to trust us, but felt outnumbered, or trapped, like he had to take the chance. The look of him, the whole feel of the situation got under my skin. Made me antsy. The helplessness, the resignation, it was *so* familiar.

I frowned at Miona, who was eyeing my comm pointedly. Right. Some leader I was. I lifted the comm up before my face. Captain Zagoni eyed me expectantly.

"You're not gonna believe this Captain. I jumped the garden wall of a burning mansion because I heard thumping and found about thirty Miarans locked in the stables. The stables were on fire and someone barred the doors from outside. They say they've been working here as slaves."

I expected the captain to be shocked. For her eyes to widen, if not her jaw to drop. Maybe she'd even gasp, disciplined, experienced and self-possessed as she was. I didn't expect her to look grimmer or to sigh.

"There is periodic slave trade out of Miara," she replied. "It's known to Sythe, but sporadic, irregular, difficult to track and shut down. I'll send a team of Force Sythers to your location, and we'll bring the freed slaves to our ship outside the city to interview them, and find out where they were taken from."

"What kind of prick leaves people locked up to die?" I asked heatedly.

"He may not be the only one. Look around you, Rarkin. How close are the smoke columns?"

It was hard to see much beyond the high fence of the manor, but I had a clear view of the sky. There were other smoke columns rising up. But none of them were huge. And they seemed spread out. It wasn't the wave of destruction we feared. This attack had been targeted. It had caused city-wide evacuation and panic, but the collars around the dragon's necks had steered them to specific targets. Why?

"You think whoever launched this attack was targeting the prick who owns this place? And pricks like him?" I asked the captain.

"They just exposed the fact he keeps thirty slaves on his manor grounds to Sythe. Had he done the decent thing and let his slaves evacuate, other Terriahns might have questioned the presence of thirty scared Miarans, who barely speak Siroan, in their midst. No matter how their boss responded, this attack would have exposed him."

I stared across the manor grounds unseeing. Using Bomber Dragons to expose a slaver? It was like using an atomic bomb to force open someone's front door. Even city-states didn't have the resources for that kind of overkill. Only Sythe had that kind of money these days…and organised crime.

But why would someone smart, and as capable and well-resourced as Mavon, take out a slaver by exposing him to Sythe? Sure, if the guy was a business rival on the black market, that would free up sales for Mavon. But why draw so much attention? Why put a whole city on high alert? Why bring Sythe down on his heels, when this situation could have been resolved another way?

We were on the ground, we had more information than during our abduction, and still, nothing made any sense.

"A ship is on its way to your location now," Captain Zagoni added. "I understand that this mission may be distressing to you all. But if you wish to understand, continuing to search the city may give you the opportunity to do so."

My face slackened. Was she implying we'd see more in person than a debrief would tell us, if we sat the rest of the operation out?

On the screen, she inclined her head slightly to my raised eyebrow.

Was I *that* easy to read today? I hated it. But I was rattled. The situation was getting under my skin and pricking at my insides. Everything about it rubbed me up the wrong way. I *needed* to know why. It was like I wouldn't be able to process it and could never let it go if I didn't. I was holding onto enough shit already...

"What do we think?" I asked my team.

"That Terriah has issues none of us knew of," Rinth replied, his jaw set as if it offended him personally. I supposed... if his dad lived here and he spent time here, how would I feel knowing some people in Bellaria used slave labour, and I never knew, and no one had ever done anything to stop it?

Amon was shaking.

"You ok?" I asked.

"My best friend is Miaran. We grew up in an orphanage here. The Syther Force couldn't locate our parents. I assumed it was because mine were dead. What if hers were slaves? What if they managed to help her escape, so she could grow up free? And they've been alive, in captivity this whole time, and that's why Sythe and my friend couldn't find them?"

"If this whole nightmare turns out to be about slavery in Terriah, I *want* to know," said Rinth. "And I want to help free the slaves. Because this situation is fucked and that's the only decent thing we can do."

Miona nodded. Amon sighed and Rinth gripped their shoulder. They bit their lip and nodded too, hesitantly meeting my gaze.

I wasn't sure what to say. It was always my life that was fucked. Most people weren't worried because they didn't know shit. And here we were, and shit was fucked up, but this time *everyone* knew. This time we were in it together. And it was worse. Even Rinth and Miona were out of their comfort zones and Amon was way out. I hated it.

But I saw that all three needed to know what was going on. From their postures, their readiness, it was clear they needed to make a bad situation right. Maybe not as intensely as I did, but enough to get somewhere with it.

For the first time in my life, I was part of a team united behind a single purpose, to make a shitty situation better. That part felt good. It felt *right*.

"We're in," I told the captain.

She gave a single nod, like she'd anticipated our response. I re-evaluated her. She was distant, cool, calm and aloof. She'd chosen to oversee others, different teams, not be part of one. But she *saw* us. She'd been watching Amon and I since our first mission. Possibly understood me better than I understood myself. And she'd seen me rattled and hating shit getting under my skin today. She understood my need to understand.

And she was offering us the choice. Like she respected us and our right to decide for ourselves. The amount of respect that showed us, a bunch of kids growing into large shoes, fast, I could get used to that. Who knows, maybe one day I'll even deserve it.

Chapter 25

Through the Smoke

A large shadow moved overhead and the Miarans backed away nervously.

"It's safe," Amon assured them. "They're weird but we've flown in them before."

"Sythe no keep promise," said the Miaran man I'd spoken to earlier, shaking his head.

"What promise?" Amon asked.

"Destroy airships after Nuclear War. Dangerous time. Too much power."

"We need that power to counter whoever did this to you," I replied.

He nodded, but I saw the reservation on his face.

The man led his people on board. Two women and a man reassured the second girl, who had woken.

"Jump on," the pilot called around the boarding Miarans. "We'll take you to the next fire."

She flew Amon, Rinth, Miona and I across our section of city, to smoke billowing near the city centre. I frowned. The fires were few, small and scattered. Targeted, just like the captain had prompted me to see.

When we descended, the Miarans thanked us. But they eyed us regretfully and the pilot uncertainly. I paused on the stairs, guessing we were the only Tarons who'd treated these people decently. "Most Tarons aren't like your boss," I assured them. "Sythe will look after you."

The man I'd mostly spoken to nodded, his mouth a firm line.

"Thank you," said the young woman. "We owe you our lives."

I smiled. "I wouldn't have had that stable situation end any other way. Good luck."

She gave me a final nod, and I stepped off the stairs behind my team, last on the ground. I surveyed the deserted street around us, as the airship took off. Most buildings lining the road were apartments or semi-detached and some were old fashioned, cast-iron terraced town houses.

We walked down another deserted street with motor carriages still parked in driveways and probably under apartments, but there was no sign of people or cats, only a few dogs barking behind fences.

"This doesn't make any sense," said Miona. "There were about six dragons, but so much of the city is untouched. I'd expect dragons to burn up whole rows of houses, if they or whoever sent them wanted to, but they haven't."

"Where is everyone?" Rinth asked, as we walked down the abandoned street.

Amon stopped in their tracks. "Bomber Tunnels! It would cause traffic jams, panic, collisions and all sorts if everyone tried to drive away. They must have ordered people to evacuate via the Bomber Tunnels. People are probably still walking out."

Wings flapped overhead and my gaze darted upwards, tracking the sound. A mular bird flew towards the smoke column downhill from us, carrying a giant sack in its mouth. As we crested the hill, the sack loosed, and water glistened as it fell.

I tensed at the extent of the flames. A whole complex of partially constructed buildings was burning on the edge of Terriah City Centre, a great domed building, half-completed towers, floors in the highest rooms gushing smoke freely, with no roofs and only partial walls to keep it in. A crowd was moving outside the base of the incomplete complex, shifting away from smoke flowing out open front doors.

We rushed downhill. People sat wrapped in blankets with their backs to us, so I didn't notice until we were closer that they were all male, and black eyed Miarans.

A Force Syther eyed us regretfully as we approached, then said, "Can you help pass around blankets? Many of our Miaran friends are in shock."

"More slaves?" I asked sharply. "Trapped in a burning building?"

She nodded. It was sick. Deceiving people into leaving their country under false pretences and using them as slaves was disgusting enough. But abandoning them to die horrid deaths just so some shits could avoid prison time made me want to toss said shitheads into the inferno. My breathing came swiftly, my fists clenched, and my torso tensed. I took deep breaths, trying to calm down. These Miarans would likely freak out if they saw an angry Taron approaching.

Miona handed out blankets. Rinth and Amon helped. But the faces they approached were fearful. Men shied or flinched away from Rinth, who squatted, because they feared his height and size. Some men had visible bruising. They'd been exploited, beaten and they didn't trust their apparent freedom at all. Eyes scanned the square they sat in fearfully, for bosses who would beat them for leaving the complex they were supposed to be hidden and slaving away in.

I knew that fear. I'd seen that pain before. Darkness writhed inside me, threatening to break free. I walked back uphill as my heart accelerated. Not now. I couldn't help the Miarans if what I was almost recalling paralysed me, and I was certain whatever it was would do that.

I tried to wear myself out with the climb, then distract myself surveying the city as I got higher, and my view broadened. The fire behind me was the largest. There were other fires, small enough to be single buildings. Was every building hit maintained or built by slave labour? Was this the biggest vigilante attack in Taros, in *Umarinaris* history? If so, the vigilantes must not have realised the slavers were callous enough to lock their slaves in burning buildings…

Miaran after Miaran walked out of the smoky, half-built complex, coughing, eying every syther nervously and sitting in tight clusters on the pavement. It was a small army of construction labourers, probably the people who built the whole complex, over years, in the heart of a Taron city, *without* being identified. How could people keep so many slaves in such a well populated area? How barbaric had their captors been to scare them into not crying out for help?

My anger roiled again and something darker churned. Grandma's face hovered in my mind's eye. A familiar sound that made me flinch. A sound about control. A sound to make you weep and scream. My fingernails dug into my palms as my hands balled into fists. I knew what that sound was, and I couldn't push it down anymore. It was time to face it, but *not* here.

I didn't register approaching footsteps until Miona asked quietly, "You ok?"

I looked away, not wanting her to see the storm raging in my eyes. But nor did I want to lie. I shook my head.

"The sythers dismissed us," she added. "We're to walk back to the captain because Bellaria's sythers have arrived. They're sending us trainees back to Bellaria."

"They don't want us to know what's going on," I replied.

I barely registered Rinth and Amon, as I led them back.

"What do you think this was about?" Miona asked.

It was hard to recall the present. Like seeing through fog, but I groped for it and found my earlier thoughts. "I think someone in Miara tracked down their loved ones who went to work in Taros and were never heard from again. They found out how badly their captors treated them and got hold of the resources to protest violently."

Miona frowned. "But the attacks *threatened* the Miarans."

"Why else would they target two places where tens of slaves worked?" I asked. "It can't be a coincidence."

Miona had no answer. "You think this was a declaration of war on slavers?"

"There's no need for war. These attacks exposed the slavers to Sythe. They'll arrest everyone involved."

"But why scare the whole city with an attack everyone thought was aimed at the general public?" Miona asked.

"Because this attack drew Sythe like moths to light. And whether it drew us to clusters of Miarans who could barely speak English in bomber tunnels, or locked in buildings, they *knew* we'd find the slaves. And free them. And track down the slavers."

"The captain said Sythe has never managed to track down the slavers or identity and free the slaves. Now they have. Thanks to whoever was behind this."

"Did a fair bit of property damage to the slavers too," Rinth added.

"Couldn't have wasted the money on more deserving shitheads," I said and we exchanged grins.

"You two have no problem with wholesale destruction of property?" Miona asked, almost smiling, while Amon nervously avoided our gazes.

"Not for people who attempt wholesale destruction of human beings," I replied. "I know what it's like to be beaten. To feel trapped and live with fear. I felt like a prisoner every day with Dad. I've a good idea how those Miarans feel. Knowing that, I think their captors got off easy."

"Why didn't you help hand out blankets?" Amon asked the ground.

"Because seeing the state the Miarans were in after how their bastard captors treated them made me furious," I replied, keeping my eyes forward.

"You *are* as aggressive as Chareck thought, aren't you?" Rinth asked.

"When it comes to bastards who treat others like crap, I'm worse," I replied honestly.

Amon remained unusually silent.

"And Sythe doesn't have a problem with that?" Rinth asked.

"I'm dealing with it and they know it. Today's an exception."

Amon kept their gaze pointedly across the city street. I made them uncomfortable. I didn't want them to be scared of me, but I wouldn't lie to them either. They had a right to know who they were working with. I just hoped we weren't too different.

Captain Zagoni met us, Merin, Zan, Joe, Johnny and Nick before a small ship on the edge of town. Only when we sat in its leather seats did I realise my feet, hips and legs were sore from hours of walking.

"How were the dragons controlled?" Merin asked the captain.

"They were fitted with large collars. Each collar contained a tracking system with a predetermined course. If the dragon strayed from that course; it received an electric shock powerful enough to make its muscles spasm and to cause it to fall a dozen paces in the air. Terriahn Sythe saw that happen as the dragons neared Terriah City. None of them wanted to fly over a densely populated area."

"Why would anyone provoke Sythe like this?" Rinth asked and I blinked in surprise.

He saw my expression and added, "They've attacked a city. Even if their intended targets *are* slavers, they've attacked across the city and forced the whole city to evacuate. Isn't that declaring war on Sythe?"

That realisation sent shock washing over me and froze me to my seat. But he was right. All Taron Sythe was impacted by the attack. Bellarian and Azmalahn Sythe were helping Terriahn Sythe clear the rubble, treat survivors and investigate the slavers. Shadowers or agents from all three cities might be tracking down the fire-bombers too.

Captain Zagoni opened her mouth, took a breath and didn't answer. Did she not know what to say? She was calm and business-like, as ever. She could talk about attacks that were a kind and scale of terrorism Taron Sythe had never witnessed, or a vigilante war, but now she was lost for words.

I didn't blame her. Whoever was behind this had poked Sythe with a different, in some ways bigger stick than Mavon had with our sytheren abduction. Had our abduction emboldened a Miaran vigilante group?

Chapter 26

Out of the Darkness

I called Glenn on our comm on the flight home. I sat tensely, nerves buzzing inside me, my chest tightening and my breaths becoming shorter. I kept telling Jay I wasn't ready to face the worst that had happened to me. But it was torture having it keep threatening to rise up and it was unsafe during missions. The only way to be free of it was to let the memories come. Let the feelings wash over me.

I was generally calmer now. I didn't need to be aggressive and I wasn't stressed about school. I was gradually accepting that I was good at field work. It was time to slay my demons and the person I trusted to watch my back, the only person I might want to talk about it to, was Glenn.

He met me at the Landing Site as the others said goodbye, Rinth leaving with his mother, Miona and the others with their parents, Amon heading into school, to the dorms.

"What's up?" Glenn asked, eyeing me with concern.

"I think the world changed today," I replied, briefly explaining, as we walked behind families heading to the motor carriage bay.

"You ok, Rark?"

"Mum used to be that scared and helpless, when Dad hit her, before Uncle Alan found out. He controlled her and kept us in that house the same way Terriahn slavers terrified their slaves into not attempting to escape. It was the same."

We climbed into the second-hand motor carriage Glenn had purchased after he got his license, but I put my seatbelt on mechanically and barely saw the Outer Farm Zone flash past as we drove. Memory fragments in my mind aligned.

I was in a different car, on a different night and Mum was driving. Mum clutched the steering wheel with both hands and kept shooting frightened glances at the rear-view and wing mirrors. Then she looked at me and her expression softened and became slightly pained. She took a tissue from her pocket and handed it to me. I held it to my nose and it came back red.

Then I was standing in our hallway.

"Toys all over the floor! No respect for my space! You little brat!"

Dad towered over me, his face covered in angry red blotches, eyes monstrous, hate-filled. He stumbled towards me, but I was too scared to move. My legs locked up. He swung his arm, pain shattered my face as my nose broke, and what I thought was snot but was actually blood trickled onto my lips.

Dad huffed angrily as I started to cry, and tremble, because I was scared he'd hit me again. Then the floor dropped away. Mum had picked me up. Dad glared angrily after us. I was so shocked I stopped crying. Mum's body trembled against mine as she slammed the front door behind us with her foot. She opened the drivers' door of our motor carriage one handed, passed me over the driver's seat, buckled me in, then shut her own door and drove off without doing up her seatbelt.

Dad stepped onto the lawn, staring. Then he ran next door, getting the neighbour's car.

It was the first time he punched me. She had tried to leave him the *very first* time. She trembled the whole time, and didn't dare speak. But she tried to shoot me reassuring smiles.

I blinked in tears. I'd wondered and worried and doubted at why she stayed with Dad in recent years, but as I let myself remember that whole evening, I knew for the first time, without doubt, that my Mum loved me.

But the memory didn't stop with Dad forcing her off the road or stuffing us both back in the car or shoving us into our rooms. I was barely conscious of clutching Glenn's passenger seat, or of his worried gaze flicking between the road and my tense, almost seventeen-year-old body in the present. In my mind, I was a six-year-old again, trembling, hiding under my bed as Dad trashed our living room, after nailing a piece of wood across my door so I couldn't get out. I curled up, feeling sick, hoping he couldn't reach me from the far side of the bed against the wall.

Then the moment I dreaded came. The rough sound of a hack saw made dust fall through the crack in my door. It swung open and Dad said, "Get out here!"

He stepped into the room and I reached for the bed post. I was too slow. He grabbed me by the ankle, dragged me across the floor and into the living room.

"SHE LEFT BECAUSE OF YOU! SHE TRIED TO LEAVE *ME* BECAUSE OF YOU! I HATE YOU!"

His grip left my ankle and the kicking started. I cried out at the pain in my stomach, clutching instinctively with my arm. So he kicked my arm instead, hard. I screamed, as my arm broke and he didn't stop.

"I'LL KILL YOU FOR THIS!"

That wasn't Dad…it was *Trent*.

The kicks stopped. I lay in agony; my vision blurred with tears. I blinked some away. Cam's older brother's friend Trent streaked across the room, while Dad stared in surprise.

Trent was wiry and thin. He looked like he'd barely hit puberty. There was a lot less of him than Dad, and Dad stood head and shoulders over him, but that didn't deter Trent. His face was hard, but I could see raw hurt in his eyes, as well as anger.

Trent sunk his fist into Dad's stomach, winding him, making him double over. He hit him in the face, punching left and right alternately.

"HE'S *SIX* FOR FUCK'S SAKE! SIX YEARS OLD YOU SACK OF CRAP! GET SOME FUCKING PERSPECTIVE!"

Trent kicked my father to the ground then started kicking him so savagely that Dad huddled into a foetal position. Trent stopped and spat on him. He stood, face flushed, eyes full of hate, of rage, panting heavily and took a deep breath, or five.

When his eyes met mine, they softened, and I gaped at him.

"It's alright now kiddo," he said softly. "Let me take a look at that arm."

I bit my lip and winced, but his fingers were gentle, and he didn't lift or try to move my arm, just touched it tenderly where it hurt and sighed.

"Broken," he said. "We'll need to get you to a healer. There's a free clinic not far from here."

I watched my memory, like a private cinema in my head, as Trent used his shirt to make a sling for my arm, handling it like a new-born babe, speaking reassuring words over my sobs, handing me tissues when he was done. Then he held my good hand and walked me to a Healing Clinic, where he told the Healer his little brother had fallen out of a tree.

I was nervous, because I'd heard strange stories about Healers. They could do magic, like the people the god Chaos made into sorcerers, who caused the Sorcery War, thousands of years ago. But the Healer was kind, Trent was patient and soon my arm and nose were fine. I was too shocked to thank the Healer, but Trent did. Then he led me home.

Mum was waiting for us at the end of our street. In the motor carriage. She was pale-faced. She nodded meekly at Trent, as she opened the passenger door for me to climb in.

"Your husband broke his arm," Trent said, his gaze hard and penetrating.

"We're not going home," she said softly, sounding a nervous wreck. "I'll take him to my brother's."

Trent nodded, as if he were my co-parent. Only then did he release my hand.

"Bye Trent," I said, waving as Mum buckled me in.

"Take care kido," he replied.

But the memory didn't end there. It jumped ahead in time. A younger Aunt Lil led me towards the garden carrying a ball to play catch. I noticed Uncle Alan's worried expression and the way Mum kept turning her pale face away from his, as he asked her what was wrong. Aunt Lil and I played catch, but then I heard raised voices.

Aunt Lil showed me a goal ring they'd attached to the fence for me to play with and showed me how to shoot for it with a larger ball, then encouraged me to practice. I shot a few times. The yelling got louder.

I put the ball down, frightened and curious. I walked quietly through the backyard and peered through the back door.

"SHE TRIED TO LEAVE ME!" Dad roared.

He strode across the room and punched Mum in the face. She cried out. He hit her again. Then Uncle Alan reached him. Fire I'd never seen before or since burned in his eyes. Dad howled, as Uncle Alan knocked him into the kitchen cupboards, then set about breaking his ribs.

Aunt Lil stood and watched. Mum was hysterical, screaming at Uncle Alan to stop, but Uncle Alan didn't listen, and Dad howled.

Aunt Lil gasped. I stood fascinated. I knew Uncle Alan was hurting Dad badly. But Dad had hurt me badly, so it was fair.

Aunt Lil led me back into the garden, but I looked back as we walked. I heard some of what happened next. Uncle Alan saw me and stopped hitting Dad, his eyes wide with shock. He blinked in surprise when I wasn't scared of him. Why would I be? He'd always been kind to me.

"Elaine, go to the police. Show them your face. Tell them about Rark's arm and nose. Get that Trent kid to testify to them and identify the Healer who healed the breaks. We took far too long to talk to the Syther Force about Dad. You know what we went through. You know what Mum went through."

"You know what they did to Dad in jail!" Mum's voice pleaded to Uncle Alan in his kitchen. "He was covered in bruises, every time I saw him!"

"Which is no more than he deserved or than your husband deserves!" Uncle Alan shouted so loudly that I could hear them clearly through the closed back door.

"I *can't* put him through that!" Mum sobbed.

It was torture, being a six-year-old and listening to your Mum cry like that. I burst into tears and Aunt Lil knelt on the lawn and held me.

"Then I should just kill him!" Uncle Alan yelled.

"*Please* Alan! *Don't*!"

"If he ever lays a hand on you again, I swear I will. Whether you want me to or not. You touch my nephew again, you'll have me to deal with, *understand*?" he barked at Dad, who grunted in reply, from where he lay on the kitchen floor.

Perhaps his jaw was broken. Trent and Uncle Alan had beat him up the same day. Guess that's what he got for being such a shit to his wife and kid.

"Now get out of my sight!" Uncle Alan yelled.

I relaxed soon after. Aunt Lil was smoothing my hair, and humming to me. She was good at calming me when I was little. She was the only one strong *and* calm enough to help.

It was odd. Parts of that day were still painful and made me flinch and feel helpless. Even seeing and hearing all of what really happened, I tensed up. But parts of it, Trent holding my hand as he walked me to the clinic and being so gentle with my broken arm, Aunt Lil soothing me when I cried, I wanted to *stay* in those moments. So soon after being so scared and so hurt, after such raw displays of Dad's instability and Mum's fragility and Uncle Alan losing it… someone had been there to calm and help me. Both times.

The worst times in my life weren't the loneliest. It was the in-between times, when I nursed bruises Uncle Alan and Aunt Lil never saw on my chest and stomach. I'd lay on my back crying, or trying not to cry. Mum would wait to comfort me, for fear of angering Dad in case he hit me again if she came too soon, knowing he would direct his anger at me, because he always did after that day. He must have forgotten or lied to himself about Uncle Alan threatening to kill him if he hit me again, because he had to have someone to blame, and treat like shit for how his miserable life turned out.

I wondered why my father didn't just kill himself. I couldn't see a single thing he had to live for.

"Rark?"

I blinked. It was like I was in a deep sleep, the kind of dream where you can barely open your eyes.

"You've been having a flashback?" Glenn asked.

I sighed and summarised for him in a daze. It was like a nightmare that holds you captive. It shifted, as I remembered an argument where he'd tried to verbally abuse me as well as knock me around, and I'd said it was time Mum and I left again. *That* was why he punched me through the window. I didn't remember the roar and rush of magic awakening within me, or lashing out this time. I remembered pain. Flying through the air with shards of glass, terrified about how much glass I'd land on and how cut up I'd get, or if I'd be impaled on a shard when I hit the ground.

The raw terror of the worst of the violence came back. Me even younger, trembling as I heard raised voices and the meaty slap of Dad's hand striking Mum. I remembered her whimpering sometimes when I was very little, trying not to cry, or cry out with pain, because she didn't want to scare me. Then she'd come and hug me in my room and tell me everything was ok, and she'd hold me till I slept.

I was so little then, and yet even then I knew Mum was hurt and something was very, very wrong. I worried it was me sometimes, that I made her sad, or that Dad hit her because of me. I worried she told me everything was ok, and held me, because she didn't want me to feel bad.

I remembered Jay's words earlier this year, "Have you ever really let go?" I'd only done that with anger and it wasn't enough. Anger was what I used to fight the pain. To be free of all the shit I was remembering, to truly move on, I had to let out the *fear*, the helplessness and the pain.

The raw hurt of meeting such hatred from someone supposed to love me. His total lack of mercy, let alone decency, on several occasions. Lack of mercy... I could hear that sound again, the one I'd heard, as I considered the helplessness of the Miaran slaves. The back of my legs burned. A belt struck them, again and again.

"Watch me punishing my wife, will you? That's none of your business. I'll teach you to be nosy!" Grandad growled, as I squealed.

How young was I? What had I seen?

Grandad, backhanding grandma across the face, splitting her lips and her cheek.

My nearly seventeen-year-old stomach turned over at the memory. Grandma was more helpless than Mum had ever been. She just sobbed and took it, as though she felt she'd done the wrong thing and he had a right to punish her, as the sick, sadistic prick had claimed.

Had someone killed him? Run him down with a car, fast enough to kill him, but slow enough for him to stand in terror, knowing he was helpless to stop his worthless life being snuffed out?

Grandad had been obsessed with control, thinking it was his divine right to beat anyone who did or said anything he disliked, because people doing or saying what he didn't want upset him, and he was such a brittle fucker that he couldn't deal with that, so he tried to beat his patheticness into the other person instead.

Dad wasn't as bad …but he was the same. Just as pathetically lashing out at everyone else for everything he was angry or upset about. A volcano forever looking for an excuse to erupt. A bottomless pit of ugly emotions, with zero accountability, and just enough positive traits for people to mistake him for a human being, and for their foolish hearts to give a shit about him, like some treacherous part of mine did, despite all the shit he'd pulled.

Chapter 27

Friends

"Do you want to talk about it?" Glenn asked.

He wasn't driving anymore. He must have pulled over.

I took a deep breath. My chest was so tight it was hard to breathe, but I suspected talking would lessen that. So I talked. I couldn't stop. And I remembered other things. "Uncle Alan got grandad put in prison because he beat Mum up badly and made her miscarry. She was pregnant with my younger sibling. He blamed himself. Said he should have fought Grandad more violently and protected her better earlier on. But Grandad was a piece of scum. The only way to protect anyone from him was to shove him off a cliff."

My insides sank. "He killed grandma. Uncle Alan got Mum out after her miscarriage, not realising grandad was killing grandma. That's why he's always hated Dad so passionately, he's always feared Dad will kill Mum and he's always wanted to kill Dad first.

"And Mum didn't want Dad to suffer. From the day he broke my arm. I think she was hiding in her room when he did that, too shocked to act, because it was so much worse than anything he'd done till then, such a sudden drop into a cesspool that she was too slow to get over the shock and get me out of there.

"He's always been jealous of me. He broke my arm because he was jealous she left *him* and took *me* with her. He's so small-minded that the only person he has room in his heart for is Mum, and she's got a damned small space, but it kept her hoping and she kept going back to it. And I kept getting knocked around. And she'd tell herself he wasn't a bad person and he should try, and I should try, and he'd pay my way through Sythe School and we could make it work."

Did she have any idea how wrong she was? Had she ever truly known? She'd been deluding herself when I started at Sythe School. When she took him back after he tried to kill me. For years, probably. And that day…

"Did Trent or Des tell you he tried to kill me early last year? Pinned me to the wall and squeezed my throat with hate burning in his eyes and watched, hungry to see the life drain out of me. And then when he apologised to Mum at Uncle Alan's, he asked her if I was alright. There was a moment when our eyes met, and I saw that he cared and then he got angry again and he looked away. And I thought that for him to care and treat me the way he did, I must be nothing at all."

Glenn's hands gripped both my upper arms and turned me to face him. "You've *never* been nothing. Hearing all that, I wonder if you can see it, but it's clear to me that your aunt loves you. Your uncle loves you. Your mother, in her flawed way, loves you. Chaos Rarkin; *Trent* loves you. He loves no one and nothing but I swear he loves you, and so do all of us.

"Your dad doesn't see your worth because he can't get past the fact he doesn't have any. Your mum loves him because she's got issues. But you've probably looked after and protected your mum better than she's done for you, and you've been doing it for years. The only reason Cam didn't get beat up at school was because everyone knew you'd flatten them if they laid a hand on him. And you bring out a side in Trent that would otherwise be dead. He's a better person for having known and tried to look out for you. So don't you tell me mate, that you're nothing."

Tears I'd kept back for years couldn't be held back any longer. It was painful to hear Glenn say all that. Part of me didn't believe him. I could hear the sincerity in every word and I still couldn't accept what he said, because I had so much pain tucked away, and I couldn't believe anyone with any worth could be made to feel so much pain. I feared Glenn was only saying it out of sympathy, not because he believed it.

I started sobbing. My tears reminded me of grandma's tears of meek, sheer misery. Mum's tears of fear and pain. The horror their husbands put them through. The horror they put me through.

I remembered the few occasions I'd cried, when it all got too much as a kid. And the many occasions when I'd felt the pain of the bruises, or the horrid things I heard people who should love each other wound each other with, and I cried like a broken kid.

Glenn, my older brother in all but blood, held me. His shoulder held my head up, because my whole body was aching, and I didn't have the strength. Then I almost choked on a thought so painful I couldn't keep it in.

"When I was a kid, it was always, 'Rarky don't do that so Daddy doesn't get angry.' *I* was responsible for making him angry. That's how she saw it. How can I… how could a kid…

"When I was about ten and I started to hit back, she'd tell me not to because he'd hurt me worse. But she didn't ask him not to hurt me… only not to hurt me too much. As if I deserved…

"And when I started getting a good punch, or two or three in, she'd beg me to stop. She'd beg *me* not to hurt *him*."

"Rarkin!"

That was Cam's voice. The door opened, and he pushed me over, so he could squish onto the motor carriage seat beside me. I was bawling my eyes out. Gods it hurt. It all hurt so much. I could barely feel Cam holding me, barely hear his soothing words over the screaming of my own pain.

"That's why I hated him so much. She thought I deserved to be knocked around a bit, or he had the right to do that to me if I made him angry. But I loved her, and she loved me, and he didn't seem to, so I blamed him for everything."

"That's not true," Cam said quietly. "I don't think she's ever believed he had a right to hit anyone. But she excused it because she loved him. She knew he couldn't control his temper, so she tried to tackle the problem from the other end, thinking you'd do a better job of controlling your actions than he would his."

"That's not fair," I said brokenly.

"Your whole childhood was bloody unfair," Glenn said fervently. "You said it yourself, that bastard had no room in his heart for anyone but your mum."

Was he so messed up that he drove away the only woman he ever loved, and hated his only kid because *she* loved *me*? I realised something I'd always known, but never been able to express; he was broken. In mind, spirit, actions, my dad was a broken man. Had been my whole life. And as much as I wanted to think well of her because she was kind when he was a prick, Mum was broken too. I'd always wondered how they ended up together. That was why. And they were probably worse together than they'd been apart.

"What's happened?" Tak's voice asked.

He and Wak were standing on Cam's driveway, their motor carriage parked on the nature strip. Des came out the front door, and I realised he'd called them.

"The Terriah firebombing dragged up a lot," Glenn answered, as he and Cam got out of the motor carriage.

I stumbled out, wiping tears off my face. Tak met my gaze. I must've looked a wreck. He reached forwards, helped me stand, pulled me into a hug and held me. I was vaguely aware we were standing in Cam's driveway, in full view of the street, but I was too exhausted to care.

Wak scanned the street menacingly, as he stepped up to screen me. It occurred to me that Tak had no intention of letting me go until I was breathing normally, and he was a hundred percent certain I was alright. Tak approached boundaries for men as set by society, Brock Heights and the normal kind, with each standard labelled in bold print, grinning broadly as he leapt over each one. Wak was protective of him and for two reasons, because his sexual persuasion was frowned on in our neighbourhood, and because Tak loved everyone he loved fiercely and was affectionate.

My gaze fell on Wak and I shivered.

Wak frowned. "What's wrong?"

"I'm nearly seventeen," I replied. "Aren't you going to tell me to pull it together?"

Wak blinked. "If anyone says that, I'll take them out."

I wasn't sure how to respond. Sometimes I felt like the weakest link, because I cried a few times and they never did. I suspected they tolerated it because they felt sorry for me. Or because I was younger than everyone. I was nervous of Wak, because he was the toughest guy present, and I was older now and I shouldn't be this weak anymore...

"Let's go inside," Des called.

We went to the lounge room, and Cam poured me some soft drink. The others drank soft drinks too. They normally favoured beer, but I wouldn't touch the stuff after growing up with a bloke who lived in a bottle, and they didn't drink that night either, out of respect for me. That put a few more tears on my face.

Glenn shook his head on my left, while Tak hugged me left-handed. I felt Glenn's hand on my shoulder and he said, "I wish I'd realised it was that bad."

Des ruffled my hair, then got Wak to budge along the couch so he could sit down. Cam sat on a kitchen chair he'd dragged into the room next to Des, and laid out another, as if he was expecting someone else.

"If you're still hurting that much and that shaken after what you saw people experience in the aftermath of the Terriah bombing," Tak said quietly, "which, after your childhood, I wouldn't bloody blame you, it's no wonder you're in this state. It might be shit, but it's logical. We get it mate. Everyone's here for you."

Cam was *tearing up*… Des hugged him, a soft expression on his face and Wak looked grave, while Glenn frowned, and shuffled so much that I could tell there was a lot he wanted to say, but he couldn't get the words out.

Someone else had words, Trent. He'd realised something was wrong, or maybe he kept an eye on the street when he was home and he'd seen us arrive. Trent doesn't have much tolerance for tears. He turned his back on the few occasions I'd cried in front of the boys. But he'd always stayed close, even with his back turned.

The others started, unsure when exactly he'd arrived, before stepping out of the shadows near the front door.

"My old man would've told you to pull yourself together, Rarkin. He'd have said get yourself a girlfriend, slap her around a bit. Take what you want because that's what she exists for and show her who's boss. Step on people who are weaker than you, crush the women, the samers, renos, andros and the stupid, sensitive, weak little kiddies. Make them big and strong and men, or else dominate them, because to be a man is to be a boss. The more destruction you wreak; the more of a man you are.

"So I took what I wanted. I stepped on someone who was weaker than me. I showed him who was boss and put him in his place. I half killed the bastard six times. Then I let him live, so he can spend the rest of his life pissing his pants about when I'll turn up to finish him off for the magic number seven.

"Don't you go giving a fuck what animals like that think Rarkin. They haven't evolved since the Stone Age. Don't you give them the time of day."

His hands were fists, his eyes a dark cloud of menace. Wak's eyes widened in alarm, while Tak's grip around my back became protectively firm. But Trent peered across the room, not at me.

He didn't like seeing me upset. He *did* want me to be strong, I could see it, but he was at war with his old man's mentality and the screwed-up version of 'masculine' shitbags our fathers believed in, because they were too pathetic to be anything else.

He hated weakness. He was *never* weak himself. But he was on *my* side in this…

He turned and walked out, letting the front door swing shut behind him. Glenn waited a few moments, then followed. He was the only one who had a hope of speaking to Trent when Trent didn't want to talk, and he'd said his piece.

Wak and Tak eyed each other.

"Bear in mind you heard that from Trent," Des said to me. "I'm surprised he could say it in front of all us, but he cares about you, Rarkin. You realise this idea you've got about keeping it together and being tough all the time, it's not unlike how your old man, or Trent's think. Trent knows it; that's what bothers him."

"You boys alright down there?" Ma Tully called from upstairs.

"Rarkin's having a rough night Ma, but we're ok," Cam replied, and I tensed, grateful the stairs were behind my couch and she couldn't see my red face or glassy eyes.

"Chocolate pudding and hot chocolate all round then?" came the reply.

"Thanks Ma," Des replied with a smile.

Mothers didn't coddle their kiddies in this neighbourhood, but if you were really upset, certain treats were allowed. And again, the fact I was nearly seventeen and she would guess, in a right state, wasn't a problem to Ma Tully either.

But what Trent and Des said… When Dad started hitting me, I had Cam's shoulder to cry on and when Des found out, suddenly I had him and his friends Wak, Tak and Glenn looking out for me too. Then Dory adopted Trent. He was the opposite of how I felt. He had the strengths I needed while being raised by my prick of a father and treated like crap all the time. I saw in him that getting hard, tough and angry made you strong. Strong enough to stand up to people you feared and to protect yourself.

Trent was what I wanted to be. What I *needed* to be. But what he'd just said about his old man… The way he'd put that bloke who was bashing his girlfriend, the pervert, my old man and at some point, his own, in their places… it *was* the same mentality, the same aggressive, guarded, angry, violent lifestyle our fathers lived. Never showing weakness, taking charge, using force to get what you want. I'd been resisting my father my whole childhood using the same thinking and tactics *he'd* used to *abuse* me.

Trent was the same. And he knew it. That's why he'd spoken so honestly, then walked out. In some ways, not the worst ones, but ones that could still cause problems, I *was* like my father. Trent didn't want me to be that way. *He* didn't think *his* way was best, as I'd believed for so long…

Trent hated better than anyone. Hate gave him the strength to battle through life alone. He didn't drink. Wouldn't touch drugs, probably because of what they did to his mother. Without them, or the support of a proper family, he depended on hatred and being hard. He could function when no one else in our neighbourhood could. But he'd done so by making himself a fortress. He was cool and distant with people he knew, and suspicious, if not outright hostile to people he didn't. And, I realised, half-closed-off even to us, when we were the only family he had. He'd had girlfriends, but they didn't last. I think he was too distant with them, and they found him too difficult to be with.

My childhood hero had all the strengths I'd thought I needed. And just as many weaknesses I'd failed to see, probably because I didn't want to. While I was living with Dad, it would've been too much. Because, if there was no hope for Trent, how could there be any hope for *me*?

But Dad was gone. Terriah was the only situation at work that had really shaken me up. I didn't need to be hard, or aggressive anymore. I didn't need to have my guard up so high. Not all the time.

Tak patted my side, and his arm moved. Then Des and surprisingly, Wak, were entering the lounge with a bowl of pudding in each hand, passing one to me and Tak, and leaving one on the coffee table for Glenn, while Ma Tully put down a tray of cups of hot chocolate.

"Let me know if you'd like another, Rarkin," she said with a smile, which I returned.

Ma Tully was hardier than my Mum, a lot hardier, but she knew things at my place hadn't been pleasant and she'd always had ways of letting me know she was looking out for me. Simple gestures, but there was meaning in them, and I appreciated them.

Glenn returned, looking troubled.

"He's done the usual?" Des asked sternly.

"What's the usual?" I asked.

"Driven north to go hunting," Glenn replied, as he sat beside me and reached for a bowl of pudding off the coffee table. "In the Wild. I called Monster Containment, and they'll keep an eye on him, from a distance."

I gaped. *That* was how Trent let off steam?

"Isn't that illegal?" Cam asked.

"My father told his former colleagues in Monster Containment a little about Trent's background," Glenn replied. "The only person he's endangering is himself, and it's better he's hunting monsters than people. Other people won't get hurt that way. That's the unofficial understanding we have with Monster Containment."

Trent held everything in and let off steam hunting monsters, on his own… he could get himself killed. I *had* to let it out, even cry. To talk about it, be vulnerable to people who cared about me, because that was the only non-destructive way to do it. I didn't like it, but I understood now.

Chapter 28

Wak and Tak's Strategy

I talked with Uncle Alan about the day Dad got too violent when I was six. He thought I'd forgotten. Said he was ashamed of how he was back then. That he hadn't realised Dad's true nature till that day, but had suspected and hadn't acted on it. It was hard, realising that neither he nor Mum were the great people I'd spent my childhood wanting to believe they were. That they were more flawed than I'd ever admitted.

Mum tried to talk to me, and I told her I was upset about Terriah and seeing people who'd been reduced to slavery. She believed me. Even now, she's still finding her feet. She never talks about Dad, but sometimes she looks at me, and I know she wants to bring it up. That makes me think she's still pretending he wasn't that bad, because she isn't ready to face it yet.

Terriah stirred up every feeling I'd ever suppressed. Memories haunted my dreams when I slept. Scenes, and feelings that matched them flashed through my mind in my waking hours. I haven't been this preoccupied since living with Dad. I'm still having flashes of Grandad and Dad's worst moments, and the memories that surfaced in the motor carriage with Glenn replay in my mind, whether I want them to or not, leaving anger, fear, sadness or exhaustion in their wake.

Jay called, checking in on me, but I wasn't ready to talk much. I was still… processing everything.

After a week, City Government downgraded the state of emergency in Terriah, but school stayed shut, to give people time to get over the shock of the first dragon attack on the continent in nine hundred years. On my first day back, after flashes of Mum's fear, Dad's anger, memories of hiding in a bedroom hearing shouting and abuse, my desk came back into focus, and I had no idea what was going on or how long I'd been zoned out. I shouldn't have come back; there was no point yet.

I slipped away at break. But where to go? It was Mum's day off and I didn't want to explain what I was doing home early. I wandered the corridors, restless, until the blue sky over the sports field appealed to me. I pushed through the external doors and ran onto the sports field. Running felt better, so I kept going round the field, faster and faster, trying to outpace thoughts and feelings, until sweat washed them away.

When I finished my third lap, Wak and Tak were waiting for me. Figures, I'd spent more time than usual with them and Glenn since school shut, and now they were checking up on me. I was glad to see them.

"You seen how lapping's done yet?" Wak asked. "By pros, that is?"

By which he meant them, of course. I had to admit; I did admire their lack of modesty.

"No," I replied.

"Then now's a good time to learn," Wak added, and Tak nodded.

They led me to the Monster Centre.

"This is less dangerous than Trent's foray into the Wild," Wak told me as we walked. "But it's *my* favourite way to let off steam."

"And you join him?" I asked Tak.

"It's not safe without a partner," Tak explained. "One partner does the lapping, the other stands by with a stun gun aimed at the monster, just in case. They also try to stay out of the way, which is the part I enjoy."

Figured, Wak liked the crazy role. I suspected he saw the same in me.

They fell quiet as we turned down the corridor to the Monster Centre. Their usual smiles were gone, and the light that often shone in their eyes had dimmed.

"We're showing you an alternative to Trent's forays into the Wild," Tak said solemnly. "He stole a car to get there. He's in prison now."

What?! "How does he usually get to the Wild?"

"He has keys to Dory and Glenn's cars. They let him borrow them whenever he needs to."

Then why did he steal a car that night at Cam's? Glenn's car had been on the front lawn… Had he lost it? Had *Trent* flipped out?

Wak and Tak must want to show me a different path, so I didn't go the same way.

"He called Dory and Glenn from inside," Tak continued. "And told Glenn to ask me to help you. He couldn't say it, but I think he meant for us to give you another strategy that works well for guys from the neighbourhood. He knows I know every guy, and a lot of girls from Brock Heights here. I've dated more than you'd expect."

He smiled, but I eyed him puzzledly.

"I know," he said. "Trent and I aren't exactly alike. But we have some things in common, including you. And he knows I'm better with feelings."

I turned to Wak.

"We're gonna teach you Brock Heights style lapping," Wak said. "I got into it after Tak brought his first boyfriend, Karlan home, and got jumped. It got me angry beyond healthy. That's the challenge for guys from our neighbourhood, managing aggression and keeping your feelings and motives healthy. What you said at Cam's the other night made me wonder how you're going with that. We know you see Jay, but this should be good complimentary medicine."

I raised an eyebrow. Tak lowered his head. Tak, ashamed?

"I uh, may have bullied it out of Des," Tak admitted, "when we wondered what you did strategy-wise and he seemed to know something."

Poor Des…

Wak smiled, "They kissed and made up. It's fine."

My jaw dropped. Tak blushed.

"You *did* kiss him? But Des is oppo?"

Wak smiled. "Rarkin, I've known noners who don't mind Tak kissing them. Tak kissing someone is kind of irrelevant to anyone's sexuality."

I shook my head. There I was worrying about Trent, who clearly did need someone worrying about him, but Chaos only knew what Tak got up to when my back was turned…

Strange calls and growls of monsters cut the air. We walked down a dirt lane between the glass enclosures of the Monster Centre. Tak and Wak seemed to know every syther wandering about the place, all of whom flicked chins as we passed them.

"These are our personal favourites," Wak said as he stopped beside an enclosure we hadn't visited in Monster Studies yet. "Gis. They're quicker than you'd expect, and their favourite attack is to punch. But if you lap them fast enough, you can make them dizzy and fall over."

I peered through thick, rippled glass and trees at a reptilian, bipedal monster at least my height, lying on its side in long grass. Its form was broadly built and the side of its body visible above the grass had *two* right arms. I was about to take on something that resembled my father at his worst, and *literally* run circles round it, until its desire to be aggressive caused it to defeat itself. Now that was clever.

"You're probably not technically allowed to take these on yet," Tak said with a wicked smile. "But Wak will give you a demo, and we reckon you're up to it."

I smiled and watched Wak swipe his ID card on the reader. The enclosure door slid upwards and the three of us entered. We'd walked past at least one Monster Centre Trainer, but when he caught Tak's eye through the glass, Tak winked, and the guy smiled, shook his head and kept an eye on us from outside.

Tak motioned me to stop just inside the door, and he waited with me, raising his stun gun. I left mine in its holster, feeling no need to protect myself. Wak advanced, and the gis sniffed the air, then stood. Its beady blue eyes tracked him across a clearing.

He walked straight towards it. Two fists drew back. Wak leapt right and ran, getting his first lap in.

The creature stepped sideways to cut off his second lap, and he moved out further, dodging a tree, then changed direction, and got a second lap in.

Tak smiled, and Wak grinned as he ran with more agility than I expected a guy his size to manage while dodging trees.

The gis was slow to understand its prey was dancing around it, but it watched Wak and tried to anticipate. It seemed capable of conscious thought, the first monster I'd encountered up close that was.

I watched Wak's alert face, the way his eyes shone, his smile broadening. Apparently outsmarting a giant, conscious creature was more satisfying than lapping one that attacked by instinct. This wasn't just a physical challenge; it was about good instincts and staying calm. That was why Wak enjoyed it so much.

Eventually Wak's breathing and dodging slowed, and the gis leapt closer to him part-way round his circuit. He feinted in multiple different directions, jumping the opposite direction each time. Tak called me, and I exited swiftly. Wak leaped through the door behind me then Tak swiped his card to shut the overhead door before the frustrated gis.

"They don't tire as fast as we do, do they?" I asked, as the gis stalked away.

Wak grinned. "Sometimes, but don't count on it. Be ready to misdirect and dodge your way out when you've had enough."

"Do you want a go?" Tak asked me.

Did I? My smile said it all.

"Are you used to running with a stun gun in hand?" Wak asked, and I shook my head. "We'll cover you from either side then. Eventually, your Trainer will ask you to run with a gun, but for now you'll move better without it."

He was probably right. I advanced in a crouch. I trusted him and Tak completely. My only worry was that I'd get in the way of their line of fire, but Wak had probably given Tak practice with that. I smiled and walked faster.

The gis was a similar size to Dad, with thick grey hide skin, large molars, and mean, intelligent eyes. It seemed to expect me to move like Wak. So I surprised it. I backed up, and got it to come at me, keeping an eye on trees and shrubs and putting them between us. Because when you put the gis in the middle of its enclosure, with trees around it, it's easier to run laps.

I couldn't tell if lapping a gis was more like playing Chase or Come Find Me. I kept backing up, or sideways, slipping behind and around trees. I tracked the creature and every obstacle in its environment, using them against it, exploiting its preference to walk forwards. I leapt, rushed and ran around it, as it growled, reached for me and missed.

I outsmarted it, again and again. My heart-rate increased, and I thrived on adrenaline, just like my first sparring match with Miona. It was the same thrill, the same freedom.

Finally, I saw Tak and Wak grinning and shaking their heads, and Wak motioning me to the exit. He swiped his card on a reader inside the enclosure and we stepped out.

"Fifteen laps," Wak said with a smile.

"More than Wak's first," Tak added.

I followed them, stopping outside the closed door, my body buzzing with energy, my muscles tight with strength.

"That was brilliant," I said.

"Then you need to come here more often," said Wak.

"And to find a lapping partner," Tak added.

I considered it. You had to focus *all* your effort on outmanoeuvering gis. It was fun, but there was more. My muscles tightened, reminding me how strong I am. How long it took me to get short of breath reminded me how fit I am. And something about the repetitive stepping and leaping got my body and respiratory system into a rhythm that calmed me, helped me relax and made me feel better. It didn't change the past, or the present, but it made me calmer and cleared my head.

I also considered a lapping partner. Miona would be good, but she's more cautious than I am with monsters. I'd seen Rinth tackle a karon with his bare hands. True, he'd been panicking at the time, but I suspected he was the only person in my class who'd volunteer to enter a gis enclosure at this point. Miona might watch from outside, but I suspect she's smarter than he is.

When we lined up for Continent Geography after break, I approached Rinth.

"Have you ever wanted to try Brock Heights style lapping?" I asked him.

Zan blinked, but Rinth looked thoughtful, then smiled. "I've wondered what it's like."

"You wanna try it after lunch?"

"You're on."

It didn't go quite as I planned. Miona wasn't the only one who wanted to watch, Zan and Amon came too, and half our class followed at a greater distance.

"What if we both lap it, at the same time?" Rinth asked, studying the gis from outside its enclosure.

Miona smiled and said, "I'll cover you."

Zan sighed and agreed to join her. He took up position, gun raised, more stiffly on the far corner of the enclosure, while Miona covered us from the near corner. Rinth and I exchanged grins, advanced either side of the gis and it didn't know where to look or who to worry about. Rinth and I had a new hobby.

***

"How are things?" Jay asked after school.

I told him about lapping and it made me feel better, but I was still apprehensive. Jay read it from my posture.

"Do you know what exactly is bothering you?" he asked.

I shook my head. I could think reasons up, if I tried, but I didn't *feel* reasons, just apprehension and maybe dread. I didn't understand it. I'd let the memories come and my feelings were coming out now too. What *else* was wrong?

"Your amygdala may still be malfunctioning. I suspect when that's happened in the past, you've dwelt on things that make you angry or stressed, because you don't know how to relax, how to be happy or grateful. I think getting worked up helped you keep your guard up and you're used to that. You're used to keeping people at arm's length and being untrusting of others. But there's no need for any of that now and I think it bothers you."

I blinked. Emotional fortress me was undergoing serious renovations, for the better. I'd reached out to Rinth today, but I hadn't told him and Amon why I wanted to be a Field Syther. I'd stood before a karon and stunned it, when I should have leapt aside and let Amon take it down, because I didn't trust them yet. Jay didn't just want me to stop holding everything in and being aggressive or unstable; he wanted me to let my guard down. I was winning a major personal battle, but he wanted me to fight another.

"How's Trent?" Jay asked.

I considered it. Trent was always guarded. He *never* relaxed. *Ever.* He'd been arrested for stealing the motor carriage he drove to the Wild Zone in, after parking the stolen motor carriage in his driveway. He'd gone with the Syther Force quietly. It was like he *wanted* to be in prison.

"Same old," I replied. "Guarded. Going back to prison."

"What do you think that does to him?" Jay asked.

"Keeps him safe," I realised, shocked. "Being guarded kept him safe from his old man. From the death of his drug addict mother. And being in prison keeps him safe from himself. Or keeps innocent people safe from him."

"Do you think he *ever* feels?"

"Too much. That's why he beat the crap out of my father."

"But he just feels anger?"

That twisted my stomach. "You're wondering if anger's destroying him, because that's all there is?"

"No. I'm wondering if anger is the only way he vents everything inside him, and if his inability to feel or express everything else, his insistence on expressing everything as anger, will destroy him."

"I'm *not* holding things in anymore!" I objected. "I bloody cried all over Glenn and Tak last week!"

"What happens when there's no tears to shed, no anger to fume, no fear to tremble with?" Jay asked. "Do you laugh? Do you smile freely, Rarkin?"

I stared across the room, unseeing. Trent never did either of those things. He could smile sometimes, but there was always pain in his eyes, or caution. His guard was *always* up, always preparing to meet another assault life dealt him. He was *never truly happy*. That was what it meant to survive, but not truly *live*. I did smile, sometimes. But it was rare and was it *ever* freely?

"In sparring or lapping I let go," I replied honestly. "When there's thrill, and not too much danger, like when we were capturing garls as Trainee Sythers and in field training with our class. I'd enjoy the thrill and the rush. Just let go of everything. I don't even know what I was holding onto."

"Are you holding onto it now?"

The truth stunned me. "Yes. I'm *always* holding onto something. Big, small. It used to be immediate, but now, the threats are distant. But I'm holding onto them. How do you let stuff go? How are *you* so easy going?"

Jay sighed. "Honestly mate, I never had so much to hold onto. My stakes were never so high, and things that got in my way in life were just road blocks; they didn't threaten to tear me apart. But tell me something, were you holding on and guarded like this when you were five? In your earliest memories?"

I thought about it. I remembered a scared kid, crying in Aunt Lil's arms. "Not when I was little."

"Then you *learnt* to hold things in. You *learnt* to put your guard up. So you can *learn* to let go and lower your guard."

I was quiet for a long time. I *had* learnt to be guarded and to hold things in, by watching Trent.

"I had Trent as a role model," I replied. "Who do I look at now?"

"Who do you respect?" Jay asked. "Is there anyone you look up to and respect, who's less guarded than you?"

"Glenn. But Glenn's Glenn. He's got a great father, and though he's never had a mother, he does alright. And Tak, but I'm not a proud aller, with loving parents."

"Is there anyone at school?"

I exhaled deeply. "Miona gets people. She's always accepted me and kept her cool in danger. She enjoys the thrill of Field Assignments and combatting monsters and doesn't get scared like everyone else. But she can laugh when Amon does fool things. I *can't* let my guard down that much."

"Why not?"

"I'd look as silly as Amon, for one thing."

"And is that such a bad thing?"

I shrugged. "*They* don't have enemies. They're an orphan. If they meet their old man in a pub one day, they'll hug him. I might need to knock mine down."

I frowned. "What are you smirking at?"

"If city centre kids could see how readily you accept Amon's gender, it would destroy their entire 'understanding' of kids from the neighbourhood."

I scoffed. "We're not all pricks like my old man. Choosing someone to hate, or to exclude them, or make them second class, just to distract yourself from *your* shittiness, or to pretend *they* have issues and *you* don't, is plain fucking stupid."

"I agree," said Jay. "There's no helping people who refuse to help themselves. But do you really need to keep your guard up for the possibility of happening across your father, some place, some time?"

I shrugged. "Our work's stressful. We saw Terriah get fire bombed just over a week ago."

"And all the other times?"

I blanched. He wanted me to let my guard down *all the rest of the time*? But that was the point of keeping it up! You never knew when an attack was coming, so you were prepared by keeping it up!

But who and what was going to attack me now? What was I afraid of? Dad was well clear. And there was always travel time on Field Assignments, time to prepare mentally and physically to face threats.

I remembered the hesitancy on classmates faces in self-defence training whenever they got paired with me. How they'd all pestered Amon about what we did when Trainer Morea whisked us off to fight serpents in Bellaria, but only Ryan had the guts to ask *me*. Merin teaching me to change my posture on guard duty and how intimidated motorists whose vehicles I had to search seemed by me, before that.

Was *that* what scared them? Me having my guard up? Was that what stopped me from relaxing, and enjoying life?

Slowly, I realised that was the last obstacle being raised by Dad gave me.

Was having their guards down what let my classmates laugh, and make silly jokes, and enjoy life, no matter what organised crime got up to? Chaos, had Wak and Tak been that way all along and I'd missed it, because I saw their strength and prowess, and assumed they were guarded, underneath their happy exteriors?

I'd always looked down on people like Amon. Thought they were silly for being soft and happy all the time, then getting hit by shock when shit went down. But shit didn't normally go down. Not for most people. Not most of the time. I'd been the exception to the rule, and I might not be, anymore...

"You think I've felt unsafe all this time, even when there's no danger, and that's why I kept working myself up and being guarded, or feeling apprehensive?" I asked Jay.

"Rarkin, I don't know if you've *ever* felt safe. And for most of your life, your home *was* dangerous. Your father leaving changed your life completely, and I believe you're still adjusting."

He was right. But if I didn't feel safe... I'd felt scared the whole time?

"What's wrong?" he asked.

"I hate being weak."

Jay's eyebrows raised. "Do *weak* people shoot karons at point blank range?"

I almost smiled.

"Do they fight off their drunken father to protect their mother? Then go to school and try to learn the next morning? Day after day? Do they fight serpents at age sixteen, in defence of their home city?"

How could you be weak, and strong, and brave, at the same time? The things I'd done, right back to helping Miona drag Kay out of the sirlon's path on our first visit to the Monster Centre, *were* brave. I *was* capable. I just wasn't strong in the way I'd always thought of strength. The way Trent embodied it …which was what made him volatile…

"I guess… I guess I've always had a skewed idea of what strength and weakness are," I replied. "Trent's father's definition of what it means to be a man is my definition of a monster and an animal. But I didn't get so far as realising that my ideas of strength and weakness, when they relate to *me* at least, are the same as his, or my father's."

That's what Tak had been trying to tell me at Cam's. It was ok to cry, because crying *wasn't* weak. It was a way of releasing feelings, like lapping and sparring, so you didn't implode. And if you weren't volatile with pent up feelings, and could come at things calmly and with a level head, the way Miona always did, and Glenn… *that* was the secret.

I'd always seen my friends as tough. But as I pictured their faces that night in Cam's lounge, Cam's always been sensitive. I've always known it. Wak *was* guarded, he was tough and protective, like Trent, but he wasn't *hard*, and I now knew he found release in lapping. Des was concerned, caring and reserved, *not* tough. And Glenn was serious and deeply thoughtful, *not* guarded. While Tak was open and caring.

I'd misjudged my friends. I'd seen too much of Trent in them. Too much of what… what I guess I'd always expected to see in males, because it was all I ever saw from Grandad and Dad. But it wasn't in my mates. And they didn't think I was weak. Just Trent. …Or did he turn away from my tears because *he* didn't dare let *his* feelings out? Was he afraid they'd destroy him, as I once was?

"I'm the only one who thinks I'm weak," I realised. "Everyone else doesn't see it that way. I think I'm starting to understand why."

"Your year level have thought you a hero since you saved Amon's neck from serpents," said Jay. "Didn't you realise?"

"No."

My mind went back to the last time someone thought I was a hero, Kay's parents thanking me in the Infirmary, after I helped Miona snatch Kay from a sirlon's path. I'd wondered then if I deserved the respect his parents had shown me. If I'd really achieved something great.

I had. I'd spent so long trying to defy Dad's pitiful expectations, but I'd struggled to expect anything of myself. To appreciate my own achievements.

And I wasn't weak. I'd been through a lot over the past year, but Trainer Lauran had already said we could sit our syther exams at mid-year, seven weeks away, when we were all seventeen, a level I once doubted I could *ever* reach.

I needed to accept what I *could* do, to keep lapping monsters to feel capable and clear my head. To focus on revision and passing my syther exams. To focus on attaining a dream qualification and believing I could. I'd have to let go of the past. Leave it there. And learn to let go of the guard I'd once kept up permanently. It was time to look to other people, and learn non-destructive ways of being strong.

Chapter 29

Syther Exams

"Sythe have confirmed that multiple inner-city apartments damaged during the Terriah Bombing were owned by proprietors of illegal, underground brothels, some of which specialise in providing underage escorts. Others have been linked to studios in which child abuse material was produced."

Glenn and I gaped at the latest report from Terriah City, on the screen in his lounge. I'd spent the second half of semester lapping monsters, seeing Jay, continuing Monster and Continent Geography Studies, in periodic lessons in Zushai and on Marksmanship to keep us in shape for the mid-year exams. And being coached as Miona, Rinth, Amon and I captured garls almost on our own, with Tali's team advising and backing us up.

I'd tried to focus on the present and letting off steam effectively, and not to worry about Mavon, or the vigilante group that had shaken up Terriah. But as mid-year approached, detailed reports on completed investigations in Terriah were being made public.

"City Government claims it is ignorant of how the attackers obtained their information or identified the child sex offenders the Syther Force have arrested over the past few months. An inquiry is underway to establish whether members of the Terriah Syther Force or Shadower League leaked locations to a criminal or vigilante organisation.

"The attacks on buildings associated with illegal brothel proprietors and child abuse material makers occurring at the same time as attacks on establishments dependent on illegal slave labour has speculation rife about a highly organised vigilante group in Terriah. Alternately, strategic analysts claim that the organisation and success of the vigilante attacks suggest that they were master-minded by underworld boss Mavon Trigate. Though why he would turn from crime figure to Terriahn Vigilante remains a mystery."

Glenn switched the screen off, as the report ended.

"Tough justice," I said immediately. "Just like I thought. Sythe and the Law Courts failed to lock up the bastards who abused those people, so someone took it upon themselves to punish and expose them."

There was a pause, and Glenn eyed me uncertainly. "You agree with the attackers?"

"They knew Sythe would detect them and evacuate the city. Sure, it's a big inconvenience everyone having to evacuate, a disruption to their day, but it put twenty-five paedophiles into the Syther Force's hands, exposed four slave owners and freed over a hundred and fifty slaves, and thirty-five children from sexual abuse. I call that worth it."

"And the fifteen people who were killed in the tunnel collapse, or the fires?" Glenn asked.

I shivered. I *liked* how the vigilantes had lashed out. It would be like me breaking all dad's bones; returning the favour. But doing so in a way that got innocent people killed... that *was* acting as callously as your abuser.

"They should have found a way guaranteed not to kill people," I replied. "Giving people what they deserve becomes a crime when you hurt people who don't deserve it."

Glenn's look reminded me of Trainer Morea's, when I said I was glad the Serenans would kill the crims who deceived them into going to war to rob them. But why have compassion for people who showed none to anyone else?

"Do you know if Mavon *was* hired to master mind the attacks?" I asked Glenn.

"We located a way station on the monster smuggling route out of Miara," Glenn replied. "We used illusion magic to fake a fire and flush everyone out. Timed it so that the smuggling ring manager —one of several suspects for the Terriah firebombing— was there. We ruled him out after questioning, but someone hired him to smuggle the convoy Sythe intercepted outside Terriah.

"We questioned him about who hired him, and he looked the shadower right in the eye, and asked if we'd shoot him dead after he talked. Whoever hired him is *dangerous* and yes —Mavon fits that description."

He lowered his gaze and took a deep breath. "It looks like a couple of people we arrested for monster smuggling were involved in your sytheren abduction. It's highly likely it was the same crime boss behind both: Mavon. The collars used to control those dragons point to great wealth and black-market connections, and we think Mavon runs the monster trade."

"What do you think he wants?"

"We still think Headmaster Zatrack went rogue. Traitor Heads are extremely rare. He was probably their greatest asset at that time, if they intended to move against Sythe. But they wasted him too, by exposing him for nothing. I wonder if, like the monster convoy, they were willing to waste him because the abduction was a test run. If Terriah was a test strike. If there's a team sitting around a table somewhere reviewing their successes, their failures, evaluating our strengths and responses, and factoring it all into something bigger."

"But how can they hope to pull more off, with the whole of Taron Sythe out to stop them?" I wondered.

"They managed to firebomb Terriah nearly six months after the sytheren abduction," Glenn countered.

I shivered.

"Their level of resources and willingness to waste them suggests that the big boss isn't in Taros. Mavon may not be as high as it goes. The big boss might be using us as guinea pigs for something they're planning on another continent. That's the only way we can explain them being willing to put us on such high alert, and still hoping to achieve their ultimate objectives."

Our abduction, the smuggling and use of firebombing to target certain criminals was practice and sacrifice for something worse in Siro, Naydah or Mavis? The idea was too big to take in. Legitimate governments *never* thought on such an international scale, not in recent centuries.

How could organised crime suddenly be thinking and acting at a level of city-wide terrorism, or war? Or was that *why* they thought that way? Because no one else did, so no one would anticipate it, or catch them out?

The mystery was my biggest test yet in accepting the past. I couldn't help wondering, or speculating with Glenn, Wak and Tak. But the situation went so far, was so obviously beyond my control, especially if our head honchos were overseas, that I needed to stay focused on what I could achieve, and that was obvious; revising and preparing for our looming syther exams.

Lapping monsters when I took breaks from revision helped me stay calm, even focused. And Rinth was good company. Somehow, with that strategy in place, and being up to date on my syther studies, exam prep was ok. I was still full of restless energy, but not stressing.

The Practical Training Centre was crowded the morning of our Syther Exams. Ryan, Lylez, Zan, Merin, Joe,

Johnny, Nick and others from our classes, and a team of trainees in the Syther Force, were there. Because it had been a stressful semester, they let us sit our coursework exam, a test for those forming our own Syther Level One Teams, and our Practical Exams on the same day, if we wanted to get it over with. Amon, Rinth, Miona and I were doing everything at once.

They split us into four groups. Once we had our gloves and padded vests on, Trainer Sirona pit me against Miona to warm up for Zushai. I crouched. Miona's skill in attacking with fists and feet, balance, speed and agility, had Trainer Sirona smiling in appreciation. But when she attacked, I watched. I anticipated. My movements flowed ahead of hers, blocking, dodging. Blocks switched to attacks when they could, and attacks to blocks if they were about to fail.

I pivoted, twisted, keeping my balance, choosing where I stepped, no matter where she was or how she came at me. She pushed me, with a smile, until I came at her, reversing the pattern of attacks.

The Trainer noticed other pairs staring and chivvied them to get warming up. Miona and I took a break, and watched Rinth and Amon. Rinth was damned strong, and forceful, but Amon had become quick on their feet, shifting their weight to dodge attacks, then targeting their attacks from angles Rinth struggled to anticipate. Instinct and brute strength let Rinth do well enough, but I was surprised how skilled Amon was becoming.

Trainer Sirona called for our attention, a new Trainer standing beside her. "You will now take on Trainer Marsh," she told us. "Trainer Marsh will test you against a range of attacks, assessing your balance, footwork and the control and effectiveness with which you dodge, block or attack. They will mark you for this exam."

Trainer Marsh motioned me forwards. I crouched before them and my heart rate increased slightly. I didn't know their style, so my anticipation was only a fraction ahead of their movements. And their face was a mask. I had to study their whole body, moving to block the part that moved, changing tack when I realised they were feinting, shifting my weight at the least sign they were on the move.

Only after a flurry of footwork in which I felt clumsy, and barely managed to keep them in sight, did I realise they'd tried to distract me and get a blow in from the side. They smiled when I kept facing them no matter how they shifted, and I realised I'd built extensively on everything I'd unwittingly learnt dodging my old man. I had this exam in the bag.

Trainer Marsh tried to catch Rinth off balance and use his weight against him, but he'd grown more careful with his footwork training with Miona, against whom that was essential, and he did well. Amon lacked confidence, but it made them cautious, dancing constantly out of Marsh's way, until they worked up the guts to throw a punch Marsh wasn't expecting, which landed solidly in the Trainer's guts and made them smile.

Miona was hypnotising. She didn't fight as such, she danced. Every step and movement of her arms flowed into the next. It was hard to tell where a block ended to become a blow, or vice versa and Trainer Marsh was smiling broadly by the time they finished.

Then our group moved onto shooting.

"Your targets this time," Trainer Dorthin explained, "will be live monsters or humans. Those of you wishing to enter Search and Rescue, Foreign Aid or Monster Containment will stun live monsters. Those of you wishing to enter the Syther Force will stun volunteers' role-playing as criminals. You will all be assessed on the same skills.

"Those of you stunning monsters will do so from inside their enclosures in a special section of the Monster Centre, having ascended into the middle of the enclosure via a lift. The lift is made of shield glass, so you will be able to look around the enclosure, before the glass descends and locate the monster before it can attack you.

"Those of you stunning humans will step through a door into a mock crime scene. Your first scene will only have fake criminals in it, whom you are to stun. Your second mock crime scene will have civilians as well as mock criminals, and the test there is to carefully evaluate who to stun before you fire.

"I will be assessing you on how swiftly you locate your target, and how swiftly and effectively you stun it. Any obstacles you overcome to reach your targets will be reflected in your test scores. You will most likely face only one target, but some students may face more. This exam will end when you have identified and stunned *every* target in your enclosure."

As Trainees, we hadn't been allowed to face more than one monster on our own yet. For anyone they pushed that way, it would be a first, during exam conditions. That made me nervous. I grit my teeth as Trainer Dorthin led everyone stunning monsters underground, through a basement tunnel to the lift.

When we lined up before the lift, Joe flicked his chin at me from the front, supremely confident as always. I smiled and flicked my chin at him, Nick and Johnny. It took a while for them to ascend the lift. I supposed new monsters had to be put into the enclosure after each student stunned one and I waited tensely.

Rinth paced behind me, while Miona stepped out to practice Zushai poses. Rinth smiled and moved to practice boxing, making me realise I was holding it in. I turned. Amon smiled and was chatting with Merin and Lylez. Everyone *did* something. We all felt stress and we all had ways of managing it. I'd never truly seen that before. It made me feel ok about seeing Jay or needing to spend so much time lapping monsters.

Rinth clapped me on the back, and Trainer Dorthin handed me a stun gun. I gripped the gun tightly as I stepped into the small, glass tube lift, my back to the line of waiting students. I held my gun in both hands, across the space before me, and tilted it slowly from end to end. It was about control, I guessed. I stopped my heart-rate from getting too crazy by exhaling deeply, keeping the tilt of my gun slow, steady, and felt calmer than before any other test.

A memory came to mind as the lift ascended. Gorn nodding to Tali. Tali shooting down a garl no one could see in a grain field, aiming by sound. That was the key. I closed my eyes and focused on what I could hear.

The lift shuddered slightly as it stopped. A mechanism retracted the glass. Leaves rustled on my right. I adjusted my gun. I pulled the trigger instinctively and opened my eyes. A medium sized, reptilian bird with a serpent-like tail dropped out of the air, and fell to the ground a few meters on my right.

"With his fricken eyes closed!" Joe exclaimed.

I turned and smiled at the far side of the enclosure's shield glass, where they stood watching. A pale blue uniformed syther swiped her card, and the glass door slid upwards, allowing me to exit. I handed her my gun and she stowed it in a gun case, then I stood waiting for the others.

"Suppose you lot are going to show us up?" said John.

"Whatever gets me a shot at the real thing," I replied, and Nick nodded, while Johnny smiled.

Amon was next. When the lift finally came back up, they stood with their eyes shut, while *three* gis walked out the shade of a tree. I held my breath, as the shield glass retracted. A twig snapped beneath a gis' foot. Amon fired. A gis growled. Amon fired again. The second gis collapsed and Amon's body relaxed. The third gis had almost reached them. It brushed against a bush. Amon put a dart in it.

"Screw Chaos!" Joe swore, shifting in surprise. His right foot tapped the enclosure's shield glass. He started as Amon's fourth dart bounced off the inside of the glass, and Trainer Dorthin called, "You're done Amon. Excellent shooting."

Amon strode out with a smile on their face.

"How did you know what height to aim at?" Nick asked them.

"I heard their footsteps," Amon replied. "Two footsteps, it had to be gis. And they know I'm a good shot, so I thought they'd push me with more than one."

Rinth's gis was more eager than Amon's. It charged as the glass lowered. Luckily, *he* had his eyes open. He dived sideways and fired several darts in mid-air. Two missed. One struck torso. The gis turned. Rinth hit the ground on his side and fired three more shots. One missed. But the second and third brought it down. He set down the gun and lay panting.

"That was harsh," Joe said to me.

"Dorthin probably wanted to check that he used his gun instead of his fists," I replied. "He knocked out a baby karon with a rock in our Field Exam."

Johnny grinned, and Nick stared open-mouthed.

"Nice," Amon said as Rinth joined us.

Rinth shook his head. "Would've been easier to knock the thing out, then stun it. Shooting isn't all it's cracked up to be."

"Except that if that gis got one punch in, it was likely to get four," Joe replied.

"Not if I clubbed it with the gun," Rinth countered.

Joe and Johnny smiled.

Miona's shooting was simpler. A wolf-like, glowing eyed, fanged hundaira moved into a crouch as the lift glass retracted around her. She took aim. As the glass retreated below her shoulders, it leapt at her. She fired. Hit it in the chest. Twice. Then she side-stepped. Its fur brushed her leg as it overshot her and landed, unconscious.

Rinth smiled approvingly and Miona's eyes shone as she returned his smile. Merin smiled too, shaking her head, and Miona grinned. Given all the admiration Merin got from guys, it was only fair Miona got some too. I suspected Merin agreed.

When Merin's turn came, a small winged creature swooped towards her. She took aim, fired several shots. One hit. But the thing flew on, swooping towards her. She rolled aside, firing two more shots from her back, and brought it down. Even rolling around with a gun, she moved as gracefully as Miona fought with her fists. I suspected Miona's developing grace was a result of extensive training with Merin. Merin had speed and grace down to an art form.

By the time everyone finished, I was fairly confident we'd all passed. Then it was into the written exam. Monster Studies and Continent Geography studies were easy because of our field work. I relied on my notes for Taron Law.

Then our group moved into the Level One Syther Team test. The things Captain Zagoni asked us to observe with Tali's team all came in handy, and it was the first written test I felt confident about. I smiled at the others when it was finished, and we joined other syther students in a celebratory meal in the Food Court.

***

A week later, the sytheren students had their exams and it was almost mid-year holidays. There was one more job, putting on my new pale blue syther uniform, and meeting my new syther team at an old hotel in Bellaria's posh district, with Mum, Uncle Alan, and Aunt Lil, who were all dressed up, because this was our Syther Ceremony.

Ryan, Lylez, Zan, Merin, half a dozen of our classmates and Joe, Johnny and Nick stood (or in Miona's mother's case sat in a wheelchair) on the dance floor of the ballroom, talking amongst themselves and their well-dressed parents, when I arrived with my family. I had no fear of Dad turning up this time, I'd had no contact with him for over a year.

Delicate piano music was playing and waiters were circulating on polished floorboards, handing out champagne. Everyone drank it this year, apparently they made exceptions for seventeen-year-olds to drink at celebrations as important as this.

"Welcome," a voice announced on stage. "Please take your seats."

Amon and their grandparents arrived just after my family greeted Miona, Merin and their families. But Amon's smiling face held my gaze. It wasn't just their joy at graduating that caught my attention. It was the pale blue eye shadow, matching our uniforms. The length mascara added to their lashes. Those lips were striking enough, but with the shade of red on them, Tak would probably be kissing them.

Miona greeted Amon first.

Rinth nudged me.

"What?" I asked.

"Say something," he said softly.

I frowned. There was no chance in Chaos I was telling Amon they looked good. Then I noticed the shy way those warm brown eyes were peering under those long lashes at me. Oh. I didn't care about painted nails, but did they worry a painted face was too much for me?

"Nice colour choice," I said, my eyes flicking to their pale blue lids.

Amon beamed at me.

Rinth shook his head.

"What?" Amon asked.

"Merin's going to be pissed she's not the prettiest person in the year level anymore," Rinth said.

Amon and I both burst out laughing.

"Maybe we should try purple next time," Merin said, stepping up beside us. "The contrast between your hair, a medium purple and your skin tone should be even more striking."

"You helped with their make up?" I asked.

Merin smiled. "Of course I did. It's not like Miona lets me do hers."

I laughed and Miona grinned. She never wore makeup. Whereas Merin's eyelids were a deep red, matching the colour of her lips.

"You both look beautiful," I told them.

Merin smiled. Were those tears in Amon's eyes? Why was Rinth grinning like that?

"Everyone, please take your seats," a voice called from the stage.

I sat between Mum and Amon, in rows of seats on the far end of the dance floor. Amon's eyes were distracting again. Their smile when they noticed me looking was even more distracting. Was I blushing? That was fireflies dancing in my chest. They'd been there when I was with Amon before. I'd always shoved them down before acknowledging them. What was wrong with me tonight?

I turned to the stage, expecting a long, boring speech before certificates were awarded and for Trainers to run the whole thing. I was surprised on both counts. The speech was short. Then curtains rolled back from the wall behind the stage, and colours split across a large screen. They showed the footage of our Field Exams that the Field Captains on the examiner panel had watched to mark us.

Ryan and Lylez smiled as we watched footage of them, Zan and another girl move in towards a family of three adult gis and two youngsters. The adult gis roared and charged. Only Lylez noticed two young ones creep outside her team's formation and try to attack from the side. She stunned a young gis, and Ryan stunned the second, saving everyone from having their thighs pummelled.

One of Amon's mates and his team forced their way into an illegal drug lab and stunned several gangsters armed with semi-automatic weapons. Then Joe's team pursued a pair of winged serpents, which flowed through the sky in an aerial dance, and were so thin they could dodge stun shots by twisting sideways.

My team's Field Exam was saved for last. Mum clung to my arm as a huge karon with segmented armour scales roared and advanced towards our group and Ine's syther team. Amon helped shoot it, while the rest of us accomplished little.

People screamed when karons of all sizes charged en mass and we tried to protect the fool adventurers. Amon gripped my hand, and I held theirs, wondering how they could be scared now, when they were the calmest of us during this mission. Joe turned in his seat to clap me on the shoulder, when I shot a karon at point blank range. It seemed sensible at the time, but I looked like a fool action hero on film.

Aunt Lil smiled at me and shook her head. Mum stared in shock.

Joe noticed Amon's hand in mine and grinned.

"Just as well Amon is a good shot," Uncle Alan commented. "Otherwise I'm not sure I'd be comfortable with you doing work like that."

Amon noticed Joe's gaze and blushed, withdrawing their hand. How had I held... bloody Merin! How had she got me semi-used to holding hands so quickly? I still mostly liked my personal space, but sometimes, some people, somehow I didn't... mind.

Everyone's gazes were mostly fixed on the screen, or the stage. I still didn't want anyone touching me when more than one person was looking at me. But when they weren't... my head began to spin, and I was happy to be distracted by certificates.

They weren't presented by a Trainer, but by Headmistress Rinas, who wore a purple Head's suit. We lined up beside the stage as our names, syther teams and the government departments we would start working for next year were announced.

My heart beat with anticipation as I lined up. It was in role order, so Amon stood at the back shaking their head in silent protest, and exchanging grins with Rinth and Ryan, who stood near the front. It was a nice change to feel anticipation for a good thing. To know that I'd made it further than I thought possible at school, despite all the odds stacked against me. And in record time.

Headmistress Rinas read out names, teams and departments one after another. I reflected on how much could change in a year and a half. On the help I'd got from Jay and the boys. Mum, selling the house to pay for Sythe School and Uncle Alan and Aunt Lil letting us live with them instead. Miona, whose acceptance had encouraged me and kept me sane in sytheren studies. Merin, who'd snuck under my guard and was corrupting how I kept people at arm's length. Amon, whose smile still drove me to distraction, who made me feel comfortable and weird and... ... who helped save my skin from monsters multiple times. Rinth lapping monsters with me, helping me to actively regulate my emotions and switch off my overactive amygdala.

"Rarkin Lormen, Monster Containment; in a new syther team with Amon, Rinth and Miona."

I'd never felt so proud as when I climbed those stairs, with a big smile on my face. It was official. I'd made it.

Headmistress Rinas smiled, shaking my hand as she gave me the certificate I intended to nail to my bedroom wall, right beside the sytheren one. I stood smiling with Rinth and Miona, and Amon eventually joined us, while our families cheered. I'd succeeded beyond fifteen-year-old me's dreams. It was time to dream new ones for seventeen-year-old me.

Acknowledgements

Firstly, thank you to my beta readers. To Steph, for feedback on introducing world building, and developing dynamics in Rarkin's dysfunctional family. And to Charlie for suggestions on pacing and sequencing to let the reader catch their breath between emotionally heavier chapters. Thanks also to Charlie for your patience with and proof reading of pesky typos, which I now realise have increased in frequency, due to the combination of my chronic illness involving brain fog and my ADHD. Thanks also Maria for back up typo detection support.

Thank you also to Bsky's Writing Community, and writers on my Writer's and Author's Discord, for your help in locating a human cover artist, in providing him with reference images not generated by ai, and helping me define the SciFi-Fantasy genre of this series with confidence. Shoutout to Kate in particular for both those reasons.

Thanks to my cover artist Lawrence Mann, for listening so carefully to my style prefs and preferences for Rarkin and Miona's appearances, for an amazing cover and your patience and consistency as communication technology woes plagued us throughout the creation of this cover.

And thanks to my family, friends, everyone on Bsky or Discord who has, and to you dear reader for, taking an interest in this book, despite that its emotionally heavy themes aren't a great match for what has been an exceptionally emotionally heavy year for the trans, immigrant and disabled communities in particular, for marginalised people in general and anyone living under certain political regimes

Please leave a review!

A few sentences of your overall impressions of Walking the Knife's Edge can indicate to other readers whether or not it's likely their cup of tea. So I'd appreciate you spreading the word by telling Scifi and or fantasy lovers in your life about it and or leaving a review on Goodreads/ BookBub/ StoryGraph/ and or a bookstore.

(QR code links via my Sythe Series books page).